Books by Edith Maxwell

A TINE TO LIVE, A TINE TO DIE

'TIL DIRT DO US PART

Published by Kensington Publishing Corporation

'TIL DIRT
DO US PART

'TIL DIRT DO US PART

EDITH MAXWELL

KENSINGTON BOOKS
www.kensingtonbooks.com

KENSINGTON BOOKS are published by

Kensington Publishing Corp.
119 West 40th Street
New York, NY 10018

Library of Congress Card Catalogue Number: 2013920827

ISBN-13: 978-0-7582-8464-8
ISBN-10: 0-7582-8464-0
First Kensington Hardcover Edition: June 2014

eISBN-13: 978-0-7582-8466-2
eISBN-10: 0-7582-8466-7
First Kensington Electronic Edition: June 2014

10 9 8 7 6 5 4 3 2 1

Printed in the United States of America

For Hugh Lockhart, the expert and hardworking restorer of more than one beautiful home and the always grateful beneficiary of food-related research.

Acknowledgments

I owe so many thanks. To my editor John Scognamiglio, able publicist Adeola Saul, and the whole team at Kensington Publishing, for nurturing this series and getting the word out about it. To my agent, John Talbot, for believing in cozy mysteries. And most of all to my readers—authors would be nowhere without you.

My fellow Wicked Cozy authors are the best support group ever. Jessie Crockett, Julie Hennrikus, Sherry Harris, Liz Mugavero, and Barb Ross are great writer companions on this journey. Look for their own cozies! Sherry Harris also worked her editing magic on the manuscript before I turned it in. Any errors remaining are certainly due to my own stubbornness. The Monday Night Salem Writers' Group—Margaret Press, Rae Francouer, Doug Hall, Bill Joyner, Elaine Ricci, and Sam Sherman—heard much of this book in person and improved it immeasurably with their gentle but firm critiquing. And, of course, Sisters in Crime, the Guppies, the New England chapter of SINC, and the New England chapter of Mystery Writers of America provided inspiration, teaching, and fun along the way.

I have several sources of farming knowledge to thank beyond my own experiences operating and co-owning a small certified-organic farm twenty years ago: Paula Chase of Arrowhead Farm, Heron Pond Farm (where we are CSA members), and the Northeast Organic Farming Association then and now. Organic farmer Julie Rawson was my garlic-braiding role model many years ago and has an anonymous bit part in this book. Farmers Darryl and Renee Ray loved the series early on and helped to spread the word on the West Coast. I want to thank, too, a special farm consultant. My son John Hutchison-Maxwell is a permaculture, organic, and nutrient-density farmer extraordinaire. He helped me with all the details about the rescue chickens: their coop, their behavior, and what to do with them. I even learned what hens really sound like at New Harmony Farm, where he's been working. Thank you, JD! I also thank Cider Hill Farm and Phat Cats Bistro in Amesbury, Massachusetts. I modeled the opening farm-to-table dinner directly on Cider Hill Farm's dinner in the fall of 2012, including the menu prepared from local foods by the fabulous chefs at Phat Cats. A version of the Sweet Potato Empanada recipe included here was generously provided by Phat Cats chef Christina Johnson. No murders are due to either the dinner or the recipe.

I thank Phil Parsons for being my geek consultant for this book, and Officer Tom Hanshaw, Detective Kevin Donovan, and Officer Ron Guilmette, as well as others from the Amesbury Police Department, for generously sharing knowledge about police procedure during and after the Amesbury Citizen Police Academy (from which I graduated in May). Any errors are of my own making. I am grateful for Karen Salemi's beautiful book quilt, which merited an anonymous mention; my late mother, Marilyn Muller's gorgeous Japanese fan quilt, also anonymously mentioned; and Jeanne Wallace, one of my biggest cheerleaders and helpers in letting the world know about my stories.

Diane Weaver is a fictional character in this book. The real Diane Weaver was the highest bidder in an auction to benefit StageSource, a nonprofit Boston theater-service organization, for the right to name a character. I hope Diane likes who she got.

The series is set in a fictionalized version of West Newbury, Massachusetts, up in the northeast corner of the commonwealth. No actual farmers or residents were harmed during the writing of this story.

ACKNOWLEDGMENTS

As always, thanks and love to Barbara Bergendorf, Janet Maxwell, and Jennifer Yanco, as well as my dear friends at Amesbury Friends Meeting. And to my sons Allan and John David, and to Hugh—thank you with a full heart for putting up with my trials and being delighted by my successes.

Nor cast your pearls before swine, lest they trample them under their feet, and turn and tear you in pieces.
—Matthew 7:6

Chapter 1

"Are we holding a dinner here or not?" A peremptory voice resounded from the wide doorway of the barn at Produce Plus Plus Farm. Irene Burr seemed to fill the space despite her petite size. Back as straight as a tomato stake and not a silver hair out of place, she wore her signature cream-colored slacks, a sweater in pale peach, and a shimmering woven shawl.

Cameron Flaherty gulped. It was the first farm-to-table dinner at her farm, and here she was, flirting with the chef in the temporary kitchen he'd set up in the barn, instead of tending to one of her most irritable customers.

Walking toward the doorway, Cam waved and greeted Irene. "Yes, of course we are. Let me show you." She ushered Irene out and walked with her toward a white tent. Late-day sunlight slanted off its top. Green fields dotted with the oranges and reds of ripe fall crops stretched beyond.

"At least the weather is good."

"Thankfully, yes. It's a rain or shine event, but I'm sure everyone will be more comfortable this way." Cam was exceedingly thankful the threatened storm had tracked farther inland. It would have been miserable for guests to sit with rain blowing in the sides of the tent, since her budget hadn't extended to renting one that included walls.

Two long tables filled the space, their white tablecloths arrayed with settings for twenty on each side. A cool breeze blew away the few mosquitoes that remained in early October. Nosegay center-pieces of bright nasturtiums and fuzzy white spearmint flowers from her herb garden decorated every couple of feet. Cam straightened a fork here, a napkin there. The dinner was to be the crowning event of her first farm season. She was counting on it to build publicity for next year and hoped it would go as smoothly as a well-oiled tiller.

"What's on the menu tonight?" Irene pulled reading glasses onto her nose and peered at the menu sticking out of one of the jars on the nearest table.

"Jake Ericsson from The Market restaurant has outdone himself. We're starting with a Shady Oak Farm mushroom tart with Valley View Farm goat cheese. He also made a killer sweet potato empanada with chorizo from Kellie Brook Farm. It's all organic, of course."

Cam was about to go on when the loud rumble of a motorcycle on the drive distracted her. She glanced back and spied two helmeted figures dismounting. The rear passenger wore a skirt.

"Why did he bring *her*?" Irene gazed in the same direction, her lips pressed in a thin line, like she'd whiffed fresh manure.

A moment later, the two sauntered toward the tent. A slim woman dressed in a black T-shirt and jeans ran a hand through spiky dark hair as she clomped in thick-soled black high-top sneakers. The man wore a hooded sweatshirt and a black pleated skirt. Cam looked again as he approached. It was Bobby Burr. In a skirt, all right, with a label that read UTILIKILTS. Cam thought about all those days over the last couple of months when the intelligent and muscled carpenter had been working on her barn from atop a ladder. She'd enjoyed going over plans and talking construction with him. Still, she was glad he hadn't worn the kilt to work, despite his curly dark hair and sweet smile and despite the pockets and hammer loops the kilt sported. What men who wore kilts thought was appropriate to wear or not wear under them was anybody's guess.

Bobby leaned down to give his stepmother an air kiss.

Irene turned her cheek. "Hello, Robert. Your attire is very unusual today."

Bobby greeted Cam, rolling his eyes. "Do you know my friend Sim? Simone Koyama, this is Cam Flaherty. We call her Farmer Cam." He swung an arm around Cam's shoulders and squeezed.

His strong arm warmed the silk on her back in a distinctly pleasant way. She cleared her throat as she eased out from under his touch and extended her hand to Sim, who looked about the same age as Cam.

"Welcome, Sim. Any friend of Bobby's is a friend of mine. He worked a miracle this summer, rebuilding my barn." Cam wondered if *friend* was a euphemism for *girlfriend* or if the two were just pals. And she wondered if Sim was thinking the same about her and Bobby.

"He's good stuff, for sure." Sim shook hands with Cam. "Nice place you have here." The silver stud in her tongue matched the piercing in her eyebrow.

"Irene, you know Simone," Bobby began, but Irene was no longer there. She was strolling, her back to them, toward the far end of the tent.

"Oh, I know Ms. Burr," Sim said in a tart voice as she raised one eyebrow. "I'm her mechanic, not that she appreciates it."

"Why am I not surprised my stepmother is unappreciative?" Bobby stared after Irene. "Oh, well. That's Irene's world."

"She brings her Jaguar in for service but seems to think I'm less than perfect because I work on all foreign autos, not exclusively nineteen ninety Jags." Sim sighed.

"You're a mechanic?" Cam looked with new interest at Sim. "Do you work on trucks?"

"Sure. SK Foreign Auto down on Main Street? That's my shop."

"Cool. I'll bring my truck to you next time it needs work."

"Happy to have the business, Cam."

Alexandra Magnusson hurried up. "Sorry I'm late, Cam." As tall as Cam, the recent college graduate and avid locavore had a flair for wearing vintage clothes in unusual ways. Today she sported a rayon housedress with a leather vest and knee-high boots. A narrow turquoise scarf gathered her long Nordic hair into a knot.

"No worries. You're set for greeting, right?" She'd enlisted Alexandra to welcome people, check their names off the list, and hand out name cards.

"I tell them to clip the name card to the menu where they want to sit."

Cam nodded. Every place setting was anchored by a pint mason jar with the menu card, a red napkin, and a clothespin. Once they'd reserved their seats, guests could mingle, get a drink, and sample the appetizers before the sit-down part of the meal started. And the jars would serve as water glasses. Mill River Winery had already set up their table. Dozens of bottles of red and white stood ready to be opened, and sparkling stemless glasses were lined up like an army of thirsty drinkers.

"What are we eating tonight?" Alexandra asked.

"Appetizers first. Then Jake has prepared salads, a local pork ragout over fingerling potatoes, and roasted root crops with rosemary. Not sure what the dessert is, but I'm sure it will include

Cider Valley Farm's apples in some form. I don't have enough from my one tree to count."

"Cam?" Ellie Kosloski, Cam's Girl Scout summer volunteer, touched Cam's shoulder. "The beer truck is here, and they want to know where to park." She pointed toward the drive.

Cam turned to see the Ipswich Ale Brewery Tapmobile idling, its driver leaning on the open driver-side door. She walked in its direction and called out a greeting.

"Follow me, Jim. Careful of the beds, okay?" Cam led the way along the wide packed-dirt path back to the tent. She'd hired the brewery to bring two kegs in their vintage red-and-white truck with the taps inserted right in the side. It was a very popular way to distribute beer.

Half an hour later the tent was nearly full. The little name cards stuck out from the clothespins, and customers holding wineglasses or beer cups chatted in small groups. Ellie and her friend Ashley, both fourteen, sported black server aprons from The Market over skinny jeans and white shirts. They circulated with trays of the bite-size tarts and empanadas.

Cam stood at the opening to the tent. She took a deep breath and prepared to be social, always a challenge for her. She began to circulate, checking in with each group. She approached her regular customer Wes Ames as he scowled down at Irene.

"It will benefit the town, Mr. Ames. I am quite sure of this." Irene shifted her glass of wine to the other hand and smoothed down a lock of hair with a pinkie finger that bent toward the ring finger at its last joint.

"Old Town Hall has been our central meeting place for decades, Mrs. Burr. It has historical significance."

"How significant can it be if the town can't even afford basic repairs on it? I'm surprised you haven't been sued for lead poisoning from the flaking ceiling falling into people's hair during

Town Meeting." Irene kept her voice even, but her jaw tightened.

"If you'd cooperate with us on our fund-raising instead of trying to buy the building out from under us, we could raise the repair money." Wes folded his arms across his chest.

Cam edged in and greeted Wes. "Where's Felicity?" His effervescent wife had reached out to Cam with support and friendship in the months since they'd met.

"Her sister in Albany is having surgery, so she's staying out there for a couple of weeks. She was sorry to miss this dinner, I'll tell you."

"It's too bad she couldn't make it. So what's this about the Old Town Hall?" The venerable building wasn't far from Cam's farm, but she hadn't had time to read the local weekly paper lately and clearly had missed a brewing controversy.

"I want to help the town." Irene's confident tone held just a touch of smugness. "I am offering to buy the building and create a textile museum in it. I'll restore it and bring tourism to our lovely town, which will bring dollars. It's a win-win."

"*Our* lovely town has been doing fine without your tourism," Wes said. "Who's going to pay for—"

"Cam! Those garnishes?" A voice boomed from the temporary kitchen chef Jake Ericsson had set up in the newly rebuilt barn. *Crud.* Cam was supposed to have cut a few last-minute handfuls of parsley and garlic chives for Jake to sprinkle on the ragout.

"Excuse me," Cam said as she turned away.

"I'll get them, Cam." Ellie set her tray down on the serving table near the entrance to the tent. "I have my knife." She headed toward the herb beds.

"Thanks, Ellie." Cam wondered what else she had forgotten to do. She went over the list of guests in her mind. Cam had comped tickets for Howard Fisher, because Jake was serving

-
d
'd
Ioward's pig farm, and for Bobby, who had somehow
rebuild Cam's barn in only three months after the
that had nearly killed her and Ellie. Her childhood
local police officer, Ruth Dodge and her twin girls
ed
ed
And, of course, Cam's great-uncle Albert. She
be a farmer if he hadn't urged her to take over the
unt Marie had died and Albert had had to have his
nd
on-
a year later. When Cam was laid off from her job,
ved
ed her the farm.
the
briskly to the barn and popped her head in its
the
She inhaled deeply. "It smells divine. Every-
trol? Ellie's getting those herbs for you." She
l his assistant, who were artfully arranging slices
e, a
bes on eighty salads laid out on a long table, sal-
ely from greens, tomatoes, and herbs that Cam
ges-
morning. Her locavore customers were going
stau-
sn't nuts about eating only locally grown foods
ubscribers, but if their obsession kept her farm
have
for it.
s head. "We are good. I think." He winked at
ehind
tly blushed right up to the roots of her red hair.
er se
Monday had been especially nice. No time to
irr
ow, though. She looked down at her green silk
jeans tucked into cowboy boots. At least she'd re-
change before people had started arriving.
red in with a bunch of herbs in each hand. "Where
hese, Chef?"
shing bin over there would be great." Jake gestured
w. "Thanks, Scout."
hea d her eyes. "My name's Ellie, Jake." She shook her
meta dropped the fragrant green bits into the galvanized

Cam reflected on how much Ellie had grown up over the sum
mer. She had been a very young fourteen in June but now looke
and acted much more like the ninth grader she was. Plus, she
grown a couple of inches.

Ellie put her hands in the back pockets of her jeans and gaz
up at the barn, rotating her head. "That Bobby dude sure work
fast. It looks awesome."

Cam agreed. Bobby had managed to capture the essence a
beauty of Albert's antique barn while improving on its functi
ality. He'd even re-created the clerestory window that had sa
Cam's and Ellie's lives a few months earlier. The rosy hues of
late-day sun filtered in through the wide window above
barn's back door.

"I'd better get back to the tent," Ellie said. "Give, lil
shout when you want us to start serving plates, Jake."

"I'd say ten minutes. We'll wheel the salads out." Jake
tured at the stainless steel cart he had brought from the re
rant.

"I should get back, too," Cam said. "I guess I'm going to
to give a little welcoming speech. I'll introduce you, Jake."

As Cam walked back to the tent, she heard shuffling b
her. She turned to see Howard Fisher keeping pace with h
eral yards back. He wore his signature dark green work sh
pants with leather work boots. The ensemble at least
clean, unlike some of the times Cam had seen him at th
ers' market. She stopped even as she wondered why he
greeted her.

"I'm so glad you could make it, Howard." Cam exten
hand.

Howard halfheartedly shook hands with a grunt of a
edgment, his rough palm barely clasping Cam's. "Glad
business."

"Your wife couldn't make it?" She had never been introduced to his wife but had seen them in public together once.

"Somebody's got to do the chores," he muttered, looking straight ahead.

Cam nodded. *Really?* Surely, the chores could wait a couple of hours. Well, it was none of her business.

Cam introduced Howard to Alexandra when they arrived at the entrance to the tent. "Howard gave us a very generous discount on the pork for one of tonight's dishes."

"Welcome, Mr. Fisher," Alexandra said. She shot an odd look at Cam and led him away, explaining to him about the seating and drinks and leaving him at the beer truck.

What was that look? Cam shook her head as she surveyed the group. The teens were doing a great job circulating with the trays of appetizers. Great-Uncle Albert chatted from his wheelchair with Lucinda DaSilva, Cam's friend and best farm volunteer. Sim and Alexandra seemed to have bonded. Bobby and Irene stood on the periphery, engaged in conversation. He frowned and shook his head while she glared at him and gesticulated.

Irene was on quite a roll tonight. First Sim, then Wes, now Bobby. Cam knew Bobby as an extremely good-natured man, a hardworking carpenter, and a bit of a flirt. Seeing him in a fight, with his stepmother no less, was new. Since the beer truck was parked right beyond them, Cam thought she might head over for a sample and maybe a bit of a listen, too. She strolled in that direction, her eyes away from the two, but her attention tuned to them.

"I am happy doing what I do, Irene, and I'm good at it," Bobby said.

"Your father wanted you to do more than carpentry, Robert. You know that."

"I have no interest in working for you, Irene. Zero. Nada. Zilch. It's not going to happen."

"You know I inherited Zebulon's assets. If you persist in this misguided vocation, you won't see a penny of them. And my real son might."

"You stole Dad's assets. For all I know, you killed him yourself. And what *real son* are you talking about?"

Cam whistled under her breath. *Whoa.*

Jim hailed her from the truck. "Try the Five Mile Rye Saison, Cam."

Cam agreed, asking for a half cup. She thanked him and savored the ale on her tongue as she mulled over what she had heard. She glanced back at where Bobby and Irene had been, but they'd moved on.

She took a deep breath. She was the farmer in charge, and it was time for her speech, whether she wanted to do it or not. She strolled to a spot at the end of the tent, between the beer truck and the wine table, and waved her arms over her head.

"Can I have your attention, please?"

Attention not forthcoming, she said it again with a rise in volume. The chatter and clatter continued. Alexandra noticed Cam's plight and stuck two fingers between her lips. A resulting piercing whistle startled the crowd into quiet.

Cam laughed. "Thanks, Alexandra. And welcome, everyone. I just wanted to say a few words before we start eating."

"Hope they're not prayer kind of words," someone behind her whispered, which made Cam almost wish she were religious solely to counter that sort of mean spirit. And then she wished she knew who said it.

She took a deep breath. "Thanks to everybody here tonight. We're going to have a really special meal. And I'd like to thank all of you who signed up as farm shareholders for my first season. You did it on faith, which I appreciate. I hope you've felt nourished by the food and by being part of this community. It's been an interesting year for you and me both." She swallowed and forced a smile.

"I particularly want to thank the volunteers who helped me keep the farm running after the fire. You know who you are." She scanned the crowd for Lucinda, Alexandra, Wes, Ellie, and others, giving each a nod.

"And there's Bobby Burr, our resident artist-carpenter, who worked like a maniac to produce a working barn again in short order." She pointed at Bobby, now standing with Sim and Alexandra, who waved his acknowledgment.

Cam looked around. Jake hadn't appeared. She caught Ellie's eye and gestured toward the barn with her head, mouthing "Jake." Ellie nodded and took off.

"I hope all of this year's subscribers will sign up again. We're going to offer winter shares this year. It'll be the first time, so I'll keep the price low and maybe expectations, too."

Laughter rippled through the guests.

"But be sure to sign up early for next year's main season. Judging by the interest here tonight, we might sell out. And early is good for a farmer. If I can get the cash for seeds and seedlings up front, we all benefit." Cam looked around for Jake again. He hadn't appeared, and Ellie wasn't back, either. What was going on?

"I, uh, had planned to introduce Jake Ericsson, our talented chef for tonight. I recommend eating at his restaurant, The Market, as often as you can. I provide much of his produce, and he works miracles with whatever he touches." Cam felt a blush creep up her neck, remembering a miracle or two Jake had wrought on her personally. "But he must be busy with the last-minute details of your dinner. Please enjoy your drinks a moment longer. And thank you all for coming."

Cam strode out of the tent in search of the chef. She slowed as she spied Irene Burr leaning over and stroking Preston, Cam's

Norwegian Forest Cat. The handsome, fluffy fellow, who usually absented himself around strangers, reared up and rubbed his head against Irene's knee as she petted him and scratched his scruff.

"He likes you," Cam said.

Irene looked up. "Animals make so much more sense than humans, don't they?" An almost sad smile crept across her face.

Cam nodded. This seemed so out of character for this sometimes domineering, usually aloof, and always controlled customer, especially given what Cam had overheard. Irene's import-export textile business was a successful one. Maybe she needed that kind of control to run it, and Bobby had told Cam that his stepmother hadn't shed a tear when her husband, Zebulon, Bobby's father, died a year earlier. But if any animal could win someone over, it would be her sweet rescue cat, Preston.

Cam excused herself and continued to the barn. As she approached, Ellie and Jake's assistant emerged with the cart full of salads.

"Good. I think people are getting hungry." Cam waved them toward the tent and entered the barn.

"Jake?" Cam looked around and couldn't see him. Where was he? The electric warming box was plugged in; fresh plates were lined up on the serving tables, waiting to be filled; and a glass of beer was mostly empty, but no chef. An involuntary shudder ran through Cam. Ever since the murder in her hoop house in June, she had found her thoughts leaping to disaster at the slightest provocation. What if something had happened to the man who was her friend and who was now starting to become more than that?

"You could at least make yourself useful," a voice boomed behind her.

Cam jumped and emitted a little shriek as two long, strong

arms encircled her from behind. "Jake, you scared me." She twisted around to look up, way up, at his twinkling ice-blue eyes. It was a treat to find a beau who was even taller than her own five foot eleven.

"It's just me." He planted a quick kiss on her lips and released her. "So, you want to help?" He was a substantial man who enjoyed his own cooking, dressed today in a black-striped chef's jacket and black pants.

"What I wanted was for you to greet the diners, but you never showed." Cam frowned.

"Hey, you want me to cook, or you want me to talk? I got work to do back here," Jake said with a tinge of annoyance. "I'll talk to them after."

"Don't you like the ragout?" Cam had watched Alexandra consume everything on her plate except the pork stew. "Mine was delicious." It had been good, although now Cam's stomach felt a little uneasy. She was sure it was from worrying if the dinner would go smoothly. Now, an hour after talking with Jake in the barn, the event looked like a success. She surveyed the relaxed faces and the mostly spirited conversation and started to relax, herself. She was happy to let others do the conversing, too. Making small talk wasn't her strong point, and she found it a strain.

"I've heard Howard Fisher doesn't treat his pigs well," Alexandra said. "He doesn't feed them enough, and their conditions are poor. I don't want to eat the meat of unhappy animals."

"Can I take your plate?" Ellie tapped Alexandra on the shoulder.

Alexandra nodded and thanked Ellie. Ashley was clearing on Cam's side of the table.

"Howard mistreats his animals?" Cam twisted in her seat to look at him. He sat at the far end of the other table. Great-Uncle

Albert sat next to him—of course, Albert knew everyone—and across from them was Irene Burr. Albert sat turned in his wheelchair toward Lucinda on his other side, while Howard leaned toward Irene and gestured as he spoke, their heads nearly touching.

"That's the information I have, and it's from a reliable source," Alexandra said.

"I had no idea about the mistreatment." Cam looked back at the younger woman.

"Who decided to get the meat from Howard?"

"I think it was Irene who suggested it," Cam said.

"You might check into your meat sources in a little more depth next time, Cam. Or assign me the job." Alexandra smiled, her expression radiating youth.

"I think the pork tastes great," Bobby said from his seat next to Alexandra. "This dinner is a big success, Cam. And you are lovely as a farmer-hostess." He set his chin on his hand, elbow on the table, and gazed at Cam with a smile.

Suddenly flustered, Cam shook her head. "Don't be silly." She felt her usual blush creep up her neck. "The dinner does seem to be going well, though, doesn't it?"

"You bet. Now, if you had some music, that would top it off. I could show you my dance moves." He winked.

Cam had opened her mouth to say she didn't dance in public when Alexandra looked over Cam's shoulder and started clapping. Others near her clapped, too.

Cam turned to see what the commotion was. Jake loomed in the entrance to the tent. She stood and clapped as she crossed the tent to stand next to him.

Jake removed his toque and bowed with a flourish as the space quieted.

"Everybody, this is Jake Ericsson, chef at The Market, who cooked all your food tonight," Cam said. The applause started up again.

After a few moments, Jake held up his hand. "Please. It looks like you enjoyed your meal. We couldn't have done it without Farmer Cam's superb produce." He put his right arm around her shoulders and squeezed a little too hard.

Another round of applause started up, despite Cam's efforts with both hands to tamp it down.

When it subsided, Jake spoke. "For dessert"—he gestured at Ellie and Ashley, who had started delivering small plates to each diner—"we have a pumpkin-crisp cheesecake. And next time you dine at The Market, let your waitperson know you were at this event and I'll try to get out front to say hello." He released Cam and leaned toward her. "What's with you and that Bobby character?" he whispered.

"Nothing." Cam frowned at him. "What do you mean?"

"I saw him drooling over you. You'd better make up your mind who you want." He turned away and began to greet the guests.

Cam took a deep breath and let it out. The jealous streak she'd seen in Jake last spring was back. Why did life have to be so complicated? She decided she'd earned a glass of wine, and made her way to the vineyard's table. Irene arrived at the same time. They both selected a glass of the pear dessert wine. Irene pulled her shawl closer around her. The fall of darkness had cooled the air considerably. Cam inhaled, catching the damp scent of fertile soil that rose up after sunset.

"Wonderful event, Cameron." Irene held her glass up. "Congratulations."

Cam clinked hers and thanked the older woman. "So did I understand you want to buy the Old Town Hall?"

Irene pursed her lips. "I have made the town an offer. I can't believe your Mr. Ames opposes the sale. Westbury needs me." She sniffed. Gone was the sad smile and affection for small animals. The imperious Irene Burr was back.

"Hey, great dinner, *fazendeira*." Lucinda DaSilva elbowed Cam with a smile. "Irene, how are you?"

Irene blinked several times and replied that she was well.

"How do you know each other?" Cam asked, looking from one to the other.

"I clean house for her. I didn't tell you that?" The Brazilian frowned with a smile.

As Cam shook her head, she felt a tap on her shoulder.

"Excuse me, Cam. We're heading out," Sim said. Bobby perched on the edge of the table behind her, gazing anywhere except toward Irene.

"So soon?" Cam smiled at Sim.

"Yeah. Hey, bring your truck down anytime," Sim said. "I'll take good care of it for you."

Irene gave a little snort and looked amused.

"Listen, Ms. Burr." Sim's voice boiled. "Have you ever, ever had a problem with my work? Your Jaguar runs like a real wildcat, and it's all my doing."

"You're not a Jaguar-trained technician is my only point." Irene raised her eyebrows and crossed her arms, the glass of wine now in the crook of her elbow.

"It's an engine. A foreign engine. I speak its language. That's all I need to know. Oh, and by the way? Ever hear of computers? Anything I don't know, I have at my fingertips." Sim planted her feet in a wide stance and folded her arms. "If you don't like my work, feel free to drive twenty miles down to the dealership and let them take your money."

Bobby pulled at Sim's sleeve. "We gotta run. Good night, everybody."

Irene nodded and turned away. Sim stared after Irene. Her face was so red, Cam thought she could see flames coming from her ears.

"I'm going to get her, one way or the other," Sim muttered.

As Wes walked by, he snorted. "Take a number, honey."

Chapter 2

Cam trudged up the worn wooden stairs of her antique saltbox several hours later. She loved this house. Growing up, she'd spent her summers here with her great-uncle and great-aunt. Marie had welcomed her like the grandchild she'd never had, and the two old farmers had enveloped Cam in love and warmth while her peripatetic parents spent months overseas, doing anthropological research. She paused at the fading photograph of Albert and Marie on their wedding day. She extended a finger to stroke Marie's image. Her great-aunt had passed away two years earlier, after sixty-one years of marriage, and some of the light had gone out of Albert. Now he seemed to be doing well, though, and was making friends in his new assisted-living quarters. He even had his own laptop computer and maintained a blog where he posted short memoirs about his life as a farmer.

Swinging aching feet into bed, Cam rehashed the dinner. It had gone well. There had been enough food, Ellie and her friend had served without a hitch, and the guests seemed to appreciate the free wine and beer. She hadn't taken time to tally the cash but thought the fifty-dollar-per-person tickets had more than covered the expenses, since Jake and the other vendors had discounted their costs so steeply. She'd certainly offer the event again next summer and fall.

Jake. He hadn't spoken privately with her after his comment about deciding between him and Bobby. Which was ridiculous. There was nothing going on with her and Bobby. The guy was a flirt. That was all.

And Cam felt uneasy at the undercurrents she'd witnessed swirling around Irene Burr. That Irene was difficult was no surprise. That she was difficult enough to spur Bobby into anger merited thought. Cam didn't know Sim Koyama at all but wondered at Irene's power to invoke her ire, too. And then the conflict about Old Town Hall's fate . . . Even mild-mannered Wes Ames was upset with Irene.

As Cam slid toward sleep, fall crickets serenading her through the open window, she was glad she hadn't experienced Irene's wrath. The distance of a farmer-customer relationship with Irene Burr was fine with Cam.

Cam threw on an old sweatshirt before heading downstairs after letting herself sleep in until almost eight. Gray clouds pressed in on the morning, and the temperature had to be below sixty. Still, the farm season wasn't over yet. She'd be working on many colder mornings soon. She took a moment to clean up an unfortunately placed hair ball Preston had hacked up during the night on the kitchen countertop, near the telephone. She shoved aside residual clutter here and there as she wiped down the counter with some liquid cleanser. Hair balls were one of the drawbacks of owning a very large, very furry feline.

She headed out to the fields to work, passing the now forlorn tent, its empty chairs and bare tables ghosts of last night's warm conviviality. The people from the rental place would be here sometime before noon to dismantle it and cart it all away.

A siren wailed in the distance. The rising and falling keen sounded like it came from the other side of the woods that formed the back perimeter of her property. Cam sniffed the air for smoke and scanned the skyline. She relaxed her shoulders, not having realized how tense she'd become at the thought of a fire. A childhood incident, combined with the barn fire, made her wary every time she heard sirens.

She threw an empty bushel basket into the garden cart and headed for the tomato field. It was time to call it a day for the crop of larger heirlooms, even though there hadn't been a hard frost yet. New England didn't offer enough sun or warmth at this time of year to ripen the crop of baseball-size green fruit yet clinging to the browning vines. She filled the basket with the pale green orbs while thinking about green tomato–apple chutney and began pulling the spent plants, laying them in the wide garden cart.

Preston sidled by and then shot off in pursuit of unseen prey. Cam worked for another hour, until her growling stomach demanded fuel. She hoisted the bushel on top of the cart full of vines. She trudged with the cart to the compost bins and carried the basket to the house. She set it down in the screened-in back porch. Extracting a key from the not-so-secret hiding place under a statue of a garden gnome sitting at a computer, she unlocked the back door and let herself in. Before getting involved in the search for her farmhand's murderer in June, she had always left the door unlocked while she was outside working. Now she locked it every time she left the house.

On the faded blue-speckled Formica of the kitchen countertop, the green light on her voice mail device blinked. The

missed call was from Ruth Dodge. Cam realized Ruth and her little daughters hadn't shown up at the dinner last night.

She accessed the message and listened, gazing at one of the dinner centerpieces on her dining table. The flower vase needed topping off with water.

"Cam, call me as soon as possible."

That was it. Cam frowned. Maybe Ruth needed some emergency babysitting. She checked the number—Ruth had called from her cell and not from the police station. Cam pressed the buttons to return the call. Ruth picked up right away and sounded relieved that Cam was on the line.

"What's up?" Cam asked. "Are the girls okay? You guys didn't come to the dinner last night."

Ruth said they were fine, that she'd explain later. "This is an official call, Cam. I'm at work."

"Did I do something wrong?" It was odd that Ruth was calling from her cell phone at work.

"Irene Burr was at the dinner, wasn't she?"

"Yes. We had about eighty guests. It was a great event—"

"Did she argue with anybody?" Ruth interrupted.

Cam kept her silence for a moment, picturing the evening.

"Cam?"

"I'm not sure you'd call it arguing. She seemed to rub a number of people the wrong way. But that's how she is. I think she probably means well."

"Any details on who she upset?"

"What's going on?"

"I need to know. Tell me who she rubbed the wrong way."

"Her stepson, her mechanic, Wes Ames, even Howard Fi You might better ask who didn't she get riled up."

"Oh?"

Cam sensed that Ruth's ears were perking up even mor

two had been friends since the first summer Cam had come to the farm, when she was six. "Has something happened?"

It was Ruth's turn to keep silent.

"Has something happened to Irene?" Cam shivered. It wasn't from the temperature.

"I have to go, Cam. I'll call you back." The phone clicked off.

Cam stared at the device in her hand, as if willing it to ring again. She set it down a little harder than it deserved and assembled a peanut butter and banana sandwich instead. Ruth wasn't going to call back. Two bites in, a bell rang, but it was the doorbell.

Hastening to chew and swallow, Cam checked the window. She opened the back door to Sim Koyama.

Sim's tough exterior now displayed a big crack. "Cam, you have to help me." Her voice quavered. She wore a uniform of black similar to her garb the night before, but her hair stuck out every which way, like a thistle plant. Dark smudges lurked under tense eyes.

"Come in. Are you all right?"

"I am, but Bobby isn't. Irene Burr is dead."

"Oh, no! That's terrible." So that was why Ruth had called. "Bobby must be really upset."

"And the pigs. My God, the pigs." Sim's dark eyes looked haunted.

"The pigs?" Had Sim lost it?

"It's awful." Sim paced toward the kitchen and back.

"Is Bobby all right? What can I do to help?"

"That's the thing. I don't know where he is. I don't even know who his friends are, besides me. I thought maybe you'd be able to find him."

"He worked for me all summer, but he didn't really talk about his personal life. I really have no idea where he would be or who

he hangs out with." Cam shook her head. "How did you find out about Irene's death?"

"My cousin's a dispatcher. She knows Bobby and I are friends. She thought I might know where he is. The police are looking for him."

"Why?"

"I don't know. To notify him, I guess." Sim's voice shook.

"Sit down. I think you need a beer or something stronger. Yes?"

Sim agreed and sat at the dining table. Cam poured them each a glass of ale from a half-full growler the brewery had given her last night. So what if it was only ten o'clock in the morning? It was five o'clock somewhere. Sim drained half her glass straight off. Cam refilled it and sat.

"What were you saying about pigs, Sim?"

Sim shuddered. Her face drew in like she'd seen a demon.

"Tell me." Cam covered Sim's hand with her own.

"The cops said Irene was found in a pigsty. Half the flesh was eaten off her legs by the pigs." Sim laid her head on her arms on the table.

Cam gasped. She squeezed her eyes shut, but the image was worse. And when she reopened them, Sim was still there. The nightmare was still there.

"A pigsty?" Cam shuddered at the awful vision. A body, Irene Burr's body, in a pigsty. On a pig farm.

Sim nodded mutely.

"How did she get into a pigsty?"

"I don't know. Somebody saw her Jag parked at the edge of the woods."

Cam's eyes widened. "Wait. Whose farm?"

"The Jag was next to a path that leads to the Fisher farm."

"Oh, no! But why didn't she get out?" Cam stared at her, the realization sinking in. "This wasn't an accident, was it? Did your cousin say—"

"Not an accident. Irene was murdered." Sim slammed her hand on the table, making the vase jump. An orange nasturtium slid away from its mates and lay beached on the old oak of the table. "Lots of people would have been much happier if Irene disappeared, me included. I wouldn't kill her, but it doesn't surprise me somebody did."

Chapter 3

Sim drove off on her motorcycle after saying she had customers waiting at her shop. Cam trudged back to work, with the news weighing as heavily on her as a bushel of new potatoes. She stopped and leaned against the southern wall of the barn, its rough wood warmed by a sun finally shining through the morning gloom, wood Bobby had hammered into place all summer long.

Poor Irene. Cam tried without success to banish the image of hungry, snuffling pigs chewing on Irene's flesh. She fervently hoped Irene had been dead or at least unconscious before that happened. Who would have gone so far as killing Irene? And why on Howard's farm?

The thought that cheery, hardworking, flirty Bobby was missing, and did not know his stepmother was dead, also disturbed her deeply. She had to admit to herself what she hadn't said to Sim: maybe he had argued with Irene and somehow had accidentally killed her. And then had left town. She shook her head. It would be the act of a guilty person, not a grieving innocent.

Cam shook her head again. She had a farm to run. It was the police's business to figure out what had happened, not hers. She grabbed a pitchfork from inside the barn and emptied the tomato vines from the cart into the bin holding the newest compost in-gredients. She forked finished compost into the cart from the last bin in the row of four. The dark crumbly matter, more valuable to the soil than gold, was the result of mixing spent plants with fall leaves, horse manure from a neighboring farm, grass clippings, and kitchen waste. Cam turned the compost as often as she could. She sprinkled it with water as she worked and then let air, microorganisms, and worms do the rest of the work of breaking down the mix. She tried to find time, or sometimes a volunteer, to shift the working compost from bin to bin every week or two, which mixed and aerated it. By the time the compost hit the last bin, all the rough ingredients were combined, broken down, and ready to nourish the soil. As long as it had enough air in the process, the friable mix smelled as fresh as newly turned soil.

This particular cartload was destined to nurture next year's garlic crop. Cam dumped it on the recently vacated tomato beds and headed back to the barn. She brought the bag of seed garlic, a small knife, and a basket out to a picnic table Bobby had knocked together for her. As she sat separating the bulbs of Music and German Red into individual cloves, she searched her mind for where Bobby might be. Maybe he'd had an accident, too. Maybe he was sick in bed. Or maybe he was a killer on the run.

One of the bulbs was particularly tight around its central stalk. This was stiff-neck garlic, the kind that grew in a single row of fat cloves around a pencil-thick stalk. She also needed to plant the soft-neck garlic. It featured several concentric circles of cloves, so some were smaller, but it kept longer than the stiff-neck vari-eties. She'd made garlic braids out of the soft-neck garlic at the end of August, and customers loved them.

Cam poked the point of the knife into the middle of the tight bulb to try to separate the cloves from the stalk. She jabbed at it as if that would get Bobby found and would bring Irene back to life. The knife slipped and pierced her palm instead. She swore as she dropped the tool.

A rumble from the driveway made her look up from her wound. The rental truck loomed. Cam pressed her other thumb to the cut as she directed the driver back to the tent. He and a helper, a young man Cam had seen bagging groceries at the Food Mart earlier in the year, set to work collapsing the tables and chairs, while Cam fetched a bandage from the house for her palm. When she returned to the tent, the driver approached her, holding something white.

"Found this under a table." He gestured behind him with his head. "Somebody must have dropped it."

Cam thanked him. It was a small envelope, unsealed, with nothing written on the outside. She opened it and drew out a slip of paper. She glanced at it and looked up with a quick movement. Had the man read what was written on it? But he had returned to his work. She read it again.

MEET ME IN THE WOODS AT ELEVEN, OR I'LL TELL
WHAT I KNOW.
YOU KNOW WHERE.

The message in all capital letters was a threat. She'd bet a bushel of heirloom tomatoes it was meant for Irene Burr. Or maybe Irene had threatened someone else. The real question was, who was it from? She slipped the paper back into the envelope and strode to the house, holding the envelope by one of its corners. She checked Albert's yellowed phone list on the wall and dialed the numbers for the Westbury police station. She asked for Ruth Dodge.

"It might be connected to Irene Burr's death." Cam tapped

the countertop as she waited on hold. *Or I'll tell what I know,* the note read. If it was for Irene, she must have harbored secrets she didn't want made public knowledge. And if it was from Irene, who in town feared a secret revealed? Cam's own life had been pretty straightforward up to now. Sure, she had a fear of fires based on an incident in her childhood. If that became generally known, it would be more embarrassing than dangerous. She was an adult. Shouldn't she have been able to master the fear by now? But a secret that would allow someone to threaten her with disclosure of it? She had nothing.

"Pappas here," a voice barked into her ear. "Who am I talking to?"

Oh, crud. "Detective Pappas, what a pleasure," she lied. "It's Cam Flaherty." It had been anything but a pleasure working with the state police detective last June. He had to be in the local station, which could mean only one thing. Irene had been murdered.

"Ah, Ms. Flaherty."

"I heard my customer Irene Burr is dead." Cam didn't want to use the words "was killed," but the fact that Pappas was on the phone pretty much assured Irene had been murdered.

"Who did you hear it from?"

"A friend of Irene's stepson's."

"Name?"

"Sim Koyama. She's a mechanic—"

"I know who she is."

Cam summoned up her inner adult, not an easy task in the face of his responses. "So I'm sure you already know Irene was at an event at my farm last night."

"Yeah."

"Well, this morning, just now, in fact, the tent guy—"

"Tent guy?"

"I rented a tent. Guys from the rental company are here taking it down. One of them found an envelope on the ground and . . ." She rushed on, worried he might be losing his patience. "It has what I think is a threatening note in it."

"You *think?*"

"Look, Detective. Am I not doing the right thing? The guy found it, I read the note, and I walked straight into my house and called the authorities. Do you want to see it or not?" *Sheesh.* He was the one who had accused her of withholding evidence after Mike Montgomery was murdered on her farm. No wonder she'd heard less than positive gossip about Westbury's finest and their statie colleagues. Although Pappas didn't live in town, this area in the northeasternmost corner of Massachusetts seemed to constitute his state police beat.

He cleared his throat. "I'll come pick it up. I wanted to ask you a few questions, anyway. Be there in ten."

Nice of him to ask if now was a good time.

Apparently reading her mind, Pappas said, "If you'll be available."

"I'm here. Separating garlic."

"What the . . . ? Oh, never mind." The phone clicked off.

Cam finished splitting the last bulb into cloves. The discarded papery sheaths from the bulbs floated out of the basket on a new breeze.

The rental-agency truck was backing out when Pappas pulled in fast, nearly ramming the truck. Luckily, the driver leaned on the horn and the detective managed to swerve out of the way. Cam winced as she watched from the picnic table. The wheels of Pappas's older-model Saab dug into the edge of the perennial flower garden Great-Aunt Marie had planted and lovingly tended until right before her death a few years earlier.

Pappas approached Cam. His shirt, open at the neck, bore a web of wrinkles, and one side of the collar hid under his sport coat, while the other point skewed over the jacket. The laces on one of his black walking shoes flapped as he walked.

"You want to sit down?" Cam pointed to the bench on the other side of the table. She didn't think she'd ever seen him so disheveled. It was kind of a nice touch. In her earlier dealings with him he had always been neat to the point of fastidiousness. He seemed more human this way, less of an automaton.

He remained standing, so Cam stood, too, and slouched against the table. She didn't know if her two-inch height advantage bothered him or not. In her experience, most men didn't enjoy having to look up at a woman.

They exchanged brief greetings before Cam said, "I'll get the note. It's in the house."

Pappas shook his head. "First, show me where the dinner took place."

Cam gestured toward the back of the farm. She didn't know what he expected to find. The tent and furniture were gone. This wasn't the scene of the crime, anyway.

"I assume the fact that you are investigating means Irene was murdered," Cam said as they walked.

He nodded but didn't meet her eyes.

The closely mowed field where the tent had stood still bore signs of trampling from the guests, servers, and rental-agency guys. Clouds threatened the hour of sunshine that had blessed the day.

"Sim also told me Bobby Burr is missing," Cam said. "Have you had any luck finding him?"

Pappas walked away from her without answering, tracing the perimeter of the field. He narrowed his spiral with each cycle until he stood in the middle, his hands empty.

"I heard this Sim person threatened Irene." Pappas turned toward Cam. "Is it true?"

Uh-oh. "Who did you hear that from?"

"Did she?"

"It was simply conversational, I'm sure. I don't think Sim would hurt anyone."

"Is she a close friend of yours?"

"No. I only met her last night."

"I'm amazed at your confidence in people you know nothing about. Did Simone Koyama say, 'I'm going to get her' in regard to Irene Burr?"

Cam nodded. Better to keep her mouth shut than get in deeper than she already was. She wondered if Sim had a criminal record. Or, for that matter, if Bobby did. He was a competent and attractive carpenter. Cam had no idea if he or Sim actually had it in them to kill someone.

"Mr. Ames was also overheard arguing with Ms. Burr." Pappas rubbed his head.

Cam looked down at the matted grass without seeing it. She wondered who from the dinner had been talking to the police so soon. This was all taking on a surreal aspect, as if Pappas had had Irene under surveillance even before her death. She shook the thought off. It was a small town. People talked.

"Ms. Flaherty?"

"Yes. Wes Ames opposed Irene's plan to buy the Old Town Hall. I'm sure he wouldn't kill her simply to stop a sale, though."

Pappas raised his left eyebrow. "By the way, what did you do after the dinner was over last night?"

"I cleaned up and—" Cam stared at him. "Why do you want to know?"

"It's policy. Need to establish whereabouts of all concerned parties." He sounded like he was reciting from a manual.

"I didn't kill Irene, if that's what you mean by 'concerned.' I cleaned up and went to bed. It had been an exhausting day."

"What time did you go to bed?"

"I think it was ten forty-five."

"Anyone else on the property at that time?"

"Not that I know of."

"All right."

"I need to get back to work. Do you want the note?" At his nod, Cam led the way to the house. They walked in silence. As they neared the house, he spoke.

"What is it with you and murder . . . ?" Pappas's voice trailed off, sounding like he was almost too tired to finish the question.

"It's nothing with me and murder! You know I wasn't involved in Mike's murder. It just happened to occur in my greenhouse. And it's not my fault people argued with Irene at the dinner. Or that she turned up dead."

"Yeah. Don't get all defensive on me. Where's this reputed note, anyway? You're not the only one who needs to get back to work." He sank onto the top step of the back stairs.

"I'll get it." Cam let the screen door slam—maybe that would wake him up—and headed for the kitchen counter. She stopped and stared. The countertop looked the same as she had left it that morning. And there was no white envelope next to the phone. She checked all her pockets. Empty except for a piece of twine and a short pencil. Cam picked up the heavy black rotary phone, which must have been new four decades earlier. No note behind it. Nothing under it. She checked through the clutter. No note. What had she done with it? She thought back. She had walked in, put the note down, called Pappas, and gone back out to her garlic on the picnic table in the yard.

Gone back out. A chill crept around her heart. Before she'd resumed separating the bulbs, she hadn't locked the house door. When she'd shown Pappas the tent site, she thought they'd be out there only a minute, out of sight of the house for only a brief time. She knew she'd left the note on the counter. But it wasn't there.

Cam groaned. Now what was the detective going to think of her? He'd never believe her story. She decided to get the scene over with as quickly as possible and called to him to come in.

He obliged, grumbling, "Just hand over the evidence, Ms. Flaherty. Some of us have jobs besides planting garlic."

She shoved her hands in her pockets. "The note is gone. I left it right on the corner of the counter. It's not here."

"Oh, criminy, Cam."

His use of her nickname startled her. He'd always addressed her as either Cameron or Ms. Flaherty.

"Where did you see it last?" He cocked his head.

"I know it was here when I called you. All I did was go sit outside and split up garlic bulbs. In full sight of the house, I might add. Then we walked out back, where we weren't in sight of the house. Maybe whoever wrote it wanted to get it back and was watching me." Cam raised her eyebrows and cocked her head.

"Jeez, Louise. Either you have an imagination fitting a fantasy writer or you're . . . Well, let me know if this reputed note ever reappears. And don't waste my time unless you have something actually in hand, all right?"

"Wait. Whoever took could still be in here." She still felt a chill unrelated to the temperature. "Would you go through the house with me?"

He rubbed his head. "All right."

He stomped through the house and down the stairs without saying good-bye.

Cam swore to herself as she slammed the door shut behind him and threw the dead bolt. She knew she wasn't crazy. But the creep factor of thinking she was being watched lingered even though her house was clear. Suddenly, the prospect of working alone in the fields all afternoon lost its attraction.

Chapter 4

Two hours later Cam was back in the fields. After lunch and catching up on some bookkeeping, she resigned herself to the fact that farming didn't harbor indulgences like fear. She stuck her cell phone in her back pocket and made sure the door to the house was securely locked. She pocketed the house key, too.

Tomorrow was shareholder pickup day. She couldn't stand up her three dozen subscribers, most of whom were avid locavores, devoted to eating primarily locally grown food. Make that one less, now that Irene would no longer be claiming her share. Cam could donate the produce to the food bank in Newburyport. Or maybe she'd accept it as a slight lightening of her workload, selfish as that seemed.

She had squash to harvest, fall greens to cut, Brussels sprout stalks to gather, beets to dig, and so much more. She could postpone planting the garlic to another day. It only had to get in the ground anytime before the ground froze in December. At least today the sun had reemerged and the clouds had burned off. The night would get cold, but for the next few hours she could use some brightness in this day.

She was bent over the kabocha squash field, cutting the squat gray-green gourds from their stems, sunlight warming the back of her neck, when a woman's voice sounded right behind her. Cam straightened and whirled, knife extended.

"Hey, *fazendeira*. It's me. Thought you might want some help for tomorrow."

"Jeez, Lucinda! You about gave me a heart attack." Cam's heart was, in fact, thumping in her throat. She took a deep breath.

"Why are you so jumpy?"

Cam shook her head. "No reason."

"I heard about Irene. Tough business, right? That why you're nervous?" Lucinda shoved back her wild black curls and tied them into a knot as she trained her eyes on Cam.

"It's really tough. Did you hear about the—"

"Pigs? Crazy bad. The poor lady. And Bobby on the lam. I bet he killed her."

"Of course he didn't kill Irene! But where did you hear about it?"

"Oh, you know. It's all over Facebook, the noon news. If somebody *didn't* hear, I would be surprised."

"I suppose you're right. Pappas was here asking me all kinds of questions about last night. Hey, at least you didn't argue with her in public. You and I are about the only ones who didn't."

Lucinda began loading the cut gourds into the cart. "I guess I have to find a new housecleaning job. Too bad. Irene paid really well, and she never left a mess."

"Is it hard to find jobs?"

"Can be. You know of anybody who needs a cleaning service?"

"What about that lawyer, Susan Lee? I doubt she cleans her own house."

"I'll call her. Good idea." Lucinda drew her brows together. "Last week I heard Irene on the phone in her office while I was dusting the floorboards in the hallway. Half the time when I worked there, she wasn't even home. But this time she was, and she sounded really unhappy with somebody. Not scared, but not her usual bossy self."

"Any idea who was on the other end of the call?"

Lucinda shook her head. "I'll keep thinking about it, though. Sometimes when I let a thought hang around the back of my mind for a while, it pops up to me later."

Cam nodded in agreement. She'd had the same experience. "If you think of it, you need to tell Pappas. Will you do that?"

"I guess. He's so not my favorite guy. Last June, when he arrested me and then gave up looking for the real killer? Not good."

"I know. But Irene's killer shouldn't be wandering around free, and he's the detective on the case."

"Cart's full," Lucinda said. "You want me to take the gourds to the barn?"

"We have to lay them out to cure. I set up a board on sawhorses outside the southern wall of the barn. Can you arrange them there?" As Lucinda headed away, hauling the loaded cart behind her, Cam added, "Meet you in the root field."

Cam trudged, pitchfork in hand, to the long beds where she'd planted beets, daikon, rutabaga, carrots, parsnips, and turnips. Some would stay in the ground for a couple of additional months, sweetening up as the temperatures dropped. The parsnips she could leave in the ground to dulcify until well into winter, as long as she loosened the slender white taproot in its soil before the ground froze. The beet crop she was digging today had been an early planting, so the red orbs were fully mature.

As she dug, she wondered if Lucinda would in fact tell Pappas if she could recall who Irene had been talking with that day. Or if the information would advance the case at all. Cam frowned. Irene had imported and exported textiles and woven rugs. She might have had all kinds of foreign enemies if she dealt with her suppliers and customers the same way she treated locals. The last thing sleepy Westbury needed was a shadowy Tunisian rug merchant or an angry Asian silk dealer coming halfway around the world to exact revenge on Irene.

Cam tossed a handful of beets in a pile. Preston pounced out of nowhere, as if a beet had animated itself into a mouse.

"Mr. P, you haven't seen any mysterious foreigners around town, have you?" Cam snorted. An exotic stranger would be as easy to spot in this provincial town as a white Blankoma beet in a basket of Red Aces.

By the time the sun approached the tall maples and birches at the back of Cam's property, she and Lucinda had made a big dent in Cam's harvest list.

"I'll do the rest in the morning. Thanks for your help."

Lucinda waved good-bye and drove off in her beat-up Civic.

After Cam washed her hands in the kitchen, she surveyed her refrigerator and her erstwhile wine rack, which was a cardboard wine box on its side. A currently empty box. Food, she had— Jake had left her a container of leftovers from the dinner. All the wine had been finished off last night, and she and Sim had consumed the small amount of beer that had been left. She grabbed her keys and wallet and walked to her truck. Such delicious food really called out for a nice glass of wine to go with it.

She left the Westbury Food Mart, wine, a six-pack of beer, and a few groceries in hand. A quarter mile later, a bad-sounding bumping started coming from the right front of the truck. She pulled over and got out to look. She swore at the half-flat tire. She knew her spare hung under the bed of the truck, but in the year since Great-Uncle Albert had given her the old Ford, she'd never had to use it. It was probably rusted in place. Dark was falling, and the temperature was, too. The last thing she wanted to do was crawl under the vehicle, free up the spare, and wrestle rusty lug nuts on the side of the road. If only this had happened at the Food Mart or in her driveway at the farm.

She spied a sign for SK Foreign Auto two doors down. Sim's auto shop. "Yes!" She pumped her fist in the air. Then worried the shop might have closed for the day. She climbed back into the cab and drove the limping truck into the lot in front of the small shop. Lights shone out like a welcome beacon.

She slid her long legs out and moved toward the door. She halted. A panel van that had seen better days was parked in the dark on the side of the building. It looked a lot like the one Bobby Burr had driven to the farm most days over the summer. He had built shelves into the back of an old Ford Econoline to hold his carpentry supplies and tools. Cam thought about seeing if it was really his, but she had a flat tire to attend to first. She pulled open the door to the reception area. Sim stood, backlit, in the door to the garage bay and was speaking to someone Cam couldn't see.

"It's a mess, all right," she said before turning toward Cam. She shut the door to the garage quickly and folded her arms over her chest. Her eyes darted once to the door and back to Cam. "What do you need, Cam?"

"I'm on my way home from the Food Mart, and I just got a really bad flat. But who were you just talking to?"

"I was talking to myself. Spilled some oil in there."

"Oh. Anyway, would you help me change the tire?"

Sim raised her right eyebrow. "I'd have bet you were good with mechanical stuff."

"I am, usually. It's just that the spare is under the bed. It's probably rusted in place given the condition of the rest of the truck." She walked out to the truck. Sim followed.

Cam gestured at several patches of rust on the sides near the wheel wells. "I don't even know if I have a jack. It was my great-uncle's truck. I've been driving it for only a year."

"No one should drive around without a jack." Sim pursed her lips.

Cam opened her mouth to speak, but Sim held up a hand.

"Of course I'll change it for you. Don't worry. Can you hang on for a minute?"

Sim disappeared back inside. The door clicked firmly behind her. Cam waited, hugging herself from the cold, wishing she'd grabbed a thicker sweater.

Several minutes later one of the wide doors grumbled its way open, and Sim appeared in the opening. She told Cam to drive in and directed her onto the lift, which clanged twice as Cam's wheels found their positions.

"Emergency brake off. Leave it in neutral," Sim called as she closed the wide door again. She sauntered to the back of the shop and flipped on a radio. Speakers on a shelf above it played the latest by the Black Keys.

Cam climbed out and stood to the side. The space smelled of oil and rubber and dust.

Sim checked a few things and pulled a lever at the side of the bay. The truck rose into the air with periodic clunks. She stopped it when the wheels were at her shoulder height, and began to re-move the tire. She ducked underneath with a big wrench to whack the rusted part that secured the spare.

"The van out there looks a lot like Bobby's," Cam said. "Did he show up earlier today? What was his reaction to Irene's death?"

"What van?" Sim kept working.

"The Econoline. It's right around the side of the building."

"It's my cousin's." The wrench Sim held slipped and clattered on the cement floor. She swore, sucked on a scraped knuckle, picked it up again.

"So you never got hold of Bobby?" Cam glanced at the door to the reception area. The glass in the top portion was dark. When had Sim turned off the light? It had been on when Cam arrived. Cam supposed she could have been Skyping with somebody. Cam used the free Internet service herself on occasion to communicate with her parents when they were overseas, which was almost always.

Sim hauled the bad tire over to an air hose and filled it. She turned it, examining the worn black rubber all over. She straightened.

"You need a new tire." She checked the other three tires remaining on the truck. "Girlfriend, you won the lottery. You need a whole new set. Treads are way too smooth for safety."

Cam groaned. This was an expense she hadn't planned for.

"I'll put the spare on for now, if it's any good. You can think about the new set, but I wouldn't wait too long. It'll be snowing before you know it." She gestured toward a grimy molded plastic chair that had started life white. "Make yourself comfortable."

It took Sim only a few minutes to add air to the spare, mount it, and lower the truck. After she tightened the final lug nut, she threw the bad wheel in the back of the truck. "It's a full-size spare, so you're okay to drive around town." Sim wiped her hands on a red rag.

"What do I owe you?"

"Nothing." Sim waved her off with a frown.

"You sure?" Cam stood.

Sim nodded.

"Can I bring the truck in for an oil change on Monday?" Cam asked. "It's overdue, and I don't think I need to go anywhere that day."

Sim checked her smart phone and gave Cam the thumbs-up. She tapped in the appointment. "Have it here by eight, all right?"

Cam agreed and thanked Sim, who raised the garage door and stepped outside. She directed Cam as she backed out. Sim waved and reentered the shop, lowering the door after her.

Cam paused to glance at the side of the building. The van was gone.

Chapter 5

A glass of red wine accompanied Cam as she settled onto the old couch in her living room. Preston settled himself onto a pile of newspapers on the floor, crackling the paper as he got comfortable. The leftovers had been perfect.

She pressed the TV remote and wandered through the channels, hoping for an old movie or maybe an interesting History Channel show. She passed the local news channel and then backed up. A senior reporter was interviewing Howard Fisher.

"Tell us again what happened on your farm this morning, Mr. Fisher." The slender woman, her silver-streaked hair perfectly arrayed around her face, held the microphone toward the farmer with a look that said she was listening only to him.

Howard cleared his throat. "I was going out to feed them. The pigs. They eat a lot, you know. And I saw her. It was terrible." The fingers on his right hand scrabbled nervously on his leg. He wore the same clothes Cam had always seen him in, but the contrast between his worn work outfit and the reporter's stylish red jacket and slim black skirt made him look shabbier than usual.

"Describe what you saw for us." Her tone implied great drama.

"Well, it was that Ms. Burr. She was lying in the sty, and the pigs was chewing on her legs. She's always wearing those nice clothes, but she was muddy and . . ." He shuddered. "She was just plain dead, all right."

"Do you know how she got in there?"

Howard shook his head several times. "No idea. She had no business there."

"Were you at a farm-to-table dinner last night?"

"It was up to that Cam Flaherty's farm. Attic Hill Farm, used to be called. Now she's got some fancy new name for it."

Cam groaned. Drag her and her farm into it. The kind of publicity she didn't need.

"Produce Plus Plus Farm. Irene Burr was there, as well. Is that correct, sir? Did you speak to Ms. Burr there?"

"Maybe." Harold tossed his head. "They were cooking my pork at the dinner, so I went. Don't like that kind of affair, generally." He turned half away, seeming to listen to someone. He nodded as he faced the camera again. "That's all I got to say."

The reporter thanked him and turned back to face to the camera. "As the authorities pursue persons of interest in the case, we'll continue to follow these dramatic events, bringing you the latest news about tragic death in the sty."

Cam clicked off the set. Her own farm hadn't gotten dragged too far into the affair. But she was willing to bet customers wouldn't be clamoring to eat pork from Howard Fisher's farm now.

Cam arose a few minutes after sunrise the next morning. She had knocked off work too early the day before and needed to bring in the rest of the harvest before the first subscribers arrived at noon. She put the coffee on, flicked on the radio, and powered up the computer. The local radio news said nothing about Bobby showing up or about Irene's murder other than "No arrest has been made in the case." She checked the news online and didn't learn anything new. She printed out her harvest list before locking the door.

She trudged to the barn, wearing her work sweater. The day would warm up later, but for now the dawn air was cool, despite the sunshine slanting over the neighbor's field. She sighed. Farming solo was a big job. When it weighed heavily on her, she imagined being in a partnership with a man who might be her lover and her fellow grower in one package. That she might find such an ideal person seemed like a fantasy at this point. Maybe she should break down and hire a farmhand instead.

With a start she realized she hadn't even given a thought to Jake yesterday. He'd been jealous at the dinner event, despite their series of very enjoyable dates over the summer. Cam had done nothing to provoke his ire. He imagined flirtation where there was none, at least not on her part. Or was there? Bobby was certainly cute. Competent. Fit. Smart.

Cam questioned again the wisdom of being entangled romantically with Jake. She relied on him to buy and promote her organic produce. The orders she delivered to the restaurant made a big difference to her business's bottom line. She couldn't afford to lose Jake as a customer, and she usually enjoyed his company. She sighed again, grabbed her field scissors and a basket, and headed out through grass wet with dew to cut three dozen bunches of greens.

Back in her kitchen at ten thirty, Cam popped a last bite of toast in her mouth and took her second cup of coffee out of the microwave. She had an hour and a half to finish up before the subscribers arrived. She sat at the computer to check the two recipes she planned to print for them, a little extra bonus she threw in every week. It particularly helped the customers who weren't accustomed to cooking a surfeit of fresh vegetables. This week she had typed up a recipe for stuffed baked kabocha squash with rosemary and shallots. Jake had agreed to share his recipe for the sweet potato empanada appetizer from the farm-to-table event, so she'd transcribed that, too. Luckily, she'd written it down a couple of days before the dinner. If she'd asked him after the dinner, he might not have been so forthcoming.

"Crud," Cam said. Rosemary. She hadn't cut the bouquets of herbs yet. Well, that was an easy job. A lot easier than being friendly and sociable to her subscribers for the three-hour window during which they drifted in to collect their weekly assortment of roots, fruits, and greens. Being chatty seemed to be a requirement of the job of a farmer with regular customers. While it was getting a little easier for Cam since she'd started, she still preferred to be alone with either a collection of software bugs or an infestation of asparagus beetles.

She hurried out the door with the sheaf of papers. She got halfway to the barn, dashed back to lock the door, and hurried to the table inside the barn where she'd already set up most of the week's offerings.

"Cam, want some help?" Ellie popped around the corner of the barn. The petite girl wore a red-striped soccer jersey, short glossy black shorts, and black and red socks pulled up over knee pads, with a black fleece thrown over her shoulders. "My dad dropped me off early so I could give you a hand. We won our second game. I even scored a goal."

"Nice job. Sure, I could use some help. Can you cut rosemary, parsley, thyme, and sage? You know the drill. Three dozen bunches. The trug is a good basket for that."

"Sweet." Ellie sauntered over to grab scissors and the flat basket with a handle from the back of the barn. "Hey, I heard that Irene lady was killed. That's wicked bad."

Cam agreed.

46

"Did they, like, catch anybody yet?" A shadow passed over the teen's cheery, chatty mood.

"As of earlier this morning there was no arrest. I feel bad for Mr. Fisher. They found her on his farm." Cam glanced at Ellie's worried look. "I'm sure there's nothing to be afraid of. It had to be someone with a grudge against Ms. Burr."

Ellie nodded. "I bet you're glad it didn't happen here. Again."

Cam agreed, then exclaimed, "I forgot the Brussels sprouts! See you back here." She grabbed a pair of long-handled loppers and hauled the cart out back. They had an hour until customers arrived, but cutting the thick stalks could be tough.

The three-foot-tall plants with their orbs clustered on them like alien eyes grew in the field farthest back toward the woods. She should leave them to sweeten up as the weather grew colder, but the shares were a bit scant this week. As she recalled, she'd planted enough for several weeks of harvest, anyway.

Cam bent over the first plant and lopped off the inch-thick woody stem right above the ground. She let it fall away and moved on to the next one. She was about to cut it when a small green cabbage worm fell onto her wrist.

Cam swore as she dropped the tool. She knocked the worm to the ground and smashed it with her boot. If cabbage moths had infested her crop with their larvae, no one would want to eat the sprouts. She examined the rest of the plant. A few leaves showed holes, but most of it looked fine, and the sprouts themselves didn't display evidence of being eaten away. She quickly strode down the row. The plants at the far end showed more worm damage, so she pulled four up by their roots and threw them as far as she could into the border of the woods.

She checked her watch. Resuming lopping, Cam counted as she went until she'd cut enough stalks. She gathered up an armful and started toward the cart.

"Cam," a voice called in a loud whisper.

Cam dropped the stalks where she stood. She looked around her with quick moves of her head. It wasn't Ellie's voice. She couldn't see anyone. Her heart thumped as her skin prickled with cold fear.

"I'm here," the voice went on. "Here," it urged.

She grabbed the loppers. The voice came from the woods, from near where she'd tossed the infested plants. There was something familiar about it.

"Who's there?" Her voice barely emerged. She tried again, and this time it rang clear. She trained her eyes on the spot where she thought the person was hiding.

A head leaned out from behind a thick maple. Bobby Burr's head.

Cam closed her eyes for a moment and let the threat subside in her body. She opened them and walked toward him until they were face-to-face.

"What are you doing here? Why are you back there?" She took a close look at him. A brown pine needle stuck out of his black hair. He was dressed in old jeans and a sweatshirt. His face bore a smudge of dirt. It was his eyes that alarmed her. They looked like he had seen the abyss.

"Are you all right?" Cam asked.

He didn't speak. His eyes darted around the field in front of him.

"You heard Irene was killed, didn't you?"

"Yes, Cam, I heard." He kept his voice low and urgent. "I also heard the police are looking for me."

"Well, sure. You're her stepson. So you talk to them. You didn't kill her, right?"

He shook his head at a funereal pace.

"So? Come to the house. You look like you could use a cup of coffee, maybe some breakfast."

"No! I can't. You don't understand."

"Make me understand."

"It's complicated." Bobby stared at the trees. "After the dinner, Irene and I—"

"Cam?" Ellie's voice called out from a distance. "Subscribers are here."

Cam looked over her shoulder, but she couldn't see Ellie. "Be right there," she called in return. She started to speak to Bobby as she turned back. But he wasn't there. He was running, crashing through the brush, disappearing back into the woods.

"Bobby, wait! Let's talk." Cam started after him, but he didn't slow and soon was out of sight. She pulled to a halt, wishing she could help him. However, she had a business to run. Still, as she returned to the sprouts, she wished he'd finished telling her what had happened between him and Irene after the dinner. And wondered if she should tell Pappas she'd seen him.

Chapter 6

About half the subscribers had dropped by to pick up their shares when Wes Ames entered the barn, carrying the market basket Felicity usually had in hand. Cam was in the middle of explaining how to roast winter squash to Diane Weaver, a subscriber who had signed up in midsummer, when she saw Preston sidle up to Wes. The cat reared up and rubbed his head against Wes's knee.

Wes quickly looked down with widened nostrils and curled lip. "Get away." He swatted at Preston with the basket.

"Hey, be nice!" Cam called. What did he have against the sweetest cat in the Northeast?

Preston stared at Wes for a moment before beelining it for the door.

Cam cleared her throat and continued speaking with Diane. Wes approached them and tapped Cam on the shoulder.

"Just one minute, Wes," Cam said before finishing her explanation. Anybody who would swat at a cat could just wait.

Diane, dressed in black jeans and a cream-colored Costa Rica T-shirt, thanked her. "I wanted to tell you that my daughter and

I put up twenty-two jars of tomato sauce last month. It was my first time canning anything." She beamed.

"That's great." Cam's mouth ached from smiling for the past two hours. Would she ever get used to schmoozing?

"I'm going to take a little walk around the fields, if you don't mind. It's so satisfying to see where my dinner is growing."

Cam assured her it was fine. Diane cast an odd look at Wes as she hefted her two cloth bags stuffed with produce. Cam turned to Wes. He glared at Diane's retreating form. Cam groaned inwardly. The last thing she needed was conflict between her customers. Or any conflict, when it came right down to it.

"What did you need, Wes?"

He started, glancing at Cam. "Oh. I heard Irene Burr died. Was murdered, is what they're saying."

"Yes, it's very sad news." Cam sniffed. She thought she detected the unmistakable aroma of marijuana.

"Did they arrest anybody yet?"

Everybody seemed to think Cam knew more than any other resident of the town.

"I don't know. I've been working all day. As of last night, they hadn't." She didn't see any reason to let Wes know Detective Pappas had been to the farm, asking questions.

"Looks like we don't lose our town hall to some museum, after all." A satisfied look on his face, Wes folded his arms.

"Wes! A woman lost her life—a person from this town—and you're thinking about town property?"

A customer bagging greens turned at Cam's raised voice.

"Well, it's an important issue around here." Wes gestured with a broad sweep of his arm. "But you're right. I should have kept my mouth shut."

Cam opened hers and shut it again. She thought she'd gotten to know Wes a bit over the summer. He was a tall, aging hippie who doted on and cooked for his wife. He also harbored a bit of paranoia about the police. But his reaction to Irene's death shook Cam.

The ding of a bicycle bell rang out, followed by Alexandra striding into the barn, blond braids swinging, eyes shining, bags swinging from one hand.

"You wouldn't believe what I just heard!"

Cam's heart sank. She hoped the news would not be Bobby being arrested or someone else dying, or anything else disastrous. *Let it not be more bad news.*

A customer selecting squash spoke up. "Did they catch that lady's killer?"

Alexandra threw her hands in the air, suddenly the focus of everyone's attention. "How would I know? I'm all about chickens. Cam, remember last month I told you I thought you should get some chickens?"

Cam nodded vaguely as she let out a breath of relief.

"I heard of a farm that's going to lose its chickens because they were neglected. We can have them for free. We can rescue them." Her zeal lit up the air with a brilliance impossible to miss. "My friend DJ and I can pick them up tomorrow."

Even as she foresaw a myriad of problems, Cam couldn't help smiling.

"Let's take it off-line, Alexandra, okay? It could work, but we'll need to discuss it a little more."

The young woman nodded. "I'll help you build the coop. I've been studying the whole chicken deal. You know you can temporarily pen them around raspberry bushes, and it's a perfect symbiotic relationship. The bushes shade the chickens and give them bugs to eat, and the hens keep the soil weed free and aerated. You really can't lose."

"We'll sit down and work it out. Just not right now, all right?"

Alexandra agreed and set about assembling her share.

"Hey, what happened to the fish shares?" Wes asked Alexandra. Earlier in the year Cam had agreed to let her farm be a pickup site for a community-supported fishery as long as it was at the same time as her shareholder pickup. Cam hadn't signed up. With everything else happening, she hadn't realized the fish truck was missing today.

"You got an e-mail survey," Alexandra said. "Not enough people wanted to renew their shares or bothered responding, so we're off the distribution route. It's our loss."

Wes, carrying a full basket, left without saying good-bye a few moments later. Cam fluffed up the herb bundles in their jar of water and straightened a bunch of flowers in the bucket on the floor. She consolidated the remaining pile of squash and made sure the greens looked fresh and sufficient. She wandered into the sunshine outside the wide door and lowered herself onto the solid bench facing the back of the farm. She closed her eyes for just a moment, inhaling the aroma of still-fresh wood, a whiff of drying herbs, the scent of chrysanthemums warmed by the sun.

"You are doing a splendid job out there."

Cam's eyes flew open. Diane Weaver sat on the bench next to her.

"Sorry. I must have dozed off. What did you say?"

"I said the fields look great." Diane gestured toward the back of the property.

"Well, they looked a lot better in late June, but thanks. The weeds have been getting away from me lately." Cam wrinkled her nose.

"I thought I saw someone back in the woods. Do you have a neighbor who hikes around in there?"

Bobby. "A neighbor," Cam lied. "Right." Had he been looking for her again?

"About Wes Ames." Diane half turned on the bench to face Cam. "Have you known him long?"

"Since last spring. Why?"

"Just curious. I've heard him speak up around town about the Old Town Hall. Did you know he's the volunteer maintenance person for the building? The town loves it because they don't have to pay anybody."

"He sure seems adamant about keeping the old building as town property," Cam said, waving good-bye to a shareholder.

Diane nodded. "Do you have any idea why he's so set on that?"

"He speaks of it like a town treasure, which I'm sure it is." Cam stood. "I should get back inside and do my happy farmer routine." She grimaced. "That didn't sound too nice, did it?"

"Hey, I'm an introvert by nature, too." Diane rose, said good-bye, and walked off.

Alexandra emerged from the barn door. A cell phone held high in the air, she turned in several directions until she spied Cam, then rushed toward her.

"Call for you on your cell. It was ringing, so I picked it up. I didn't know if you left it inside on purpose, but—"

"Thanks." Cam reached for the phone, but it dropped in transit, stirring up a miniature mushroom cloud of dry dirt where it fell. It stopped ringing.

"Crap. Sorry, dude." Alexandra reached for it and retrieved it from the dirt. She handed it to Cam.

The display was dark. She pressed a few buttons, tried to turn the power off or on, rubbed it on her shorts. No response.

"That might have been the last straw for this old girl," Cam said. "It's a first-generation smart phone. They don't live forever."

"Put it in a bag of rice in the freezer. Sometimes that revives them." Alexandra looked hopeful as only an idealistic twentysomething could.

"I think that's for when they get wet, isn't it? The rice draws out the moisture."

"Whatever. Anyway, I'm all set with my share. When can we talk about the chickens? It's pretty urgent. They needed rescuing, like, last week." She set fists on hips.

"Oh, boy. I was hoping to relax a little tomorrow. But I admit, hens would be a great addition to the farm. Everybody seems to want local eggs. Your idea of fencing them around the raspberries is good, too, at least during the day. Can you wait until the last customer picks up? Then we'll open a beer and go through the issues."

"Righteous." Alexandra thumbed her own smart phone and looked up. "I'll bring up the pictures for you."

Cam silently echoed the younger woman's "Whatever."

By the time the last shareholder had straggled in, collected his share, and left, it was almost three o'clock. Cam proffered a glass of local beer to Alexandra and motioned her to a lawn chair. Grasping her own glass, she lowered herself into a matching chair under the old sugar maple in the yard. Sure enough, the day had warmed to the high seventies with the Indian summer sunshine. Most of the leaves had turned a brilliant red, and a scattering of them decorated the grass under the tree.

"Cheers." The two women clinked glasses and sipped in silence for a moment.

"So give me the scoop about the chickens that need to be rescued." Cam hoped it wasn't a crazy scheme. She liked Alexandra and her enthusiasm for all things local. Plus, she was a strong, dedicated volunteer. Cam didn't want to lose her.

Alexandra leaned in. "I'm active in an underground rescue league." She looked around and lowered her voice. "That's how I knew about Howard Fisher mistreating his pigs. And last night I got a text alert about a farmer who's been busted for neglecting her chickens. Penning them up, starving them. The health inspector wants to destroy the birds, but it looks like our group can save them. Are you in?"

Cam sat back in her chair. She took another cool sip before she responded. "I really admire your tender heart, and I would love to have chickens on the farm. Everybody always wants to know when I'll have local eggs. But how do we know we can save the hens? Does your group do it legally?"

"Don't worry. It's legal. We have it under control."

"Are the birds diseased?" Cam wrinkled her nose. "And do abused hens ever lay eggs again after they get happy, or whatever their tiny brains understand as happiness? I wonder if you've thought about these issues."

"Well, they aren't diseased. If they were, they'd have to be put down. Like I said, we can pick them up tomorrow."

"Who's *we?*"

"Me, DJ—he's a dude who works on urban farming issues—my sister, and a couple others. And from what DJ says, hens usually recover really well once they're well nourished and protected."

"And we'll have to build a coop. That's going to cost something." Cam felt tired even considering the new venture. "How many birds are we talking, anyway? Ten or a hundred?"

"I think there are three or four dozen. You'll need a covered run, too, so they won't be picked off by hawks and stuff. But I told you, we have a team, and we're going to do all the work."

"It's a lot to take on. I'm kind of overwhelmed by my workload even without chickens."

Alexandra stood. "Are you in or not? These poor hens are going to die. Do you want their deaths on your head?" Hands on hips, she fixed Cam with a look that wasn't hostile, but it certainly challenged Cam to answer.

"As long as you build the coop, find the food, and tell me how to take care of them, yes, I'm in." Cam also stood. "Are you in for spending the day tomorrow building whatever our rescue fowl need?"

The younger woman beamed as she nodded.

"And will you go home right now and research what they eat? I need you to take the lead on this project."

"You bet. I'll borrow a car and pick up whatever the Agway down in Middleford has in stock for feed. Then we can figure out the most cost-effective place to order more from." She reached out and wrapped her arms around Cam and then released her. "Thanks! I know you won't regret it." Alexandra hoisted her pack of produce onto her back and headed for her bicycle.

"Wait a sec. What local farmer is neglecting fowl, anyway?" Cam asked.

Alexandra paused for a moment and turned. "Bev Montgomery. Not good news, I know."

Cam frowned in dismay. The mother of the man murdered in Cam's hoop house earlier in the year was a troubled woman, but Cam wouldn't have thought she'd be so hard-hearted as to starve a collection of chickens.

After Alexandra cycled away, Cam wandered out behind the barn. She had to figure out the best place to locate the chicken coop. Probably near the barn, so it would be easy to get to their feed. She'd need to install a small refrigerator in the barn to keep the eggs cool, too. Wait. Several dozen chickens? She might need a full-size fridge. She realized she had no idea how many eggs a few dozen hens would lay once they were healthy.

Even if Alexandra was positive this venture would work, Cam wasn't so sure she should be taking on so much extra work. She'd been invited to share a guest table at the thriving Newburyport Farmers' Market the next day as a trial run. The Tuesday market in Haverhill had started out the year as a bustling enterprise, but by the fall customer interest had dwindled. Some of the farmers had stopped coming, so then even fewer customers showed up. Cam didn't know if it was the fault of Bev Montgomery, who was the market manager. Cam relied on a heavily traveled market day to bring in cash throughout the season. She might have to switch to the Sunday market instead. Bev wasn't going to like hearing that Cam was both getting her hens and withdrawing from the market.

What the guest table also meant was that her day wasn't over yet. She pulled her phone out and tried it. Grateful to see it working again, she checked to see who had called her when the phone dropped earlier. A message was from Lucinda, who said she'd be happy to come back and work for a couple of hours. There was one problem solved.

Chapter 7

Shadows were long by the time the two women called it a day.
Cam would cut and bag salad greens, as well as herbs, early in
the morning, before heading to the market's opening at nine. She
and Lucinda had loaded the truck with several bushels of squash.
Leeks poked their pointy leaves out of a bucket of water in the
barn. Buckets of kale and chard also stood ready, as did a basket
of cured garlic. A flat box held berry boxes of Cam's prize gold
cherry tomatoes.

They'd even picked a half bushel of what Cam would adver-
tise as "Organic Sauce Apples." The fruit from the one antique
tree on the property was mottled and dimpled, but it had a deep,
old-fashioned flavor that made Cam want to wear a long skirt and
have her beau take her riding in a surrey. She reminded herself
once again to ask Albert if he knew what the apple variety was.

She thanked Lucinda for coming as they sat on the bench outside the barn. "Kind of nuts to do a market the day after pickup
day, isn't it?"

"You planted enough stuff, so you'll be okay. I've been to the
Newburyport market. It's pretty amazing. Besides the produce,

they got cheese makers, bread, wine, even live music. All local. And lots of customers, too. Feels kind of like a festival."

Cam's thoughts turned to Bobby popping out of the trees this morning and disappearing back into them.

"Can I ask you something?" Cam said. "You housecleaned for Irene." She described the threatening note the tent guy had found the day before. "I'm thinking it has to be either for Irene or from her, right? Do you have any idea, you know, from being in her house, what that might have been about?"

Lucinda's laugh was a peal of bells. "Seriously? I think she had a good heart, but she didn't know how to get along with people. Everybody seemed to do the wrong thing in her eyes. I was the only one she wasn't mean to."

"Why?"

Lucinda raised both hands. "I didn't let her push me around, I guess. She told me once I reminded her of her younger sister."

"Maybe that was it."

"I guess. But you shoulda heard some of the stuff she said about other people." She shook her head. "Whoa."

"Like what?"

"Like Bobby was a weasel, that he wanted her money without working for it."

"I overheard something like that at the dinner. After she said it, he even suggested that maybe Irene had killed his father."

"Yeah, she was always going on about that. She said, 'Poor dear Zebulon, bless his heart.'" Lucinda had switched into a perfect imitation of Irene's clear Boston Brahmin pronunciation. "'He died of natural causes, and that Bobby shouldn't soil his memory.'" Lucinda snorted.

"But Bobby is such a talented carpenter. Look at this." Cam gestured to the barn. "Why would she even want him working for her? And doing what? Selling textiles?"

"Irene was about seventy. I think she saw her own death coming. She didn't have any children of her own. She built up the business by herself, and I think she wanted to leave it to somebody. But Bobby's not the right one."

"Who else did she mention when you were around her?" Cam asked.

"She had some kind of relationship with Fisher, the pig guy. I don't know what it was. I overheard her talking about money to somebody named Howard once, and another time his truck was driving away when I arrived."

"She probably bought pork from him."

"Yeah."

"I overheard Irene mention her real son. Did she ever talk about him?"

"No. But that Sim girl? The mechanic?" Lucinda wrinkled her nose. "Irene needed her to fix the Jaguar, but she was always ragging on Sim. Irene would pick up the car and call Sim once she got home, yelling that there was a scratch on the door or a bit of dirt on the floor mat. Once Irene gave me a ride home. We stopped by Sim's shop, and Irene chewed her out. 'Don't you know this is a nineteen ninety Jaguar?' " Lucinda again imitated Irene's patrician diction. She shook her head. "No wonder somebody killed her."

After Lucinda left, Cam fixed herself a quick omelet with sautéed leeks, a bit of chopped rosemary, and the end of a piece of Brie. As she ate it with sourdough toast and washed it down with a glass of red wine, she reflected that sometime soon she could be making omelets with eggs from her own hens. An intriguing thought.

The temperature was falling. She went around closing windows, making sure they were all locked, before pulling on a thick sweater. She was beat, and tomorrow's alarm would ring early. She sat at the computer and pulled up her e-mail to find a new one from her former colleague, fellow geek, and friend Tina, which read, Call me! So she did.

They chatted for a few minutes. Cam answered Tina's questions about the murder, which she'd seen described on television, including the reference to Cam's farm.

"So I got laid off last week," Tina said. " 'Reduction in force.' "

"You're their best coder. They're idiots to do that. But you won't have any trouble finding something else, I'll bet."

"It's an occupational hazard of working in high tech. Anyway, I have some feelers out." Tina laughed. "And for sure, I'm not taking up farming instead."

"Hey, it's working for me. Of course, having a great-uncle who offered me his farm right after I was laid off last year did help."

"I've been meaning to say something about that goofy farm name you chose. You take a perfectly good name, Attic Hill Farm, and change it to Produce Plus Plus? That's crazy stuff, Cam."

"I know, but now I'm stuck with it."

"Are you sure? You know we haven't even coded in C++ since you left. It's C Sharp now."

Cam groaned. "Great. Maybe I'll change it back to Attic Hill. I never did get around to getting a sign made for the road, and business cards are cheap." Cam snapped her head to the right. There was a soft rapping on the glass of her back door. She checked the time. Seven o'clock.

"Hey, I gotta run," Cam said. "Somebody's here."

"Hot date on a Saturday night?"

The rapping sounded again.

Cam called out, "Just a minute," in the general direction of the door. "Not a chance," she said to Tina. "I don't know who it is, actually." They said their good-byes, promising to get together soon, and disconnected.

Cam walked to the door and pulled aside the white lace curtain, another of Great-Aunt Marie's touches Cam hadn't seen any reason to change.

Nobody was there. But someone had stood near the house recently. The motion-detector floodlight illuminated the back porch and the brick patio beyond it. She unlocked the window next to the door and opened it slowly. She stuck her head out and looked both ways. She couldn't see a soul.

"Hello?" she called out into the cool darkness beyond the pool of light. No answer.

Cam closed and locked the window. Maybe it had been Bobby, coming back to ask for help. Why hadn't he stayed? He might have thought she had guests because she was talking on the phone. Who else would be rapping on her door if not him? She shuddered and shot the dead bolt.

Chapter 8

At two minutes before nine the next morning, Cam finished setting out her business cards on her table at the Newbury-port Farmers' Market. The other guest vendor had canceled, the market manager told her, so she was able to spread her wares out. A white tent top identical to the several dozen others shielded her from the morning sun. She fluffed up the lettuce heads and was straightening the bunches of leeks when the gong rang, signaling the start of market. Customers already milled about, chatting with vendors, hefting a fat eggplant here, a bunch of scallions there. Once the gong rang, business commenced.

The Herb Farmacy was across the way. The farmer, who Cam had met at the Locavore Festival last spring, gave a quick wave before turning to a buyer. Cam greeted the cheese maker from Hickory Nut Farm next to her and proceeded to sell two squashes and a bunch of oregano, rosemary, and sage to an eager customer.

She had been selling for about an hour and was tapping her foot to a bluegrass tune this week's band was playing when two big hands covered her eyes.

"Guess who?" a deep voice whispered in her ear.

Cam grabbed Jake's hands off her eyes and turned toward him. His smile was devilish, particularly combined with one raised eyebrow. He wore his usual today—black-and-white checked pants paired with a white double-breasted chef's shirt. He carried two cloth shopping bags.

"How's my favorite farmer?" He bent his head down until their noses nearly touched.

The usual rush she felt when she was next to him heated her cheeks. He seemed to have gotten over his snit from the night of the dinner.

"I'm fine," Cam said. "This is a great market, isn't it? I'm thinking of switching to selling here instead of at the Haverhill market on Tuesdays."

"It rocks. I usually stroll down here to see what's special on Sunday morning and then revise my menu accordingly." Jake's restaurant was only a few blocks away.

"How much is the kale?" a young woman asked. She stood with her arm around the waist of another woman.

As Cam turned back toward the table, Jake gave her own waist a little squeeze. "See you tomorrow night? It's my turn to cook." They'd made a habit of having dates on Monday nights, the only night the restaurant was closed. "Six o'clock."

"It's two dollars a bunch." Cam watched Jake out of the corner of her eye as he left even as she took the customer's money and thanked her. He sampled the goat cheese at the next table and bought ten logs. He strolled to the specialty vinegars and olive oils. Despite his height and heft, he moved with a flowing grace she could watch all day. She didn't really focus on her table until he disappeared around the corner of the aisle.

A young man with a baby boy in a carrier on his back handed Cam four SNAP tokens in exchange for a bag of mixed greens.

"I already swiped my card with the market manager." His look of tired patience indicated he had explained the system more often than he cared to. "They're dollar tokens—"

"I know." Cam smiled at him. "We welcome tokens. I think they're great." But he was the first customer to use the Supplemental Nutrition Assistance Program at Cam's table since the market had opened. She reflected that Newburyport attracted a different demographic than Haverhill, where customers using food stamps for fresh produce were much more numerous.

Ruth Dodge appeared with her daughters, Natalie and Nettie, during the prenoon lull. Every market had its lull point. The Newburyport market ran from nine to one, so the end of the eleven o'clock hour was quiet. Cam was sure it would get frantic in the last sixty minutes. People came after church fellowship hour. An absentminded type might remember the farmers' market, check the clock, and head down here. Bargain hunters knew many vendors lowered their prices during the last fifteen to thirty minutes. Whatever the reason, the lull period was a good time to take a quick bathroom break, straighten up the display, or actually sit for a few minutes before it got busy again.

"Hey, Ruth. Hi, girls." Cam stood to greet them.

"Hi, Ms. Cam." Nettie bounced on her heels, her dark curls bouncing, too. "Can I have a tomato?" She reached for one of the gold cherries.

"Nettie, those are for sale," Ruth said, staying her daughter's hand. Ruth, clearly off duty, wore her Mom uniform of jeans and a pink Red Sox T-shirt. "But I'll buy us a basket. Natalie, do you want one, too?"

The blond-haired twin hid behind her mother as she shook her head.

"You don't have to buy them," Cam said. She picked out the best-looking basket and handed one of the tomatoes to the girl. "Natalie, is there anything here you like?"

Natalie nodded slowly. She pointed to the kale, its dark gray-green leaves curled around purple veins.

Cam glanced at Ruth, who smiled.

"Let me help you get a leaf out. That's a healthy food to like," Cam said. She extracted a stem and handed it to the little girl, who wore a red tracksuit and miniature sneakers. Her more adventurous sister was decked out in striped tights, a denim dress, and a little fleece vest.

"This is a great place to shop," Cam said to Ruth as the girls munched their snacks.

Ruth nodded absently. She glanced around the crowd. She was clearly in the habit, uniform or no uniform, of someone accustomed to having her radar up for wrongdoing.

Cam lowered her voice. "Any news about the case?"

"Not that I can share. Detective Pappas is in charge, so unless he asks us directly, we let him take the lead. The fact that Bobby Burr is missing is worrisome, I can tell you that much. I've heard talk of it being a double homicide. I don't know what the motive would be for killing them both."

"Oh, it's not. I saw Bobby—"

Ruth focused her attention so keenly on Cam, she felt like a laser shone into her eyes.

"You *saw* him?" Ruth's whisper rasped on Cam's ears. She grabbed Cam's arm.

"Yesterday. It was weird." Cam shook her head. "He came out of the woods at the back of my farm. He looked terrible. I think he was about to tell me something, but he split when he heard Ellie calling me."

"Cam! Did you tell Pappas? They're looking for Bobby everywhere."

"I was so busy the rest of the day, I didn't even think about it. I meant to call him, but I forgot."

"I'd better tell him right now."

"He's going to hate me. Let me call him when market closes. I'll phone him at one o'clock, I promise."

"He's still going to hate you." Ruth pulled out her phone. "I need to do this. Watch them for a minute, will you?" She gestured at the girls, who were sidling toward the bread samples two tables down.

Nobody was near Cam's table, so she moseyed behind the twins. The baker beamed at them and extended the flat basket of sourdough squares.

"No gluten allergies, Mom?" The baker smiled at Cam, eyebrows raised.

She opened her mouth and shut it again. Why get into explaining she wasn't their mother? It was kind of a nice feeling that she was assumed to be. She simply said, "No."

At the same time, Nettie pronounced, "Our mom is over *there*. This is Ms. Cam. She's a farmer."

Cam introduced herself to the baker. The girls munched bread, the tomato and kale apparently forgotten.

A customer fingered a bunch of leeks at Cam's table, so she ushered the children back. As she explained how to clean the leeks by slicing them vertically halfway through and rinsing the dirt out of the white part, she heard a plaintive question from Natalie.

"Mommy, I miss Daddy. When's he coming back?"

Ruth, now off the phone, saw that Cam had heard. She leaned down and murmured something to Natalie, stroking her hair.

Before they left, Ruth said in a soft voice to Cam, "I'll tell you later."

Chapter 9

Two bicycles, an old pickup truck, and a Prius with a THINK GLOBAL, EAT LOCAL bumper sticker occupied Cam's driveway when she arrived home. Sounds of hammering echoed off the house. When she rounded the corner of the barn, her mouth dropped open. The chicken coop was already half built, an A-frame structure sitting on a two-wheeled trailer base.

Alexandra, another young woman, Wes, Ellie, and a young man with a scruffy beard and a wide-brimmed hat were hard at work. They were measuring, sawing, hammering. The guy in the hat examined an oversize piece of paper that looked like a building plan. It lay spread out on a makeshift table. A bale of hay sat next to a large bag labeled CHICKEN LAYER/BREEDER MIX. The air smelled of fresh sawdust.

"It's a coop raising!" Cam said. Alexandra had called early that morning, asking if it was all right to go ahead, and Cam had said it was, but she hadn't expected this kind of progress. "Ellie, you're here, too."

"Alexandra called and asked if I wanted to help. I said, like, 'Of course.' It'll help me get my Voice for Animals badge, too."

Cam thanked her. "Did your dad drop you off?"

"Mr. Ames gave me a ride."

"Thanks, Wes," Cam said. "I appreciate you helping out."

"With Felicity out of town, I have a little too much time on my hands. Happy to do it."

Alexandra introduced the other young woman as her sister Katie and the young man, named DJ, explaining he was one of the rescue league members. "He's the one I told you about."

The *Star Trek: The Next Generation* theme song rang in Cam's pocket. "Excuse me a minute." She turned away and checked the ID on her cell phone. Pappas. Might as well get this call over with. She strolled back toward the house before answering.

"Where are you?" he started in without preamble.

"Good afternoon, Detective. I am at home. At the farm. Why?"

"I'm on my way to talk with you. I'll be there in five minutes."

She barely had time to agree before he disconnected. Yup, he hated her now.

In even fewer than five, Pappas roared into the drive and parked directly behind Cam's truck, as if he were blocking her exit. He climbed out and rested one hand on the car.

"Bobby Burr was on your property. You spoke with him. And you didn't think of calling it in?"

"I'm sorry." She put down the empty basket she'd taken from the back of the truck. She turned toward him. "Saturday is my shareholder day, and I was working without a minute's break all day long. Really."

"Tell me exactly what happened."

She related her encounter. "I asked him to come in, to have something to eat. He looked like he might have slept outdoors or somewhere rough. But he said he couldn't. He was about to tell me about the night of the dinner when he heard someone calling me. And then he split."

Without trying to be too obvious, she checked Pappas out. Once again he presented a slightly disheveled front. He wore jeans, which was certainly appropriate for Sunday afternoon, but his pale green shirt bore the remnants of a meal, possibly pizza, and he'd missed shaving a patch near his chin. She wondered what was going on in his personal life.

"We would very much like to speak with Mr. Burr, as you can imagine. More and more as time goes by. At least now we know it wasn't a double homicide." He wiped his forehead with a purple handkerchief retrieved from his back pocket. "If you see him, hear from him, catch a glimpse of someone who looks like him, call me. Will you do that?"

"Yes. I suppose you searched Irene's house and he's not hanging out there? I would assume he has a key."

He nodded. "Bobby isn't there." He took a few steps away down the drive and turned back toward her. "We need to work together. I'd like you to keep your eyes and ears open."

Cam nodded. This was an intriguing new development. The detective asking for her help.

He walked up until he faced her. He could have reached out and touched her. "Any bit of information you think might be related to Ms. Burr's death, I'd like to know. All right?"

His tone was friendlier than Cam had ever heard from him. It was almost plaintive. His eyes seemed to implore her to help him.

"Sure, Detective."

"I can't be everywhere, and we've had staffing cuts. And, um, Cameron?" He cleared his throat and mustered a smile. "You can call me Pete. If you want."

"Thanks, Pete." Cam conjured a smile back at what looked like a sudden case of nerves. They might have more in common than she had imagined. She watched him climb into his car and waved to him before he drove off.

She resumed unpacking the truck, singing "I Feel Good," à la James Brown, under her breath. It had been a great market day. She had nearly sold out. She was going to have chickens on the farm. And now Pappas—Pete—was even being nice. When she was done, she called in an order of pizza to be delivered for the coop crew, donned her own tool belt, and joined the project.

An hour later, Alexandra and DJ said they were going to go fetch the chickens.

"I have the letter from the board of health authorizing us to take them." Alexandra brandished a white envelope. "And the inspector is going to meet us there."

"Let me come with you. I know Bev. Maybe it will make it easier." Cam wasn't sure about that but thought the respectful thing to do would be to accompany the rescuers.

Alexandra exchanged a look with DJ, who nodded. "Okay," she said. "But you're not going to let her talk us out of taking the hens, right?"

"No. I won't." Cam shed her tool belt and dusted off her hands.

Cam and Alexandra squeezed into the cab of DJ's truck. Cam directed him to the Montgomery place across town.

She was shocked when she saw the state of Bev's farm. The fields beyond the barn, which used to be neatly planted with corn, were now choked with weeds. The pumpkins curing in their patch sat small and misshapen. The faded blue paint on the farmhouse was peeling, and the patch of lawn out front hadn't been mowed in some time. A whiff of sour anaerobic manure wafted by.

Alexandra followed Cam up the steps to the side door and waited while Cam knocked.

Bev opened the door. She frowned and squinted at them. Cam greeted her and introduced Alexandra.

"Hello, Bev. This is Alexandra Magnusson, one of my subscribers. Alexandra, Bev Montgomery."

Bev looked back and forth between them. "What do you

want?" Bev had looked worn and tired ever since Cam had met her the previous spring, but new lines were etched deep in her face and the light had gone out of her eyes.

"We've come to give your hens a new home." Alexandra proffered the letter. "The board of health authorized it. Oh, there's animal control." She backed down the stairs to stand with DJ.

A woman climbed out of a van labeled WESTBURY ANIMAL CONTROL and walked toward the house. After she stopped and conferred with Alexandra and DJ, they began unloading large cages from the back of the van.

Bev snatched the letter. "My girls are going to you?" Her voice rose as she stared at Cam. "You oughta pay me for those birds. They're good layers. Or used to be."

"As I understand it, they're about to be put down," Cam said.

"I don't know what Madeline Fracasso is doing here." Bev glared at the animal control officer as she approached. "Joe at the board of health is an old family friend. He never would have carried through on that letter."

"That's not the way I heard it," Madeline said from the bottom of the stairs. "The hens are reportedly very thin and are missing most of their feathers. The board said you aren't feeding them at all."

"Oh, hens scratch and find worms and such. Just because I'm a little short on cash right now doesn't mean I should lose my prize layers."

"Mrs. Montgomery, we're here to collect the hens," Madeline said in a firm voice. "Please don't make any trouble."

Bev shook her head and glared. "You can't just take them, you know."

Cam knew Bev was an old-style farmer who didn't see the wisdom in organic practices or growing what she called "fancy" salad greens, like mizuna and arugula. But thinking her malnourished chickens were fine seemed to border on delusional. Maybe

Albert could convince her to get out of the business, for her own sake.

"Let's get this over with," Madeline said. She picked up a cage and led Alexandra and DJ with theirs out behind the house, toward a barn that listed more than the Tower of Pisa.

"It's called robbery! Taking my property without paying for it." Bev pointed a shaking finger at Madeline's back. Her red face glistened with anger.

Cam cleared her throat. "I also need to tell you I'm not going to be able to sell at the Haverhill Farmers' Market anymore."

Bev whipped her eyes back to Cam. "Not going to be able to or don't want to?" She spit out the question.

"It's a business decision, Bev. With the customers dropping off, I'm not making the kind of money I need to justify spending an entire afternoon there."

"How do you expect us to keep the customers if farmers like you stop coming?"

"I'm sorry." Cam did feel bad about abandoning the lower-income customer base, but she had her own income to consider.

"Maybe you'll be even more sorry soon." Bev stepped back into the house and slammed the door behind her.

Chapter 10

By the end of the afternoon, the coop was finished. A ramp led up to a small square door in one end, with a more human-size door next to it. The crew had set up orange plastic temporary fencing around the area and had placed a metal feeder and a metal water receptacle on the ground near the ramp. The cages of utterly miserable-looking chickens waited inside the fence, in the shade of the barn. Their scrawny little bodies were missing most of their feathers. They clucked and preened in the most pitiful of ways.

"Thanks so much, everybody," Cam said. "These poor girls don't look too happy."

"They sure don't." DJ knelt next to one of the cages. He stuck a finger in and stroked the head of the nearest hen. "They'll need food and care, plenty of fresh water always available, and a proper home so they can range and scratch. In our experience, most rebound fine if they're given the chance. It's really criminal what that lady did."

"Why didn't you guys offer to help Bev take care of them instead of bringing them here?"

Alexandra shook her head. "Board of Health getting involved

made that impossible. We had to move them to keep them from being slaughtered. And they're your birds now," she added. "Why don't you introduce these girls to their new home?"

Cam unhooked the door of the closest cage. The hens cowered, shrinking away from the open door. DJ squatted easily in front of it. He spoke in a soft voice and reached in, gently grasping one of the birds. He set her on the ground in front of the cylindrical metal feeder. He scratched a finger in the feed in the flat dish that spread out below the cylinder.

"Come on out, ladies," he murmured to the rest of them. "Open the other cages," he said to Cam with a big smile. He made a clicking noise and patted the ground in front of the first cage. One of the hens ventured forth but tripped on the bottom lip of the opening. He gently lifted her out.

"They're not too smart. But they'll be fine," DJ said. "You'll be fine, won't you, gals?" he said to the hens now stumbling out of the cages.

Katie positioned herself in front of the next cage and mimicked DJ's clicking sound. When the first hen hopped out, Katie smiled and beckoned to the next one.

Soon all the birds were clustered around the feeder, some pecking each other instead of the food. DJ rose and scattered a couple of handfuls of feed on the ground. He made the clicking noise again until the birds noticed the extra food.

"You're the chicken whisperer," Cam said.

DJ doffed his hat with a flourish and a smile.

"This calls for a celebration," Cam said. "Alexandra, grab some chairs from the lawn and the barn. Ellie, help me bring drinks out from the house, okay?"

When they were settled in a line of chairs outside the fencing a few minutes later, Alexandra raised her bottle of beer toward the enclosure. "Here's to healthy hens!"

"To healthy hens!" resounded throughout the group. Ellie

clinked her bottle of natural root beer with Cam's and DJ's beer bottles. Ellie seemed enchanted by the young man and began asking him questions about the rescue league and where he had learned how to talk to chickens.

Cam turned to Wes on her other side. "When is Felicity coming back?"

"It'll be another week or two. Her sister had some complications." He set his beer bottle on the ground.

Alexandra turned in her chair on the other side of Wes and looked at Cam. "Have you heard any news about Irene's death?"

Wes jerked in his chair. His right knee bobbed up and down repeatedly, knocking over his beer.

"Whoa," Alexandra said. She grabbed the bottle and handed it to him. "Relax, Wes."

"I haven't heard anything," Cam said. Why did Wes react that way?

"I wonder if Bobby will continue with Irene's plan to buy the town hall," Wes said, staring straight ahead, continuing to jiggle his knee, as if he were bouncing a baby.

"They'll have to find him first," Cam said.

"Is he missing?" Wes asked. He whipped his head to the right. "How do you know?"

Cam nodded. "Heard it around. I hope he'll reappear, and soon."

"My mom says opening a textile museum would be a great thing for the town," Alexandra said.

Cam remembered that she'd moved back in with her parents after college to save money.

"It would bring in jobs and tourists," Alexandra continued. "The town would get some money for other projects, like low-cost housing, which we're really short on. It's a cool idea. It's too bad Ms. Burr died, but I hope her stepson keeps going with the plans."

"And where would we hold Town Meeting, young lady?" Wes gave her a stern look.

"High school auditorium?" Alexandra raised her eyebrows. "I'm sure there are plenty of places. It's not like it gets a huge turnout, anyway. Dad told me last time they needed a quorum for a vote, the police stopped cars on Main Street, asking if they were residents. If they were, the cops basically ordered them inside."

Wes shook his head in exasperation. Cam decided to extricate herself from the conversation and turned back to Ellie and DJ. They seemed to be involved in an intense discussion of permaculture, so she rose and bent down to stroke Preston instead, who stood outside the fencing. He gazed with intense interest at the hens.

"Mr. P, those are *not* your next forty dinners."

Katie walked over. "He's one sweet cat." Not as tall as her sister, she wore her dark hair at shoulder length.

Preston reared up and rubbed his head against Katie's knee, emitting his tiny mew. She scratched his head and gave him a few firm strokes.

"You should keep the cat away from the ladies for a week or so," DJ called from his chair. "But usually farm cats are fine with chickens. It's foxes, coyotes, and stray dogs you need to worry about. Herd all the girls into the coop before it gets dark for the next couple of days. After that they'll probably start going by themselves to roost, but latch them in every night, to be safe. And even though it's on a trailer, we'll keep it here next to the barn for a week or two so they get used to one place."

"Why is it on a trailer?" Cam asked.

"If you leave it in one place, the droppings get pretty nasty. You can rotate it around to any field or area you want fertilized and weeded and leave it there for a few weeks."

"That's cool. What do I haul it with?"

"Your truck can pull it. And we'll build the covered run next weekend, right, Alexandra?" DJ leaned his head in her direction. "The run attaches to the coop, but you can easily pick it up and move it. With a friend, anyway. With a covered run they can range in safety and hawks won't be able to pick them off."

Alexandra nodded. "Remember what I said about the raspberry patch, Cam? We can position it there for a week or two and put the covered run over the bushes."

"Got it."

DJ walked into the enclosure and beckoned to Cam to join him. "Go in and take a look at your new chicken motel. There isn't really room for two of us in there."

Cam followed him. She opened the larger door, which wasn't even as tall as she was, and leaned in. Two levels of nesting boxes lined the back wall. Dowels stuck out every foot halfway up the end walls. Fresh wood shavings covered the floor and lined the boxes. The vents on either end would provide air circulation.

Cam pulled her head back out. "Tell me what the dowels are for."

"They're roosting bars," DJ said. "The hens sleep on them."

"Won't they fall off?" Ellie piped up.

DJ laughed. "You'd think so, right? Chickens are descended from jungle fowl. Sleeping off the ground has kept them safe for a really long time." He angled his head at Ellie and smiled. Ellie, in turn, blushed.

"It all looks great," Cam said, closing the door. The coop looked sturdy, protective, and, she imagined, inviting, if she were a hen. All it really needed was a little framed sampler of embroidery reading COOP, SWEET COOP.

"For tonight let's leave some food and water inside since they've been so neglected, but take the food out tomorrow. It's better if they eat away from where they nest."

"So how exactly do I herd them in?" Cam asked. "Flap my own wings and say, 'Shoo!'?"

DJ looked at the sky. "It's getting pretty close to dark now, anyway. Let's do it together. I have to return the truck to my friend Tyler tonight, so I can't stay much longer."

She and DJ surrounded the hens. Cam tried to persuade them to walk up the ramp and into the coop. "Time for bed, chickens."

DJ's method was more successful. He walked, half crouched, with his arms out and low to his sides, shooing the hens ahead of him up the ramp, clicking as he went. Cam picked up the last straggler and plopped her inside.

"They had a coop at Mrs. Montgomery's, so they know how to walk up. It's just that it was filthy inside and they were so under-fed." DJ frowned.

"She was really steamed about us taking them," Alexandra said. "But she was going to lose them, anyway. This seems like a four-way win to me. You get egg layers. Bev doesn't have to feed them anymore. Board of Health doesn't have to turn extermina-tor, and the girls have a nice, safe home and regular meals."

DJ carried the food and water into the coop and latched the door. "It'll take time for them to remember how to live like real chickens. I'll get you more information on how to take care of them and how to rotate the chicken tractor to prepare new plant-ing areas."

"What tractor?" Ellie asked.

"Yeah, I don't own a tractor," Cam added.

"Right. It's a coop on a trailer, but people call the whole sys-tem chicken tractoring," DJ said. "When you move them to a new area, it'll take them just a couple of weeks to clear it of weeds and fertilize it. You can plant right away, but chicken ma-nure is pretty hot, so it's best to let it sit a few more weeks. You don't want to burn your seedlings."

"I have a lot to learn," Cam said. "Thank you, DJ and Alexan-dra, for rescuing these gals, and all of you for making a nice home for them."

"I'll be back tomorrow to check on them," Alexandra offered.

"Bring me the bill for the supplies," Cam told her.

Alexandra assured her she would.

As DJ headed for the truck, he called out, "And, Cam, if you ever need an extra hand around here, I'm an able body and I love growing stuff. Text me. Alexandra knows where I am."

"That'd be great, DJ. Volunteer Wednesday is every Wednesday." She laughed at her redundancy. "Anyway, I'd love to contact you for special projects, too. Bye, everybody!"

DJ pulled out, the sisters rode off on their bikes, and Wes promised to deliver Ellie home. Cam peered into the grated window in the human door of the coop. The birds looked cozy and sated on their roosts.

She whistled as she walked to the house. Young people interested in farming and animal welfare. A great new farmers' market gig. Forty new female companions out back, no matter how dim witted. Life seemed pretty rosy today. As long as she didn't dwell on a gruesome murder close to home or a missing carpenter now, apparently, under suspicion himself.

In the formal dining room at Moran Manor Assisted Living that evening, Cam poured Great-Uncle Albert a glass of the chardonnay she had brought and then poured for herself. He wore a tweed jacket over his sweater vest, his nod to the Sunday night dinner dress code imposed by the facility. Cam hoped her sweater and slacks were nice enough to pass muster.

"What's this I hear about a murder happening after your splendid dinner last week?" Albert asked, setting his glass on the white tablecloth.

"Howard Fisher found Irene's body in the Fisher farm pigsty. The authorities can't find Irene's stepson." Cam decided not to go into the whole story of Bobby's brief appearance on her farm and his subsequent disappearance. "Wes Ames seems positively delighted that Irene's plan to buy the Old Town Hall has fallen through. And the police were asking about her mechanic, Sim Koyama, who was heard arguing with Irene at the dinner. I'm glad it's not my job to sort out that puzzle."

"Yes, at least the death wasn't on your farm again."

"Small blessings."

"I know Simone well," Albert said. "She used to service Marie's Honda. A lovely girl when you get past the black clothes and all those piercings. Although it doesn't surprise me she has a bit of a hot temper."

"I'm taking the truck in to her shop for service tomorrow. I know you preferred taking it to the dealer, but I'd rather patronize somebody in town."

"I don't care about that." He shooed away the distinction with his hand. "Now, tell me about your day, Cameron. It was pretty quiet here. Folks who need assistance living don't make much ruckus. And I like a little ruckus now and then. Short of a murder." He smiled under snow-white eyebrows whose bushiness threatened to take over his kindly face. "Although I do have a bit of news of my own when you're done."

She described the Newburyport Farmers' Market and her decision to sell there instead of at Haverhill. "It's such a vibrant market, Uncle Albert. You remember Lucinda?"

He nodded.

"She told me it was like a festival. And it was. Live music, baked goods, even wine and beer tasting after noon. There was a boy, couldn't have been older than twelve, demonstrating his beehive."

"And lots of customers, I assume?"

"Absolutely. I sold out. Although not so many were using SNAP tokens."

"An excellent program. Poor people need more healthy food."

"And now we have hens at the farm, too." Cam sighed. "I think it's a good thing. But they're going to be a lot of work." She described the rescue venture, the brand-new coop, and the forty new residents.

"I approve. Why, we had chickens for some years, don't you know. Oh, your great-aunt Marie loved to feed them out of her apron. She made a little clicking sound that brought them running."

"That's the same sound DJ made."

Albert nodded. "Chickens are smelly things, though."

"The chickens must have been before I started coming to the farm," Cam said. "I don't remember any."

Albert agreed it must have been. "Do you have a rooster, too?"

"No, a male wasn't part of the package."

Their dinners arrived, and they ate in silence for a few moments.

"Where'd you say those chickens were rescued from?"

Cam hadn't said, on purpose. "You're not going to like it. They were Bev Montgomery's. The board of health was about to destroy them. I guess she wasn't feeding or cleaning them. They're skinny and look miserable. I went over there to help pick them up. Bev wasn't happy about it."

"My poor friend Beverly. She has gone through so many hurtful times. And now she's hurting pin-brained birds." He put his fork down. "I wonder what I can do to help her. She was an angel to us when Marie was dying. I believe I told you. An angel."

"Maybe she should sell her farm and come live here," Cam said. "I'll bet her property would go for a lot. She's all alone on the property now."

"Why, that might be just the ticket, Cameron." Albert's eyes lit up.

"I wonder if she's old enough, though."

Albert took a sip of his wine. "She's over sixty. Which qualifies her for independent living. And the assisted living area doesn't have a lower age limit."

"Do you think she'd do it?" Cam said. "I mean, sell the farm and move here?"

"She's stubborn, but I do believe she is also down and out. I'll pay her a visit sometime soon and see if I can convince her. Now, what else is new with you?"

"Well, my programmer friend Tina says my name for the farm is already out of date. Nobody uses the C++ programming language anymore. I'm thinking of changing it back to Attic Hill Farm. What do you think?"

"I'd be pleased with that. It was the farm's name for two centuries before you changed it. I wanted it to be your enterprise, my dear. That's why I didn't object. And it is your farm, but I'll admit I'm happy to hear the old name will be restored."

"Good. I'll do it."

"Now, what about the fair? You are going to enter the vegetable competition, like we talked about, aren't you?"

"I'm a beginner." Cam shook her head. "How could I win a prize against veteran farmers?"

Albert patted her hand and kept his age-spotted, knobby hand on hers. "My dear, your Sun Golds are the best tomato I have ever tasted, bar none, including all those so-called heirlooms, which used to be the only kinds we grew. And your garlic braids? You used big, plump cloves, braided them expertly, and they're organic. Nobody else will come close." Cam had brought one over to show him a month earlier.

"I had a lot of fun learning how to braid garlic. If I hadn't gone to the organic farming summer conference in August, I couldn't have done it. A farmer was sitting there one afternoon, braiding and teaching anybody who wanted to learn. She was getting her own work done and sharing knowledge at the same time."

Albert nodded.

"So I thought I'd give braiding the soft-neck garlic a try. They do look pretty nice, don't they?"

"And you'll take them to the Middleford Fair?" Albert leaned toward her, as if trying to pull the yes out of her. "It will be great experience in any case, and you'll get a sense of who else is out there. Remember, too, a blue ribbon is a perfect marketing tool."

"You talked me into it." She smiled at the man who'd spent his summers teaching her about growing without her even knowing she was in class. And who was now her marketing guru, as well. "I already printed out the entry forms. I'll head down there Tuesday morning. Wish me luck."

"Break a leg, Farmer Flaherty."

"I never heard what your news was. Tell me." Cam patted Albert's hand.

He was about to speak when their server appeared at Albert's side, a high-school girl in tight black pants and a white button-down shirt barely covering her midsection. She cleared their plates onto a tray. "Can I get you some dessert tonight?" She proffered a small menu card.

"Cameron?"

"Sure." The assisted-living facility had a remarkably capable baker on staff, and Cam never turned down dessert here. "I'll have the apple tart with vanilla ice cream. Those are local apples, aren't they?" *Listen to me*, she thought. *Those locavores have converted me.*

The girl caught herself halfway through rolling her eyes. "I'll check for you. Do you still want it if they aren't local?"

"Actually, I do. But I'd like to know, okay?"

Albert ordered the sugar-free ice cream. "Damn diabetes."

"You've never been overweight," Cam said. "How did you get diabetes?"

"It's hereditary. I inherited a curse from my father, is how I see it. That's how I lost my foot, you know."

Cam nodded. Their desserts arrived, with an aside from the server that the apples were from Cider Valley Farm. Cam thanked her.

"Now, then. Time for the news I heard yesterday." Albert cocked his head. "Howard Fisher has run into a spot of bad luck lately, I've heard."

Cam raised her eyebrows. "What kind of spot?"

"He's not been managing his business well. He might lose the land to foreclosure."

"That'd be so sad. Are people just not buying pork anymore?"

"Perhaps. Or maybe he's just a bad businessman. If he loses the land, he loses everything."

Cam whistled. "How'd you hear that?"

"Our friend Bev. She and I, we like to keep up on the goings-on in town."

Chapter 11

Cam checked the hens when she arrived home. The coop door was latched, and all seemed well under a waxing moon that was already past quarter full. A screech owl called from the woods with its eerie whistling whinny, and dewy grass dampened her sneakers as she headed for the house.

She ushered Preston in and locked the door. Providing a new home and nourishment for hens that had been on their way to the executioner's block had been a great idea. She hoped they wouldn't add too much to her workload. But even so, they would be an asset to the farm. She would have a great source of nitrogen for compost and could offer eggs for sale whenever the hens started laying again.

The success of the hen rescue turned her thoughts to Howard's pigs. Maybe they needed a rescue mission, too. The scope of that would be totally different, given the size of the rescuees and the demands of an appropriate living space.

Cam sat at the computer to check her e-mail before bed. She also looked at the Comments page on the farm's Web site. An inflammatory comment a few months earlier had forced her to moderate the messages, and she saw one message sitting in the administrator's mailbox. She opened it and frowned.

Leave other people's livestock alone. Mind your own bizness, or else.

Well, that one was going straight into the trash. No, on second thought, she saved it to her own e-mail and forwarded it to Pappas, with a note explaining Project Rescue Chicken. The comment qualified as a threat in her mind, whether he thought so or not. On further contemplation, Cam forwarded it to the Westbury police, too. It didn't really pertain to the murder, or so she hoped, but was a threat nonetheless.

The sun was creeping over the top of the woods when Cam opened the coop door the next morning.

"Good morning, ladies. Come on out whenever you're ready." She lifted the feeder and the water receptacle and carried them down the ramp, setting them at the edge of the fencing where they would be shaded at least half the day. .

One groggy hen stumbled down the ramp, making Cam wonder if she should have brought out a tray of tiny espresso cups, instead. She replenished the food from the sack in the barn and carried the water basin to the hose. The girls had made a dent in the contents of both vessels overnight. As Cam herself would have if she'd been continually underfed.

The rest of the hens made their way toward the fresh food. Cam laughed at the sounds they made, a cross between crooning and gargling. She hadn't noticed their vocalizations the day before. Maybe they'd been too shell-shocked to talk. One with a goofy topknot stuck her neck out and ran straight toward Cam, then slowed and made the same funny sounds, which were nothing like the *bock-bock-bock* one heard in popular culture.

Cam's phone rang in her pocket. She checked the display. Alexandra.

Cam greeted her. "What's up?"

"I can't stop thinking about those pigs at Howard's. I want to see for myself. But I don't really want to go alone. He's kind of a creepy guy."

Cam agreed but added, "Are you sure you want to confront him?"

"I don't want to confront him, exactly, but I feel like I need to see the animals. Do you have time to go over there with me?"

"I don't know. We'll need some kind of story. We can't just show up for no reason."

"Can we get there through the woods? I sure don't need to talk with Howard."

Cam checked her watch. "I don't have time to go for a hike. But I do need to go out to drop the truck at Sim's garage for service, anyway. I'll drive us over there for just a minute. We'll think of some excuse when we see him. He and I are both farmers, after all."

Alexandra said she'd meet Cam in the parking lot of the Food Mart in ten minutes, and they disconnected.

No way would she be willing to host rescue pigs right now, but Alexandra deserved to know the truth about the swine's living situation at the farm. And Cam wouldn't mind getting a good look at Howard's pigs, too.

At five before eight, they pulled into Howard's drive, if one could call a rutted gravel path a drive. White housewrap covered the left wall of the mid-nineteenth-century farmhouse, one corner flapping in the wind. Paint had chipped off the clapboards on the front. But tidy blue flower boxes hung from the railings of the side porch, with well-tended red geraniums reaching for the sun and bright nasturtiums spilling out like a waterfall. The lawn was mowed and free of leaves, despite a towering sugar maple nearby.

The drive widened as it curved around behind the house, so Cam drove on. She wasn't quite sure where the farm area was but assumed she'd run across it. Sure enough, some yards back, the drive ended at an open area ringed by outbuildings and a ramshackle barn. She parked the truck.

"What are we going to tell him we're here for?" Alexandra asked. She didn't sound worried, simply curious.

"I'll think of something. Let's go exploring." She hoped this wasn't too crazy of an idea.

They climbed out of the cab. Woods lined the left side of the area, and cornfields stretched out as far as Cam could see behind the outbuildings and the barn. Pork and corn seemed to be the extent of Howard's enterprise. Plus, he sold rhubarb in the springtime, she remembered.

No one seemed to be around. An old dog moseyed up without barking, sniffed at Alexandra, and ambled toward the house. It was early, but Cam had never yet met a farmer who wasn't already hard at work at eight in the morning.

"Hello?" she called. "Howard?" No answer. She thought she heard faint snorting sounds from the farthest outbuilding, so she and Alexandra headed that way. They picked their way along a dirt path around the left side of the building, which was more a collection of random boards and pieces of corrugated sheet metal cobbled together than a planned structure. The air smelled of rotten eggs and ammonia.

The back of the building was open to the air but was ringed with yellow police tape. Three fenced areas extended several yards back from the roofed area. In one, a sow suckled what looked like a dozen piglets, two of which seemed excluded and kept climbing over the others to get to a teat.

Alexandra drew in her breath sharply and moved toward the nearest of the other two enclosures.

Five or six pigs laid about in the mud in each area, but these were not the fat animals one saw in discussions of "the other white meat" or in children's books about farm animals. These beasts, while not exactly thin, looked mangy, with lackluster eyes and spots on their skin. To Cam's inexpert gaze, they appeared malnourished. She felt like she was seeing the hens from the day before but writ large. She covered her mouth and nose to filter the stench.

Then it slammed her. These were the pigs that had chewed on Irene's legs. Cam's bile rose, and she had to swallow hard. She looked at the back part of the fence. Even though the police had left the tape up, they must have already examined the fence. She didn't need to. It was bad enough imagining the scene. She didn't know if Irene had been dead and dumped into the sty, if she'd been stunned and pushed in, or if she somehow . . . Cam shook her head. It was no use conjecturing, and it wasn't her job under any scenario. Wind shook the tops of the tall maples and chilled her. She took a deep breath.

"It's criminal what he's doing to these poor animals." Alexandra wiped away a tear.

Cam nodded. "And they never would have attacked Irene if they weren't so hungry."

"Wait'll I tell DJ about this. He's really going to be steamed." The sadness on her face turned to a titanium resolve. "The police must have been here. I wonder why they didn't report Howard for animal cruelty?"

"Maybe they did. Bureaucracy can take a while. Let's get going."

They made their way back to the truck. Cam completed two parts of her three-part turnaround and had her eyes on the gearshift.

"Uh-oh, here's trouble," Alexandra said.

Cam heard a bang on the hood of the truck. She looked up to see Howard Fisher's angry face in the driver's-side window. She put the truck in neutral and rolled down the window.

"What the hell do you think you're doing on my property?" The spittle flew from his mouth, and he waved a rifle in his left hand.

Cam recoiled and tilted her head inward. "Hey, Howard." She attempted a smile. Alexandra gave a little wave from the passenger seat.

"Yeah. Good morning." His gruff voice edged toward friendliness. "What do you want?" He lowered the rifle.

"I've been so sad about Irene's death. You must be, too, and I wanted to see how you were doing. I called out when we drove in, but nobody was around. I assumed you were out back, feeding the pigs or something." Cam tried to smile.

"We're a little short on feed just now." Howard's brows knit together, and his eyes sagged. "But they get plenty of slops. Oh, they're fine. Very happy pigs, you might say." He mustered a cheery tone with what looked like difficulty.

"Well, great." Cam cleared her throat. "You're carrying a gun. Do you have problems with trespassers?"

"Maybe." His eyes shifted toward the trees to the left, behind the outbuildings, and back to Cam. "You know the police are saying it was murder, don't you? Mrs. Burr's death wasn't no accident."

"I guess I did hear something about that."

"If you ask me, it was that stepson of hers. He wants her money."

"Really? Bobby wouldn't hurt a soul."

Howard snorted.

"Hey, Howard." Alexandra leaned toward the driver's-side

window. "I heard your land is being foreclosed on. It would be awful for you to lose your farm."

He glared at the younger woman. "Where'd you hear that? I'm not losing the farm." His voice shook as he shouted. "You tell whoever said so, they're out of their consarned mind, you hear me?" The rifle came up again.

Cam decided this would be a good time for them to get out of there. "Sure. Gotta run," she said, putting the truck in gear. "Didn't mean to alarm you."

He looked like he might have been about to speak again, but Cam smiled as she drove away, elevating her hand in a wave.

"He's one unstable dude," Alexandra said. "I'm sorry to drag you into that, Cam."

"It's okay."

"I wish there was something we could do for the animals." Alexandra shook her head.

"Me, too." Cam swung onto Main Street. "But you should know, I'm not ready to host starving pigs, as well as chickens. At least not yet."

"I know."

"How'd you hear about his land being threatened?"

Alexandra threw a hand up. "It's all over town. One of the joys of living in a village, I guess."

They rode in silence the rest of the way to the Food Mart, where Alexandra got out and headed for her bicycle.

When she arrived at SK Foreign Auto, Cam sat for a moment in the cab. Things hadn't quite gotten ugly at Howard's, but an angry man with a rifle in his hand? Something she could do without.

Sim sauntered out, wiping her hands on a red rag. "Ready for a spin on the bike?"

Cam halted halfway out of the cab. "On the bike?"

"You're leaving the truck for the day, right?"

Cam said that she was and that she would walk home. "It's only two miles. I can use the exercise."

"I'll give you a lift. Ever ride bitch on a Harley before?"

"What?"

Sim laughed. "You know. Shotgun. On the back."

Cam shook her head. She wasn't totally sure she wanted to, either.

"It's fun. Come on. I have a spare helmet. All you have to remember is to lean into the curves. Don't fight them."

Cam handed over the keys to the truck as she wondered what she'd gotten herself into. She slung her handbag over her head and across one shoulder.

Sim handed her a heavy helmet. "I don't believe in those half helmets dudes wear. They think I'm a wuss for wearing true protective gear. I think they're idiots for not protecting their brains."

Cam dutifully fastened the helmet while Sim put on her own. The thick foam liner pressed in on her forehead, and the strap rubbed against her throat. She fumbled with the strap adjustment but couldn't loosen it. She was glad the helmet didn't have a plastic visor covering her eyes.

Sim pulled on leather gloves before climbing onto the hefty bike painted with a bold red lightning strike on the back. She swung it off its kickstand and motioned Cam to get on behind her.

"Put your arms around my waist," Sim called through the helmet. "I promise I won't lust after you."

Cam set her left foot on what looked like a rear footrest, threw her right leg over the back, and set each hand on Sim's leather-clad waist. Sim fired up the machine and eased onto Main Street.

When they turned onto Attic Hill Road, Cam leaned into the curve. Sim sped up. The engine roared in Cam's ears and vibrated beneath her. She hung on to Sim's waist with increasingly cold fingers. The familiar fields and woods dotted with houses sped by in a blur. And Cam's own familiar house sped by, too.

Where was Sim taking her? Why had she ever agreed to this crazy idea?

They turned again, onto Moulton Street, and raced around the reservoir. They sped over to Indian Pond Road, charged up the steep Middle Street hill, and flew down the other side, narrowly missing a passing Jeep. They finally rejoined Attic Hill Road.

The engine slowed as Sim turned into Cam's drive and came to a stop.

Cam dismounted and removed the helmet with shaky hands. "That was quite a ride."

Sim stayed on the bike but flipped up her face shield with a wicked smile. "Was that fun or what?"

"I guess. I don't think it's really my thing."

"I love speed." Sim looked into the distance like she'd rather be out on a highway in Wyoming, going ninety miles an hour. "And I had to distract myself from thinking about Bobby."

"Did you test-drive Irene's Jag like that? I'll bet they go pretty fast." Cam actually had no idea how Jaguars drove. But Lucinda had put the idea of Sim as a suspect in her mind, and Cam wanted to see what she had to say about Irene.

"That witch? She accused me of taking it on joyrides. I told her I had to take it out on the road after a tune-up. There's no substitute for a road test to make sure a car is running smooth. But she hated the idea of anybody else driving her baby. She even threatened to charge me for every tenth of a mile I drove it."

"You're not going to miss her business, then." Cam handed the helmet to Sim and rubbed her cold hands together.

Sim didn't look up as she turned to fasten the spare helmet to the back of the bike. "No. I am not."

"Any word from Bobby? I'm worried about him."

"Me, too." This time Sim met Cam's eyes. "He's gone underground. I don't know where, and I don't know why."

"What do you mean by *underground?* How do you know?"

"I just mean that I haven't heard from him."

"Has Detective Pappas been by to speak with you?"

"Yes. I really don't like that guy."

"He had mentioned to me that maybe it was a double homicide." Cam knew it wasn't, but wanted to see if Bobby might have contacted Sim in the same way he had appeared at Cam's farm.

Sim shook her head with a fast movement. "No, no. It can't be. I—" She cleared her throat and, looking down, fiddled with her glove.

"You what?"

"Nothing. I'm sure he wasn't killed, that's all. Let me know if you want a lift back this afternoon. Should be done by three."

Cam thanked her for the ride and said good-bye. She hugged herself, still chilled from the windy ride, and watched as Sim roared down the hill, the smell of the exhaust trailing behind her. She wasn't quite sure why she hadn't simply told Sim about Bobby's appearance on the farm. She'd bet the price of the Harley that Bobby had contacted the mechanic, too. But where was he now?

Chapter 12

Cam worked the rest of the morning and all afternoon, taking only a quick lunch break in the house. She finished planting the stiff-neck garlic. She harvested a dozen ripe crops, including the gold cherry tomatoes she'd take to the fair the next day. She split apart the soft-neck garlic bulbs she hadn't braided. She selected only the fattest cloves for planting, saving the smaller ones for cooking in her own kitchen. She'd come to realize that what ended up on the farmer's own table was never the biggest, most beautiful examples of what came out of the fields.

She took the basket of cloves and a pitchfork to the field. She loosened a large bed that had held bush beans earlier in the season, so it was now rich in nitrogen from nodules on the legume roots, and covered it with several inches of finished compost. Kneeling, she pressed a clove, root side down, about an inch into the loose, rich soil. The next clove went in four inches away. She continued that way along the length and width of the bed, every clove a hand's width from its neighbor. Preston sidled by to visit and sat on a bale of salt marsh hay to watch her work.

The wind kept up, ruffling her hair, and the sun warmed her back. She knew she was blessed with good health. She had a kind great-uncle who had given her this land and this livelihood. She possessed a smarter-than-average brain, at least when it came to writing software. And what was software but elegant solutions to everyday needs, solving problems with logic?

As she worked, she thought about this current problem of Irene Burr's death and the associated events and reactions. Bobby's disappearance. Sim's apparent hatred for Irene. Howard's maltreatment of his animals and the challenge to his land, not to mention his farm being the scene of the crime. Wes's opposition to Irene's proposed enterprise.

Surely, Cam could try to find an elegant, true solution to this problem. It wasn't that different from writing and debugging software. You tried one thing. If it didn't work, you tried another. You eliminated possibilities. But this particular problem involved humans, not "ifs" and "thens." She shook her head. It wasn't her problem to solve, anyway, as Detective Pappas would be the first to point out.

At four thirty, Cam climbed on her bicycle and coasted down the hill to town. She had looked in on the hens before she left. They seemed fine, if pecking around the yard was fine. She gave herself a mental nudge to spend some time reading about normal chicken behavior and best rearing practices. She'd be back before dark to herd them into their coop.

At the shop, the truck was parked in front, and Cam hoisted her bike into the back. Sim strolled out, wiping her hands on a rag.

"It all looks good." Sim pointed at the tires. "Remember, though, I recommended you get a whole new set. Winter's coming, and you have to make it up quite a hill to get home."

Cam promised she would get tires and paid Sim. As she backed out, she spied the corner of a van parked around the back. This time she decided to follow up on her hunch that it was Bobby's van. She stopped her truck, climbed out, and strode to the rear of the shop. A dark-haired man was slipping through the back door. Cam caught the door and followed him in.

"Bobby!"

He whirled in the narrow hallway. He tried to push past her toward the door, but she blocked his way. His hair looked like it hadn't been washed in a week, and his clothes were in an even scruffier state.

"What are you doing?" Cam asked, extending her arms. "Nobody's after you. Why are you on the run?"

Sim burst through the door from the garage. "You're back!" She threw her arms around him with a big smile.

"Back?" Cam asked, watching them. "You were here before, weren't you?" she asked Bobby. "Last Friday?"

Bobby nodded, but he looked trapped. He detached himself from Sim and edged toward the door. "I gotta go."

Sim moved to block his way.

"I think we have to do an intervention with this guy," Sim said to Cam. She took him by the arm and led him into the garage bay. Bobby let himself be led. Cam followed.

Bobby leaned against the workbench. "I think you're right." He picked up a wrench and tossed it from one hand to another. He looked from Sim to Cam and back. He pushed his hair off his forehead. He leaned his back against the wall and exhaled a heavy sigh.

"The police just want to talk to you, dude," Sim said.

"I guess I'm ready to do that now. I've been living in my van at Salisbury Beach. But I have to get back to work. Got a big job starting end of this week."

"Why have you been avoiding the cops?" Cam cocked her head.

Bobby's smile was wry. "I started to tell you when I saw you at the farm. That night at the dinner, Irene was pressuring me. I don't know why she was so set on having me take over her business when she hated me so much. I told her I didn't want to. I was trying to be polite. But then she started threatening me, said she wouldn't leave me any of her money. It's my dad's money! Which she stole from him. She said she wouldn't give me any of it if I wouldn't work for her. Can you imagine what kind of hell that would be? At this point I don't care about her damn money."

Sim nodded.

"But I couldn't figure out how to tell her, so I walked away."

"Did she give you a note telling you to meet her someplace?" Cam asked.

"No." Bobby looked confused. "Why would she?"

"Never mind. Go on about why you've been in hiding. It's not a crime to argue with your stepmother."

"After the dinner, after you dropped me off, Sim, I was still steaming. I drove to her McMansion down by the river. I hate that house. I sat out front and planned what I was going to say. I decided to tell her if Dad's money meant so much to her, she could keep it and go to hell. I got cold feet and was sitting there stewing when Westbury's finest came by on patrol and started questioning me. I suppose a van like mine looks suspicious parked on the street at ten o'clock at night in the richest part of town."

A siren approached. Bobby's suddenly tense eyes darting to the door were those of a cornered animal.

Sim laid her hand on his arm. "Relax, man. They're not after you."

The siren grew closer. It stopped. Car doors slammed. A hand pounded at the back door.

"Westbury police. Open up!"

An instant later the door from the reception area opened. Chief George Frost marched toward Bobby with another officer behind him.

"Robert Burr?"

Bobby nodded, his face gone pale.

"We need to take you in for questioning about the murder of your stepmother, Irene Burr."

Bobby's knuckles whitened on the wrench. He raised it as he said, "I didn't kill her!" He took two quick strides toward the back door. He turned and started back toward the chief, gesturing with the wrench.

The officer raised his arm and fired. Bobby cried out as he fell.

Chapter 13

Cam disconnected the phone. On his way out in handcuffs, after recovering from being tased, Bobby had asked her to call a lawyer for him.

"Did you reach the lawyer?" Sim asked. "What'd he say?" She paced back and forth in the small office.

"*She* said she'd go down to the station and talk to him." Cam rose from the chair behind the desk.

"The lawyer's a woman? How do you know her, anyway?"

"Susan Lee is an old friend of my great-uncle's. Albert said he used to babysit her. Don't worry. She's a force of nature." Cam smiled. "Wait until you see her. She was my friend Lucinda's lawyer last June, when she was falsely arrested."

"Bobby shouldn't have been taken in, either! He didn't kill that witch." Sim punched a fist into the palm of her other hand over and over. "Do you think they'll arrest him?"

"They will now. I'm sure they thought he was going to attack them with that wrench. But I wonder what evidence they have against him for the murder," Cam said, staring out the front window of the shop. "It can't be merely because he was sitting outside her house in his van. Do you remember him being in a bad mood when you drove him home on the motorcycle?"

"It's kind of hard to tell somebody's mood when they're sitting behind you with a helmet on."

"I guess."

"What do we do now?" Sim asked. "How do we get him out?"

"Based on what happened with Lucinda, they'll hold a bond hearing in front of a judge tomorrow or the next day. They won't let him out on bail if they think he might try to bug out. His hiding for four days probably won't help him."

"We have to spring him, Cam."

"Wait a minute, Sim." Cam held up a hand. "This isn't the Wild West. You have to let the process play out. If you ask Susan Lee, she might be able to get you in for a visit."

Sim nodded. "Yeah, I'd like to visit him."

"The best thing you can do is be completely honest with Detective Pappas when he comes to ask you questions, because he definitely will. Tell him everything you know about the dinner, about Bobby, about Irene."

Sim straightened the papers on the desk, tidied a pile of pens, shut a file drawer. She looked everywhere but in Cam's eyes.

"They can't keep Bobby if they don't have evidence that he killed Irene," Cam went on. "But they need all the information you have. Okay?" Cam felt like the heavy. What did she know about crime fighting? Nothing, really, but her involvement earlier in the year had given her experience she might as well draw on now. And she had a sneaking suspicion Sim was hiding something.

"I have an idea," Sim said, finally looking at Cam. She dangled something from her finger.

Cam took a closer look. It was a key chain with a tiny silver hammer and a single key.

"Bobby's apartment. He gave me the key a while ago, when he had to travel for a job. Wanted me to water his plants."

"Okay. You have his key." Cam waited. "And?"

"Let's go over there. Maybe we can find some clues or something." Sim frowned and nodded, convinced of her own idea. "He lives right across the river in Merrimac."

"Now? Don't you have regular hours here?"

Sim batted the idea away with a brush of her hand. "There's nothing left for today. I'll put a note on the door. No problem. Let's go. You in?"

"I don't know, Sim. This isn't *CSI*, and you're not Sherlock Holmes. What kind of clues do you think you'll find? And what if the police show up while we're there?"

"How do I know what we'll find?" Her voice rose. "I have to help Bobby. Are you coming or not? We should hurry. The cops are for sure going to go over there themselves after they book him."

Against her better judgment, Cam agreed to go on the condition they take her truck and not the Harley.

Twenty minutes later they stood in Bobby's one-room apartment, a renovated shed behind a large antique house on the Merrimack River. The interior walls were planks of natural wood, and the back of the living space was a wall of glass. The approaching sunset had dyed the river pink, and it seemed to fill the room. It was stunning.

Cam wandered throughout the large room, which was punctuated by a half dozen healthy-looking houseplants. Hooks near the door held coats, shirts, and pants. In one corner a Southwestern-patterned spread covered a platform bed that held brightly colored bolsters and pillows. The small kitchen at the opposite corner of the space was clean and tidy. A wide couch faced the river, with a flat-screen television off to the side. A coffee table displayed the only signs of disorder in the apartment: an empty beer can, a wineglass with a trace of desiccated red in the bottom, last week's newspaper, a bowl with dried bits of cereal stuck to the inside. She poked her head into the small bath, which featured a glass shower enclosure and red and yellow towels.

Cam turned back to Sim, who was bent over a broad desk, rifling through a stack of papers.

"Are you sure you should be going through his stuff?" Cam asked.

Sim abandoned the pile and started yanking open drawers. "Maybe there's a letter from Irene here somewhere that threatens him. Or his bank statement, showing he didn't need her money. I don't know, Cam!" Sim looked up with tears in her eyes. "I'm worried about him. He's my best friend."

"Hey, don't worry. He's going to be all right." Cam walked over to Sim and gingerly patted her on the back. She rarely had the need to comfort a fellow human, and it didn't come naturally to her.

The outer door creaked. Cam twisted her head to see Detective Pappas standing in the entrance, staring at Sim. He did not look pleased.

"What are you doing here? You have no business in the home of someone under suspicion of murder." He raised bushy eyebrows.

Sim straightened up. "I have a key. He asked me to water his plants." Sim's stance was as defiant as her tone.

"And he keeps houseplants in his desk drawers? Right. What were you looking for?"

Sim shook her head.

Cam backed up a few steps. It wasn't enough to escape Pappas's attention.

"And you, Cameron? Can't keep your nose to yourself. You should know better."

"Now, wait a minute, Detective. There wasn't any yellow tape up," Cam said. "We didn't break in. We have a key. Bobby is a friend to both of us. A good friend. Why shouldn't we be here? And aren't you supposed to have a warrant to search a house?"

Pappas shook his head in exasperation. "Get out."

"Lemme see the warrant." Sim set her hands on her hips and glared.

Sighing, Pappas drew a piece of paper out of his pocket. He held it up in front of him.

Sim read it from where she was. "All right, we'll go."

"And I'll put up the damn tape. They brought him in only an hour ago. Didn't think I needed to quite yet." He watched them hesitate. "Get!"

Chapter 14

Cam and Sim were almost back to the auto repair shop when Cam glanced at the clock on the dashboard. Her eyes widened as she swore.

"What is it?" Sim asked.

"I have a dinner date. I forgot all about it."

"When are you getting picked up?"

"I have to meet him in Newburyport. At six." Cam pointed to the clock, which read 5:50. "And I have to get home and change." She gestured down at her work clothes from the day, old jeans and a long-sleeved T-shirt decorated with dried mud and plant stains. She groaned, pulling into the parking area of Sim's shop.

"Sorry to make you late." Sim opened her door and climbed down. "And thanks for driving."

"No worries," Cam said, shoving the gearshift into reverse. "Stay away from Bobby's place, okay?" she called out the window.

Sim held a hand up as she walked away. Cam noticed the mechanic didn't agree. But she didn't have time to worry about that. She drove home as fast as was safe in the gloaming. When she arrived, she left Jake a quick message that she was running late, and tore through a high-speed shower, wondering as she washed why he hadn't picked up his phone. He was probably in the middle of some complicated sauce. She threw on clean black jeans and a soft pale blue sweater, since the evening threatened to cool down even more before she returned home. She ran a comb through her hair, pulled on her cowboy boots, and was about to dash back out when Preston looked longingly at his dish.

"Gotcha, my man." Cam scooped dry food into his dish and ran him some fresh water.

After she'd rung the doorbell to Jake's flat for the third time, Cam checked her phone. *Uh-oh.* It was 6:45. She was really late. And Jake wasn't coming to the door. She stepped back and checked the second-story windows. They were closed, but light from his apartment pushed out into the night like a bloom of welcome.

He lived above his restaurant. Since it was Monday, The Market was dark and the big exhaust fan on the side of the building was quiet. Cam shook her head. In the short months she'd known Jake and fallen partway in love, she'd also experienced his volatile moods and occasionally incendiary temper. Maybe this was one of those times when Cam's being late had sent him into a minor rage. Wait'll he found out why she was late. Anything involving a threat, in Jake's mind, of Cam becoming interested in another man had sent him through the roof in the past. She made up her mind not to mention Bobby and her little field trip to his house with Sim. If Jake ever opened the door.

She rang once more. She heard the peal from within and was rewarded by the sound of heavy footsteps clattering down the stairs.

Jake pulled open the door. He wore a big grin, a silky black shirt, and jeans, with enormous bare feet poking out.

Cam let out a breath she didn't know she was holding. He wasn't angry with her. *Good.*

He pulled her into an embrace and nibbled on her ear. "How's my farmer?" His voice was husky and sensual.

Cam hugged him and delivered a quick kiss. She pushed him away gently, trying to ignore the parts of her body he had just lit on fire. "Hungry, that's how she is." She smiled up at him.

"All business, all the time." He shook his head, tsk-tsking her.

"I rang the doorbell a bunch of times." She hoped that didn't sound like whining, but wondered why he hadn't responded to the bell until now.

"Mmm." He ushered her up the stairs ahead of him.

He followed so closely, she could feel his heat. When she paused in the living room to drop her bag, he gracefully passed around her, letting his hand linger on her waist.

"Come and taste." He stood over a large pot on the stove, where a divine aroma surrounded him. He held a full spoon over the pot and gestured her closer. "Bouillabaisse. What do you think?"

Cam tasted the stew. She closed her eyes to savor it on her tongue and opened them again.

"You've done it again. Fabulous, Jake. It's rich and subtle and light all at once." She shook her head. "I'm amazed. If I tried that, it would never come out so good."

"Hey, I've been saving seafood shells—you know, lobster, shrimp, mussel. I boil them in court bouillon to make a seafood stock. And with the fishes, I put your leeks and herbs. Your red pepper and garlic go into the rouille. So it's a collaborative meal."

"I can't remember what rouille is," Cam said.

"Think of it as a spicy cream sauce, but without the cream. I blend olive oil with bread crumbs, garlic, saffron, and hot peppers."

Cam murmured her approval. She was getting weak in the knees. Could a person swoon over the mere description of food?

Jake pulled a loaf of crusty bread out of the oven and asked Cam to slice it while he ladled the stew into two wide bowls. He spooned the rouille over the top and placed one bowl on each red place mat. A simple green salad in a wooden bowl and an open bottle of Côtes du Rhône Blanc already graced the table, along with two slender green tapers in glass candlesticks.

"Sit, Cameron." He held her chair for her. "Now, what did I forget? Ah, yes, candles." He headed for the coffee table to fetch a lighter and returned to bring flame to wick.

Cam waited, wondering again why he hadn't answered her first several tries at the doorbell. She was glad he wasn't in an angry mood. And further wondered what she was even doing with a man whose moods she had to worry about.

Jake poured them each a glass of wine and dimmed the lights in the kitchen area. The candlelight softened the crags on his face. He sat and reached for Cam's hand. "We should do this more often." He squeezed and let go.

Cam raised her glass. "To bouillabaisse."

Jake frowned. He arrested the movement of his glass. "I didn't mean more French fish stew. I meant more intimate meals together with you, Cam." He took a sip without clinking his glass with Cam's or meeting her eyes.

"Which sounds good, too." Cam hoped that would be enough to smooth his Swedish feathers. Or maybe they were his dysfunctional-background feathers. Feathers reminded her of the hens.

"Guess what? I have chickens at the farm now."

Jake's face switched from whatever mood he had been in to instant delight. "How so?"

Between bites of the savory stew, Cam explained Project Rescue Chicken, how Alexandra had found birds in need, and how her friends had chipped in to build the coop. "When you saw me at the market Sunday? Alexandra and her crew were all at the farm, setting up a new home for the girls."

"Where did you get the birds?"

"There's the unfortunate part. They were Bev Montgomery's. She wasn't feeding them or taking care of them. The board of health was about to exterminate the lot. Alexandra's friend DJ helped get them out. He seems to understand chickens and can kind of talk to them."

Jake rolled his eyes. "Are there any guys out there you aren't attracted to?"

"I didn't say anything about being attracted to him." Was Jake jealous of DJ? "He's young, like Alexandra, and he knows what he's doing. I appreciate his talents. That's all."

"Hmm," Jake said with a toss of his head.

"Anyway, Bev isn't too happy about the rescue mission. She claims we stole them from her. She's deluded about that, since the board of health was going to take them, anyway, and those pea-brained ladies would have been dispatched to the big coop in the sky. Uncle Albert said he is going to try to get Bev to sell her farm and move into his assisted-living place. I think it's a wise move."

"Will you have eggs to sell?" Jake tore off a piece of bread and dunked it in the stew.

"I will after they recover from . . . oh, crud." Cam smacked her forehead.

"What?"

"Great chicken farmer I am. I forgot to get them into the coop before I came over here."

"What? Is a fox going to get them?" Jake laughed.

"One might, actually. Or a coyote." Cam couldn't believe she'd forgotten to make sure the girls were safe for the night.

"You were late getting here. What was up that you forgot about the hens, too?" Jake's face turned serious again.

Cam sipped her wine. "You probably haven't been following Irene's murder investigation, but her stepson, Bobby, has been missing."

"Was he killed, too?"

Cam could swear he looked almost hopeful. She shook her head. "When I was at Sim's, picking up my truck—"

"Who's Sim? Somebody else I have to worry about?"

"Hey, you must have seen Sim. She's the mechanic who came with Bobby to the dinner."

"Maybe. I can't remember." He waved a hand and nearly knocked over his glass.

"Jake, stop it. Listen to me." Cam covered his hand with her own. "I like you. A lot. I'm not looking to be involved with anyone else. I run into a lot of people in my work. You can't keep imagining reasons to be jealous of every single man who is remotely in my age bracket."

Jake pulled his white-blond brows together. He didn't look convinced.

Cam retrieved her hand and sat back. "As I was saying, when I was picking up my truck at Sim's auto repair shop—at *her* shop—Bobby showed up. He had started to tell us why he had been staying out of sight when the police swooped in and took him in for questioning about Irene's murder." *Oops.* She'd planned not to mention Bobby. Why couldn't she think before she talked for once?

"I never liked that guy. Glad they have him behind bars. Why'd he kill her? For her money?"

"Who said he killed her? I don't think he did, and Sim certainly doesn't."

"You can't deny he was flirting with you all summer. Then he shows up at the dinner in a goddamn skirt." Jake looked like he'd tasted a piece of rotten halibut.

"The skirt was his choice." Cam had liked the way it looked on him. And she had to admit she had enjoyed the months of flirting with the handsome carpenter, but she wasn't about to mention that to Jake. "Anyway, Sim wanted to check out his house. She had a key and wanted me to go with her, so I did. That's why I was late."

"So you chose Bobby over me."

Cam stared at him. "I'm done." She laid down her spoon and took a last sip of wine. She stood.

"Where are you going?" His voice was almost plaintive.

"I'm going home. My affection doesn't seem to be enough for you. If you want to spend time with me, I can't be stuffed into a box or kept on a leash. I'm an adult woman with a life outside yours. You have a choice." Cam grabbed her bag and started for the door. "Get used to it, or go find yourself somebody else, somebody meek and retiring."

"Don't go." Jake stood and followed her, arms outstretched. "I'm sorry, Cam."

Cam paused. He did sound sorry. But they'd been through this before.

"Please?" He grabbed her left arm, his huge hand encircling it completely. He closed it tighter, squeezing her bicep.

"Let go of me." Cam unfolded his fingers with her right hand. "Think about what I said."

When she reached the bottom of the stairs, she glanced back up. The sad look on his face had turned to stone.

She let herself out and stood for a moment outside the door. She shuddered. She'd playfully called him Lurch earlier in the year. The more she got to know him, the more often she glimpsed a monstrous side to him. She didn't like it. Not at all.

* * *

113

At home, Cam drove behind the barn and angled the truck so the headlights shone at the chicken yard. She let herself into the fencing and shooed the hens up the ramp and into the coop.

"Come on, ladies. Time for bed."

She couldn't tell if they were all there or not. She glanced around the yard and didn't spy any bedraggled creature lurking in the shadows. She'd have to count them in the morning. When she picked up the water receptacle and the feeder, she thought she felt a feather caress her hand, and her heart sank. She hoped a fox hadn't invaded their space and made off with one of them. She placed the receptacles inside and secured the door, checking it twice.

Tomorrow she'd rig an outdoor light on the barn wall. For tonight she'd just earned an F in Hen Management.

Chapter 15

The next morning dawned foggy and cool. After Cam pulled herself out of bed at six, she donned work clothes and an old sweater.

As she let the chickens out of the coop, coffee mug in hand, Cam tried to count them while they tumbled and staggered out. The one with the topknot flew out the door, startling her. Except for that one, they all looked pretty similar, and she thought she'd counted forty as she brought out their food and drink and replenished both. Preston stood outside the fencing with his ears perked up, but he didn't try to get into the enclosure.

"You leave the girls alone, Mr. P. They aren't your girlfriends or your lunch, you hear?"

She could have sworn he shrugged as he turned away. She yawned as she trudged out to an empty bed she'd raked smooth the afternoon before and carefully dropped hardy spinach seeds into three shallow furrows. It was too late for the plants to mature this fall, but she'd read the crop overwintered easily.

Over the bed she started to erect a knee-high mini hoop house. She set out heavy wire arcs spaced a foot apart. She fetched some floating row cover from the barn and laid it over the half hoops, anchoring it on the ground with lengths of lumber and pinning the ends to the wires with clothespins so they wouldn't flap in the wind.

Later in the season, after the ground froze, she would mulch the bed with salt marsh hay, much like she did with the garlic, and would replace the floating row cover with thick plastic, stretched tight to keep the snow from collapsing the hoops. The plastic would raise the temperature enough to keep the crop from dying off completely, and when spring came, it could resume growth. At least, that was the plan she'd read about in a book on growing in all four seasons.

On her way back to the barn, a breeze brought the flutter of a feather from the direction of her neighbor's property. Cam glanced to her right.

"Oh, no." She strode to a sad little heap on the ground. It was the remains of one of the hens. So she hadn't counted an even forty, after all. A mostly stripped skeleton lay abandoned near the boundary between her farm and Tully's meadow. The beak and claws, if that was what chicken feet were called, were intact, as were the bones. Most of the flesh had been eaten away.

Who or what had done the hen in? Cam guessed it could have been any predator, from a hawk to a fox to a coyote. Through her own negligence Cam hadn't been able to protect all the ladies, after all. She knew it was only a tiny-brained animal destined to become stew one day, but she felt sad for it and a failure for not being able to keep it safe. Plus, what would Alexandra and DJ think of her?

She drew her phone out of her back pocket to check the time. *Crud.* Now she was negligent in another direction. She was almost late if she wanted to get to the Middleford Fair on time. She blew the carcass a kiss and loped to the house, promising to give the dead girl a burial later in the day.

Cam quickly washed her hands and face and dumped her

work clothes in a pile on the floor. She threw on her vegetable-print vest over a black shirt and the same black jeans she'd worn to Jake's. She tied her black sneakers and checked the clock. Nine twenty. It was a thirty-minute drive south to Middleford. She had to submit her entry at the county fair by ten o'clock at the latest. She had barely enough time. She clattered downstairs and grabbed the completed entry forms from the desk. She winced at her farm's name, which was increasingly striking her as ridiculous. She'd change it back this winter. Albert had certainly expressed his approval for the move.

In the short walk from the house to the truck, Cam could feel the fog dampening every strand of her hair. Yet another reason to wear it short. It dried quickly, and humidity didn't really affect it. Hurrying, she loaded her three most perfect, most uniform garlic braids and four baskets of her sweetest, roundest gold cherry tomatoes into the cab of the truck, glad she'd harvested them in the sun the day before. They were so small, the temperature at harvest time made a big difference in their flavor. A warm, sunny day really brought out the sugars, while cooler or cloudy days made them taste more acidic.

She climbed into the truck and maneuvered into the navy-blue rain jacket she kept ready for days like these. As she drove, cutting across back roads to pick up Route 1, she rehashed last night's conversation with Jake. Why did the two of them seem to light up fireworks every time they were together? The romantic kind along with the conflicted kind. Her life was difficult enough. She didn't think she needed a contentious love relation-ship on top of it, no matter how weak in the knees Jake made her.

Her thoughts turned to Bobby, sitting in a jail cell. She hadn't heard from Sim this morning or from Susan Lee. Poor Bobby. Fi-nally, when he'd been willing to come out of hiding and talk to the police, he'd been abruptly taken away instead. And tased, too. Cam had heard about the stun guns, but she'd never seen one used. Bobby had cried out as he fell like a giant rag doll. She had at first thought the police had shot with a bullet, and was immensely relieved when Frost looked at her and said, "Taser."

She drove through the Great Marsh of Newbury. The fog cloaked the salt marsh haystacks. These weren't modern hay bundles shrink-wrapped in white plastic. Instead, they evoked earlier times with their traditional mushroom-like mounds elevated on wooden racks. She made it through the traffic from the Rowley strip mall shoppers, and up and down the wooded hills through Middleford. She hoped this weather would keep the crowds down at her destination. Even on a Tuesday morning the county fair had the potential to snarl traffic and clog the pop-up parking lots that bordered the fairgrounds.

She would never consider going near the fair on a weekend. People flocked to it for all kinds of reasons. 4-H teenagers hoped to win a blue ribbon for a prize goat or steer, even in these modern times. Other teenagers wanted to neck on the carnival rides. Adults came for the music venues, to watch the tractor-pull event, or to browse the blue-ribbon quilts and best-of-show family farm exhibits. And children everywhere clamored for sugary fried dough, a chance to play a shooting game, a spin on the most thrill-inducing ride. But flock there they did. Cam, on the other hand, didn't enjoy crowds one bit.

She stopped behind two other cars at a red traffic light. The light turned green, and the first car accelerated. A truck running the red light zoomed out from the crossroad. It swerved around the first car and sped away. The first car slammed on its brakes. The car behind it crashed into it. Cam jammed on her own brakes. She thanked her lucky stars she always left a large space between her and the vehicle in front. Her heart beat so hard, she could barely breathe.

She rolled her window down as both drivers exited their cars. Neither looked seriously hurt. They conferred about insurance and excoriated the red-light scofflaw, now long gone. Should she get out and leave her name as a witness? Another car pulled over, and Cam heard the driver call out that she'd seen the whole thing. She dug a farm business card out of her bag and handed it out the window to one of the drivers, apologizing for not staying but asking them to call if they needed her testimony.

Cam drove around the cars and continued to the fairgrounds. She had to make the deadline to submit her vegetables, and she could easily get stuck in traffic up ahead. Her heart rate gradually returned to normal, and her resolve to proceed very cautiously at intersections was reinforced.

She snagged what seemed to be the very last parking space in a grassy lot across from the fairgrounds, a spot at the back bordering a band of brush. She backed the truck into a tight space between an SUV and a beat-up Civic that must have been two decades old. She slung the bag of garlic braids over her shoulder with care and lifted out the flat box holding her tomatoes. She slammed the door with one heel. No need to lock the old rust bucket.

She stood in a group of fairgoers waiting for the police officer on duty to signal them to cross the busy two-lane highway. Howard Fisher walked through the parking lot, toward her, with his head down. He glanced up and saw her. He abruptly changed direction.

"Howard! Hey, Howard!"

His reluctance was obvious, but he turned back and shuffled up to her side. "Morning."

"How are you?"

He grunted, hands in pockets. "I'm all right." He gazed across the road at the acres of bustling fair.

"Do you have an entry here?" she asked.

"Yup. Bacon."

"That makes sense." As long as no one judging the bacon

knew Howard's current pigs had been gnawing human flesh. A little shudder ran through her. And he couldn't very well enter one of his emaciated swine in the judging, so maybe bacon was his only option. Winning could provide him with good publicity, the same reason Cam was entering.

The police officer in his electric-yellow vest motioned the group across the highway. Howard split off from Cam, barely saying good-bye, as soon as he was on the other side. Cam asked a volunteer in a green vest where the produce barn was and followed his directions. She glanced at her watch. Could have stopped at the accident, after all. She was ten minutes early.

The fog hung even more heavily here in the flat valley between the hills. It didn't dampen the fairgoers' spirits, from what Cam could see. The aroma of fried dough beckoned to her, as did sausages frying at a different booth. She stopped. Wes Ames and another man stood right beyond the Sausage Gal booth, each digging deep into a messy sub with oily peppers and onions trailing out of the roll every which way. Wes's friend was short, a bit thick through the middle, and wore a gray ponytail tied at the nape of his neck.

"Hey, Wes," Cam called.

He looked up and waved.

Cam approached the two as Wes turned back to the booth, grabbed a handful of paper napkins, and wiped his chin.

"Cam, how are ya?" Wes grinned. "Want a bite of sausage?"

She declined and greeted the other man.

"Billy's an old college buddy. Lives in Idaho. I thought I'd show him some local color. Homegrown, you might say." The men looked at each other and began to laugh.

Cam didn't get the joke but wished them a good time and moved on. If she didn't know better, she'd say they were acting like stoned college students. Maybe they were stoned. She didn't care.

A few moments later, she stood at the entrance to the warehouse-size produce barn with butterflies in her stomach. The end of her first year of farming. What had she been thinking, entering a competition? She was certain more experienced growers would be the blue ribbon winners, not her. But, as Albert had said, it would give her experience in the process. Plus, her gold tomatoes were exceedingly tasty and organic, too.

She squared her shoulders and marched in.

Chapter 16

After leaving her produce and her entry forms, she had two hours until the judging decisions were announced. She strolled through the vegetable area. First, she checked out her competition in the cherry tomato and garlic braid area and hoped she had a chance. Two of the braid displays looked a little pathetic, with small bulbs and uneven braiding. She kept walking through the barn. Some of the family farm displays went all out, including knitted tea cozies, handmade baskets, deep ruby jams, and bright green pickled beans, as well as the usual array of squashes, onions, and sheaves of cornstalks. She'd never have that kind of display unless she hooked up with a grandmother or two.

She moved to the next building, the quilt barn. Perusing the displays, she was amazed by the artistry. One wall hanging looked like a basic patchwork with narrow rectangles, until she looked closer. It was actually a bookcase, with each block a book, complete with title and author embroidered on the spine. A blue ribbon hung from another, a beautiful and complex rendering of interlocking Japanese fans in shades of gold and turquoise.

Cam ventured into the animal barn. To her surprise, Vince Fisher and a pig occupied one of the pens. The skinny teen wore khaki pants and a white polo shirt with WESTBURY 4-H embroidered on the chest. He was grooming a huge swine that didn't look like it could get much cleaner or much fatter.

"Hey, Vince. How's it going?"

"Yo, Ms. Flaherty. I have to, like, show this big guy in an hour. I'm pretty nervous."

"He looks well fed." This pig was so healthy and fat. Where had Howard Fisher been keeping it? Clearly, it got special treatment, which had to be to the detriment of the rest of the pigs Cam had seen the day before.

Vince looked up with a smile, his skinny, acne-ridden face half hidden under a lock of sandy hair. "For sure. Buddy here gets nothing but the best."

"That's great. Are all your pigs so big?" She was curious what he would say.

A shadow passed over Vince's face. "Well, not all of them. We're a little short on feed right now." He brightened. "But if Buddy gets Best of Show, we'll get some money, for sure."

"Really? I didn't know the fair offered award premiums."

"They don't usually, but some rich guy put in a bunch of money for prizes this year."

"What time are you showing him?"

"At noon."

"Well, good luck, Vince. I'm sure you'll do great."

"Thanks, Ms. Flaherty. Hey, can I ask you a question?"

"Sure."

"I was just wondering, like, about Ms. Burr's killer. Do you think they're going to catch him soon? It kind of weirds me out. And she was such a nice lady."

"Did you know her?"

"Yeah. I mean, sort of. She came to the farm one time. She seemed interested in me, asked me about my classes and what I like and stuff."

"It's very sad she's gone. I'm sure they'll catch someone soon, Vince." Cam hoped she sounded confident. "Don't worry."

"Wicked. Stay cool, Ms. Flaherty."

At least this time he hadn't addressed her as "dude," as he had earlier in the summer. Cam smiled as she walked back to the produce barn for her own judging. He was a good, hardworking kid with a difficult father. She hoped Buddy would win. Interesting, too, that Irene had taken the time to get to know Vince a little. More proof that Cam really hadn't known her at all.

Outside the barn, she checked her watch—three minutes until the announcement. She took a deep breath and walked in.

Farmers of all ages and sizes stood arrayed in an expectant semicircle. They faced the judges, who clustered at the end of the display tables. A photographer dressed in black tapped his foot, poised to capture the awards. Cam slid in at the end of the line of growers. She glanced around but didn't recognize any of them, which didn't surprise her, being the new girl on the block.

The head judge introduced himself and began by announcing the winner of the winter squash entry. The farmer, a woman younger than Cam, walked up and shook the judge's hand. She posed for a picture with him, her acorn squash, and her blue ribbon. He moved on to the next vegetable category and repeated the ritual. When a winner wasn't present, the judge laid the blue ribbon on top of the display. This could take a while.

An hour later it was time for the garlic braids. The judge announced the third and second place. Neither was Cam's. He held up a braid.

"This one incorporates the fattest bulbs and the best braiding. Unfortunately, we had to disqualify it because a string was used in the braiding." He went on to award the blue ribbon to a farmer from Essex. The handshake and photograph were accomplished.

Cam had used a string in her own braid. Had it been the erstwhile winner? It looked like hers. She made her way over to the garlic table, where the judge still stood. She introduced herself.

"I'm sorry. But rules are rules," the judge said to Cam. He held out her braid.

She took it. "I didn't see anything in the guidelines about not using string." She thought she had studied the online booklet in detail.

"The rules clearly say all entries must be produced on the farm. It was a wild guess you didn't grow the cotton and spin the string."

"So if I had sheep and spun my own yarn, it would be admissible?"

He raised his eyebrows. "Yes, I suppose it would."

Disappointed, Cam turned away, garlic in hand. It was a very fine braid.

Half an hour later the same judge approached the cherry tomato division. At least half the audience had already left. Some farmers, apparently, stayed only until their own entries were announced, and then they cleared out. Cam wiped her sweaty palms on her pants. Why was she so nervous about this? It was only a silly ribbon, and she was a freshman farmer, for Pete's sake.

He announced third place and then said, "Cameron Flaherty, Produce Plus Plus Farm, Westbury." He held up the red ribbon.

Cam's eyes flew wide open. *Cool.* A red ribbon on her first time entering. After the blue ribbon was awarded to a Groveland farmer, she picked up her own award.

She trudged toward her truck. The energy of the crowds had sapped her own, and even the second-place ribbon in her bag for the tomatoes didn't restore her spirits. She'd spent a day away from work for a minor award. To lose the garlic blue ribbon on a technicality was apparently one of those live-and-learn experiences. As she passed the Sausage Gal booth, the aroma of sizzling pork, which had smelled so enticing earlier, now made her feel a little nauseous.

The fog had lifted somewhat, but a fine mist continued to envelope the world. She climbed into the cab at the same time that a tall man folded himself into the Civic next to her. She followed him to the exit and waited in line next to him, checking her watch. It was already one thirty. She flipped on her turn signal to go left into the flow of traffic heading north on Route 1 until she saw it was moving at tortoise speed.

A Harley formed part of the line of cars inching up the hill. She squinted. It had a red lightning bolt on the back and a slender driver. What was Sim doing here in the middle of the day? If that was even her.

Cam glanced to the right. The southbound cars were driving at a normal rate. She could head that way and cut over to pick up Route 95 north. She'd probably get home faster, even though the distance was longer. Maybe she could salvage some of the rest of the day's work hours. She could call Sim when she got home and find out if it had been her. Cam shifted the truck's position a little and switched her turn signal so the traffic cop would know which way she was headed. He finally let her in, looking a little annoyed at her turning right from the left lane of the parking lot.

The road climbed up out of the valley. It leveled off for a dozen yards and crested at a forested area before a steep downhill stretched for a half mile. Fields and marshes lined the road and its narrow, crumbling shoulder. Cam was reaching down to switch on the radio when she realized her cruise control wasn't holding her speed back. She pressed her foot on the brake pedal. Nothing happened. She pumped it. No response. The speedometer read seventy-five and increasing. The Civic from the parking lot drove in front of her, creeping along, probably going exactly the speed limit to conserve gas. The gap between them was narrowing fast.

Cam pushed the brake pedal to the floor and swore when nothing happened. Her hands dampened on the steering wheel. She leaned on the horn. She grew closer and closer to the Civic. It didn't speed up. Its driver didn't hear her. Cam was about to crash into it. She reached for the emergency brake under the dashboard, but her hand slipped off. She was out of time. She saw a wider bit of shoulder ahead, near the bottom of the hill, and steered for it.

She fought the wheel as her tires found the shoulder, narrowly missing the Civic to her left. The truck wrenched right. But what had looked like a solid shoulder wasn't paved. The tires spun on the tops of marsh grasses. The Ford launched airborne. She gripped the wheel with all her strength, but there was nothing left to control. The truck crashed down into the marsh. Cam was jerked up, her hands torn off the wheel. The seat belt cut into her shoulder. Her head whacked against the roof. The engine cut out. All went silent.

Chapter 17

"Miss? Miss?" A knocking sound. Cam opened her eyes. She turned her head a little, but it hurt. A man was knocking on the window.

Where was she? Who was this guy? She looked around as far as possible without moving her head. Okay, she was in her truck. In a marsh. Cattails and tall grasses stuck up all around, interspersed by the invasive brilliance of purple loosestrife. *Wait a minute.* Her truck was in a marsh?

"Miss?" The guy made a cranking motion with his hand. He looked desperate. "Can you roll down the window, please?"

Cam stretched out her left arm and cranked down the window. "What am I doing here?"

Relief washed over his face. "You must have been speeding down the hill, and you ran off into the marsh. I'm so glad you're all right!"

Cam stared at him. It came back to her in a flood. "I wasn't speeding! My brakes didn't work. I didn't want to crash into the car in front of me. I tried to alert him, but he didn't hear my horn." She took a closer look. "Wait. You're the guy in the Civic."

The man, a thin fellow with salt-and-pepper hair and a white

Vandyke beard, looked abashed. "Right. I was playing my music really loud. I'm so sorry. I didn't even see you until right before you crashed. I don't use my rearview mirror." His look turned to concern. "Hey, are you all right? Your head is bleeding."

Cam put her hand up to her head. Sure enough, it came away covered with blood, but nothing hurt in an acute way. "I think I cut it when I hit the roof."

"I called nine-one-one. They're on their way." The keen of a siren sounded in the distance.

Cam tried to open her door, but it wouldn't budge. "Can you open the door for me?"

"That's not going to happen. You're stuck in the muck here. So am I." He gestured down. Cam leaned her head out to see that his legs vanished into a thick mud from mid-thigh down. She groaned and pulled her head back in. She closed her eyes. The fecund smell of marsh muck washed over her.

"Miss, you need to keep your eyes open. I learned that in an emergency training session at my workplace. Please look at me and keep talking. In fact, tell me what year it is and who the president is."

Cam sighed but obliged. This fellow was trying to help her.

"How many fingers am I holding up?"

"Four. What's your name?" Cam asked.

"Brian Walsh. What's yours?"

"Cameron Flaherty. Cam."

"So we're both Irish. Were you just at the fair?"

"Yes." She felt for the ribbon on the seat next to her, but it was missing. "Where's my ribbon?" She gestured to the wreckage of the cab. All the junk she usually kept on the seat, the floor, or the dashboard had played a game of musical chairs and switched places.

"What ribbon?" He frowned.

"Oh, the ribbon I won. Second place. For my tomatoes."

He smiled with crinkles around his eyes. "You grow vegetables? How amazing. I'm a software engineer. I couldn't grow a vegetable if you paid me."

"Well, I wrote code, too, until about a year ago." Cam tried to laugh, but that hurt, too. This guy was good at distracting her if she was actually trying to laugh. "And now I farm. Who knew?"

After being extricated from her truck and transported by ambulance to the hospital in Newburyport, Cam was scanned, x-rayed, poked, and evaluated. She wondered why they were taking even more blood out of her, until she was asked to give the state police permission to examine it for alcohol. Her shoulder sported a big bruise from the seat belt, and she had a surface cut on her forehead. She sat on the edge of the bed in an emergency department bay. A big clock on the wall read 4:40. There went any thoughts of working today, owing both to the time and to how she felt.

"You were lucky," the doctor said. "Although I wonder why your head hit the top if you were wearing a seat belt."

"It's a pretty old truck. I'm lucky it even has seat belts."

The doctor cocked her head, shiny black hair following. "How do you feel right now?"

"Like I was hit by a truck. Which I guess I was."

"Do you live with anyone?" the doctor asked.

"My cat."

"You probably have a mild concussion. I'd advise asking a friend to spend the night. A human friend. But if that's not possible, do this. When you find yourself getting sleepy, set a timer for two hours. You want to wake up every few hours and make sure you continue to see and think clearly."

"Do you think clearly when you're awoken every two hours?" Cam asked. "I sure don't."

The doctor laughed. Although she looked younger than Cam,

her dark eyes creased at the corners. "Good point, although I don't think I've slept for more than two hours in a row in years. All right, set your timer for every four hours. Get as much rest as you can. And refrain from physical activities for a few days."

"I'm a farmer! I can't not work. It's ninety percent physical."

"Do your best." The doctor looked over her glasses at Cam. "All right? You're released to go home." She made a note in the chart, saying Cam should call her personal doctor the next day and schedule a follow-up appointment. "Oh, and there's a police officer here who wants to talk with you before you leave."

Cam had called Lucinda to pick her up from the hospital. She was trying to tie her left sneaker without lowering her head when a man in uniform appeared at the entrance to the curtained bay holding her bed.

"State police, Ms. Flaherty. I'm Officer Russo. I need to speak with you for a moment, ma'am."

"Now? My ride is waiting outside." She grimaced at hearing herself whine.

"Yes, ma'am. Permission to record the interview, ma'am?" He switched on an iPad and lightly pressed a few icons.

Cam nodded, which made her head hurt again.

"I need you to acknowledge permission out loud, ma'am."

"I give permission to record this interview."

He noted the time, date, and location, and identified himself again. "Please describe in your own words what happened on Route One earlier today."

Cam told him about the truck speeding down the hill, about her brakes not working, about the car in front not seeing her. About the shoulder and how she landed in the marsh. "I'm grateful the truck didn't flip and that there wasn't a big tree waiting to greet me."

"You were fortunate, ma'am. Had you been having problems with your brakes before?"

"No. In fact, on my way to the fair this morning, I had to apply them suddenly because some idiot ran a red light. The car in front of me crashed into the car in front of her, but I had enough distance and my brakes stopped me in plenty of time."

"I was called to that event. You didn't stay to provide a witness statement." He looked up from his tablet with a stern expression.

"I know I should have stayed, but both drivers seemed fine and another witness had stopped. I gave one of the drivers my card. I had to get to an appointment at the fair." She smiled wanly and hoped he'd understand.

"What year is the truck you drive?"

"It's a nineteen eighty-five, I think." At his look of surprise, she went on. "It was my great-uncle's. It's only really used for farmwork and driving around locally. He always maintained it well, and it has pretty low mileage."

"Do you know the last time the brakes were replaced?"

Cam said she'd have to check. "But I'm sure it was done when it was needed. Albert is meticulous about that kind of thing. And I had it serviced yesterday."

"Where?"

"SK Foreign Auto in Westbury."

The officer, who looked about Cam's age, looked up again. "Wait. You're a farmer. Is your uncle Albert St. Pierre?" He smiled.

"Yes. Do you know him?"

"I do. Our families were—" He cut himself short and wiped the smile off his face. "Yes, I do. And admire him greatly. Now, since no alcohol was found in your blood—"

"They said they were testing for that."

"Of course. It's routine in any hospital transport after a motor vehicle incident. As I was saying, since you were not under the influence and no one else was injured, you are free to go. This interview is concluded." He switched off the recording app.

Lucinda pulled up in Cam's driveway and hurried around to open the passenger door. "I'll come in," she said as she helped Cam out and held her elbow while they walked toward the back door. "Let me make you some soup, *fazendeira*."

Cam thanked her. "I'm okay. I think I have a can of soup in the cupboard. I only want to lie down on the couch and do nothing."

"Are you sure?"

Cam eased herself onto the couch with a groan. "I'll be fine."

Lucinda set a glass of water and Cam's bag on the end table and stroked Cam's shoulder. "Call me if you need anything. I still owe you big-time." She pulled the door shut behind her with a soft click.

As Cam reclined with a blanket on her lap and a throbbing head, the crash played over and over in her mind. Why had her brakes gone out? They had been fine earlier in the morning, more than fine. Could someone have tampered with them? The thought made her shiver. She pulled the blanket up around her neck. It had to have been someone at the fair. She'd seen Howard and Vince. She'd run into Wes. She thought she'd seen Sim on her bike. She considered all of them friends. Why would any of those people want to do her harm? O would some evil stranger have done it just for kicks?

Her head hurt more than before from hashing through all the possibilities. She felt sleepy and realized she should call her great-uncle before she snoozed in case her crash made the early news. She reached for her bag and dug the cell phone out.

"I guess you're at dinner, Uncle Albert," Cam said in reply to his voice mail greeting. "I was in a little accident today in Middleford, but I'm fine, so don't worry. Oh, and I won the red ribbon for the Sun Golds. Talk to you tomorrow. Love you." Speaking with him about her suspicions would have to wait. She made a mental note to tell Sim to check for malicious tampering with her brakes. Which wouldn't do much good if Sim herself had done it. Or maybe she should tell the police.

As she lay there, Cam acknowledged that her blessings ran to luck, too. She could so easily have killed someone else—the nice guy in the Civic—or been killed herself. If she were Preston, one of her nine lives had just gotten used up, she thought as she slipped into sleep.

Chapter 18

A sound. Music. Cam pulled herself up out of a dream. She looked around. *Oh, yeah.* She was on the couch because she'd been in an accident. Sunlight angled low and weak through the window facing the back. So the fog must have burned off at last. The music sounded again. *Star Trek: The Next Generation.* She finally came fully awake. It was her phone ringing, which was parked on the end table. She sat up quickly, reaching for the phone as a sharp pain shot through her head. She closed her eyes, succeeding in knocking the phone to the floor.

Crud. By the time she retrieved the phone, it had stopped ringing. She peered at the caller ID. Alexandra.

Cam hit SEND with one finger while pressing her other hand to her temple. Alexandra picked up immediately.

"Cam, I was looking at Wicked Local News online and saw your name. You were in an accident? Are you okay?"

So the news was already online. *Great.* "Yeah. Well, sort of. My head hurts."

"I was going to come by and check on the hens. I'll check on you, too. See you in a few, all right?"

Cam agreed and disconnected. She was glad she'd have some help getting the birds in before dark. No way did she want to ever see another chicken carcass on her property. She rued having to tell Alexandra about the dead bird. At least it was only one.

Gingerly was the only way to put it: how she stood, used the bathroom, drank a glass of water in the kitchen. She eyed the prescription pain pills Lucinda had picked up for her on their way home from the hospital. Cam hated to take drugs. Now might have to be the exception. She shook out two and downed them with another glass of water.

It seemed like only a minute later that Alexandra rapped on the door. "I whipped you up some healing muffins." She extended a basket broadcasting a delicious smell from a green-checked cloth.

Cam thanked her as she pulled back the cloth. Steam arose from crusty brown muffins dotted with blue and green flecks.

"Whole-wheat blueberry with mint. I picked the blueberries last summer and froze them. They have local honey and butter in them, too, and the wheat is from western Mass."

"They smell delicious. I feel better already."

"So how'd you get run off the road, anyway?"

"What's more important is the story of Bad Farmer Cam." She told Alexandra about her lapse of the night before as they strolled slowly out back to check on the birds. She added how she'd found the dead hen this morning.

"I'm really sorry," Cam continued. "Things got complicated at the end of the day yesterday, and I forgot about the chickens until well after nightfall. I promise it won't happen again." The air, as they walked, had turned warm and mild, and a slight breeze brought the scent of a recently mowed lawn. Weather in New England. What was it they said? "Wait an hour, and it'll change."

"Cam, don't worry. I'm just glad you're all right. And, you

know, the hens were all going to die, anyway. So we saved thirty-nine instead of forty. That's still huge."

The two women rounded the corner of the barn and observed the hens pecking inside their fenced area. It looked like only about half of them. Cam's stomach dropped. Had the predator been back and made off with half the flock?

Alexandra peered inside the open door of the coop and counted for a moment. "There are eighteen of them in here. Just hanging out." She extracted her head with a smile. "You can almost imagine them with little chicken e-readers, catching up on their reading lists now that they know they don't have to fight all day to find food."

"Wonder what they like to read?" A giggle bubbled up in Cam.

"Probably not *Chicken Soup for the Soul*. Maybe *Fifty Shades of Feathers?*" Alexandra's laugh turned into a snort, which made them both laugh more.

"*The Girl with the Chicken Tattoo?*" Cam couldn't stop giggling. She felt punchy.

"Or *The Hen Whisperer?*" Alexandra wiped her eyes. "Seriously, DJ said they like to roost at the same time every night, right around dusk. That's why half of them are already in."

Cam, a little high now on both laughter and pain meds, helped her shoo the rest of the birds into the coop. Alexandra counted to be sure twenty-one marched up the ramp before she shut the door and latched it.

"We'll work on a covered run this weekend. DJ said he'd have time, and I will, too. And one tip? It's probably better to get them in early rather than late, you know, if you're pressed for time."

"Got it. Do you want to come in for a cup of tea or a glass of something stronger?" Cam asked.

Alexandra said she'd like a cup of herbal tea. When they were settled at the dining table with tea and the muffins, Alexandra narrowed her eyes at the bandage on Cam's head.

"Now tell me about this accident."

Cam, in the middle of a bite of muffin, held up her hand. She swallowed and said, "These are great. I didn't realize how hungry I was."

"I just threw them together." Alexandra tossed a braid back over her shoulder.

"Is there anything you can't do?"

Alexandra laughed, a light crystal peal. She straightened her already perfect posture. "Now. Out with the story."

Cam relayed her tale, right down to the Civic driver who made her say who the president was and how many fingers he was holding up. "Good thing I can count, right?" She laughed weakly.

"Wait. So your brakes were fine before you got to the fair and totally didn't work after? How'd that go down?" Alexandra knit her brows.

Cam raised her own eyebrows. "Question of the day. I don't know. It doesn't seem possible they would go bad on their own in such a short period of time." She mentioned the people she'd run into at the fair and seeing Sim's Harley on the road. "I had the truck in for a service to Sim yesterday. But she couldn't have tampered with the brakes then, because they worked fine on my way to Middleford. Besides, why would she?"

"Sim, Wes, Howard, Vince." Alexandra ticked the names off on the fingers of her left hand. "Or a random somebody. Crazy."

"With the crowds the fair draws, anybody could have seen me or my truck. Why anybody would tamper with the brakes is the real question."

"What do the police say?"

Cam wrinkled her nose. "About somebody trying to kill me? I didn't talk to them about that idea. They seem to think I wasn't driving carefully. They even tested my blood alcohol at the hospital. Which was zero. And I always drive with care, anyway."

"I think you should tell them you suspect tampering. Where's the truck now?"

"At Sim's garage. You know, right in town. I asked the police to have it towed there."

"And where's your cell?"

Cam pointed to the end table where she'd left it.

"I'm calling the cops." Alexandra fetched the phone and pressed some numbers.

"You know the police station number by heart?" Cam was surprised.

"An old boyfriend works there. I memorized it a while ago." She extended the phone to Cam.

Cam was opening her mouth to object when someone answered on the other end. She identified herself and asked to speak to Chief Frost.

"He's not in, ma'am," said the dispatcher who answered. "Can I help you?"

Cam asked if Ruth was on duty, but the dispatcher said she wasn't.

"It's about an accident I had today in Middleford. I think . . . Well, could you have Chief Frost call me? I think there might have been foul play." Cam squeezed her eyes shut at the cliché and opened them again.

The officer agreed to leave the chief a message and took Cam's information.

Cam disconnected and gazed across the table at Alexandra. "I'm sure she thought I was some kind of lunatic. *Foul play.* Right." She should probably call Ruth at home and tell her. The effort to do that seemed overwhelming at the moment.

"What about asking Sim to check the brakes for you?" Alexandra asked.

"I'm really tired. I'll call her tomorrow. I need to rest again."

"What can I do for you before I go?" Alexandra stood. She frowned and smiled at the same time.

"Actually? You can bring the timer on top of my stove over here and set it for four hours. The doctor said I need to keep waking up to be sure I can see straight and focus." Cam pushed up from the table. She grabbed another muffin and made her way slowly back to the couch. Dark was falling fast. She switched on the lamp.

Alexandra set the timer on the coffee table. She added Cam's phone and a glass of water as Cam pulled the blanket up under her chin again.

"Well, call me if you need me, Cam. I can borrow my mom's car and come back. I can even stay the night if you want."

Cam smiled. "I really appreciate it. But I'm sure I'll be all right."

"I'll come early for Volunteer Day tomorrow. I can coordinate everybody."

"Volunteer Day!" Cam groaned. "I totally forgot about it. Thank you. That would be a big help. I'm sure I'll feel better by then. You be careful on the road, okay?"

Alexandra shook a little light on a head strap at Cam. "Always do," she said as she walked out. A bicycle bell dinged from outside a moment later.

As Cam sampled the second muffin, she hoped she'd feel better tomorrow. Right now every bone in her body ached and her head throbbed. She realized she hadn't seen Preston since she'd been home. He must be taking a long nap somewhere. She didn't need to worry about him. He had his own entrance to the house, after all, the cat door in one of the basement windows.

She also realized the human door was unlocked. She couldn't summon even an ounce of strength to get up and bolt it. If an intruder wanted to come in and whack her over the head, well, she could hardly feel worse.

* * *

Cam opened her eyes. The television cable box read 8:15. Her head hurt. She was hungry again. And it was too quiet. Why wasn't Preston lobbying for his six o'clock treat? He was always in the house well before now, demanding his daily spoonful of canned food. She eased herself off the couch.

"Preston, treat," she called. "Preston!"

She opened the back door. The long dusk of a New England autumn had lost its last rosy light. The evening air continued mild, but the moon hadn't yet risen. She called again, adding the high-pitched soft whistle—*schwee-schwee-schwee*—he always responded to, no matter how far out in the fields he was.

No cat. Where was her Buddha buddy, who never roughened the edges of her life, like Jake did, or rejected her, as her former boyfriend had? Mr. P was one of her constants. As she gazed out into the dark, Cam racked her brain to think of the last time she'd seen him today. It had to be this morning, before she left for Middleford. Which seemed like a week ago. But had he been around this morning? She struggled to remember.

She took a deep breath. She reminded herself that he had stayed out all night before and had appeared the next morning, looking for breakfast, as if it was perfectly normal to put his human through a night of tossing and turning. But now? Life seemed so much more tenuous. Irene had been murdered in a horrific way. Bobby had disappeared and then had been arrested. A hen had been killed. And someone had tampered with the brakes on her truck. Could the fox have taken Preston, too? The thought of him being harmed made it really hard to keep the faith that he would show up happy and hungry at dawn.

Cam laced up her work boots on the back porch the next morning. The steam curling up from her coffee brought the rich aroma to her nose but did nothing to soothe her heavy heart. Preston wasn't sleeping on the sunny living room windowsill, as he usually did in the mornings. He hadn't come when she called. His dry food dish, a ceramic bowl with kitty footprints all around it, was as full as she'd left it the night before.

Despite having downed two more pain meds with a muffin, her head hurt and her body ached. But it was nothing in comparison to the empty space beneath her hand where her faithful cat should have been. She paced out to the road. Scanning up and down brought no sight of a puffy figure lying too still, as she had feared. She'd never seen Preston try to cross the country lane, which some residents liked to treat as a speedway. When he roamed, he always headed for the fields and the woods out back. Which held their own menaces, as the dead chicken attested to.

Speaking of chickens, it was time to let the girls out for the day. Cam opened the coop door, latching it ajar. She topped up their food and drink and made sure the fence was secure after she let herself out of the enclosure.

Her cell phone rang as she approached the barn. She dug it out of the back pocket of her work pants and noticed Westbury PD was the caller ID. Chief Frost himself was on the line. He asked her about the message she'd left the day before.

"Did you hear about my accident?" Cam asked.

"Yes. I hope you're feeling all right."

"Thanks. I am, sort of. About the accident, I didn't mention it to the state police, but I think someone must have tampered with my brakes. I was driving safely, and they worked fine on my way to the fair."

"Are you sure?"

"Yes! In fact I had to apply them suddenly when some idiot ran a red light. I know it's an old truck, but there was nothing wrong with the brakes."

"Where is the vehicle now?"

"I had it towed to SK Foreign Auto, right there on Main Street."

"Ms. Koyama's shop." He drew out Sim's last name like he didn't give her much credibility.

"Right. She's a good mechanic. She serviced the truck on Monday, in fact."

"Oh? Maybe she's the one who messed with the brakes."

"No! Why would you say that?" Although, of course, she'd had the same thought.

He cleared his throat. "I'll send someone over there to take a look. I'll get back to you."

Cam thanked him and disconnected as Alexandra sailed up the drive on her bicycle for Volunteer Day.

"How's the head?" Alexandra asked, dismounting.

Cam shrugged. "I've been better, but I'm up and around. It actually feels good to be moving again. But Preston is missing." She knew what a huge heart the younger woman had for animals.

Alexandra looked stricken. "That's terrible. Are you sure he's not out hunting?"

"I haven't seen him in twenty-four hours. He's usually back eating by now when he's stayed out all night before. Which he rarely does, anyway."

"We'll make posters and put them up everywhere." Alexandra placed hands on hips. "Did you call Madeline?"

"No, but I guess I should." The animal control officer kept a menagerie of found, foster, and abandoned animals at her own farm, including several rescue sheep.

"You don't think he's been kidnapped, do you?"

Cam stared hard at her. "You mean somebody might have taken him?"

"I don't know. There's been a lot of bad stuff going down around here lately, right?"

143

Cam's core turned to ice. The thought of Preston being in malicious hands was even worse than picturing him lost in the woods. "Who would do something like that?"

A car pulled up, and three shareholder volunteers piled out. Lucinda arrived in her own car right behind. Their eager faces and energetic stances reminded Cam she had a farm to run.

Alexandra patted her arm. "He'll be back."

Cam nodded. "Will you organize out here? You know what needs to be done. I'll go in and call Madeline and print up some posters. I have a nice picture of Preston I took a few months ago."

Alexandra nodded and turned to greet the arrivals.

"Good morning," Cam called to them as she headed for the house. "I'll be out in a couple of minutes. Alexandra will get you started."

After a quick conversation with Madeline, Cam e-mailed her Preston's picture. She created a file for the poster. She pasted in the picture of Preston standing on the back porch that she'd taken on a sunny morning in July, and added a big heading that read, LOST. LAST SEEN AT 8 ATTIC HILL ROAD. PLEASE CALL OR E-MAIL IF YOU SEE PRESTON. She finished with her cell phone number and the farm's e-mail address. She sent ten of them to print in color and on the highest-quality setting. To heck with how much ink cartridges cost.

The house phone rang from its anchored spot at the end of the kitchen counter. Cam couldn't quite bring herself to give up the old black phone, its receiver connected to the heavy base with a curly cord. The telephone, the numbers on its rotary dial now faded, had been there for as long as she could remember. When she'd first been at the farm, they'd only had to dial the last four numbers to reach someone in town, and now she had to include the area code to call somebody across the street.

The device was a connection not only to the farm's past but to her great-aunt Marie. Cam could still picture the petite woman, a

144

flowered bib apron tied around her tidy midsection. She would take a quick break between farm chores and making dinner to chat with a friend as she sipped a cup of coffee. Since the cord didn't stretch too far, she'd either stand at the corner of the counter or pull up a chair. A sharp pang nicked Cam's heart. She missed her great-aunt, who'd been more of a mother figure to her than her own mother. Marie had been unfailingly warm and nurturing, firm and fair, present and loving. Mom, on the other hand, had barely been present, even when she wasn't off on a research trip with Cam's father on the other side of the world.

Cam walked the few steps from her desk to the counter. The only people who used this number now were the older residents of town. Everyone else called her on her cell. Even though she'd added a voice mail service to the line, she nearly always picked up when it rang. The device couldn't display caller ID, but she could trust that a friend would be on the other end.

"Uncle Albert, how nice to hear from you." Cam smiled at the phone. Friend or family, that is.

"I'm surprised you're indoors on such a beautiful morning, Cameron."

The weather hadn't even registered on Cam this morning. Was it a beautiful morning? Were her troubles so many that her farmer's instinct to pay attention to the weather above all else had crumbled like a dry leaf?

"How are you?" Albert went on. "You said something about an accident."

"I'm all right. A little sore. I have a crew of volunteers out there and was inside . . ." Cam realized she didn't feel up to sharing her woes about Preston right now. "Uh, getting something."

"Well, now, why don't you stop up at the place here when you get done this afternoon? I think we have a few things to catch up on."

Cam agreed. "I'll ride my bike over at about four o'clock."

Before Albert disconnected, he added, "And bring me a six-pack of that Ipswich beer you like so much, will you?"

Cam raised her eyebrows but agreed. She hung up. She knew he liked a glass of wine with his dinner, but didn't think she'd ever seen him even taste a beer. A late afternoon Ipswich IPA with her favorite octogenarian? Well, why not?

Cam borrowed Lucinda's car and posted Preston's picture at the Food Mart, the library, and the post office. She stapled five more to telephone poles and signposts at intersections. She added one a mile down the road in either direction from the farm.

She'd just arrived back at the farm when Pappas pulled in behind her. Cam unfolded her long legs out of Lucinda's car and leaned against the open door, watching him.

"Nice car, Detective. I mean, Pete," Cam said as he approached.

Pappas, in a crisp plaid shirt and dark slacks but no tie, turned and glanced at the Saab with a little smile and then turned back to Cam. "It's my indulgence." He cocked his head. "And it's twenty years old."

"Looks like you take pretty good care of it." The car, like its owner today, was tidy, clean, and without dents or scratches. Cam looked down at her black Johnny's Selected Seeds T-shirt and her work pants, with stains on the left knee and a hole in the right, the knee she routinely knelt on. She suddenly felt like the odd woman out.

He stretched his left hand out to rest on the open driver's-side door of Lucinda's car, effectively blocking Cam in. She glanced at the untanned band on his ring finger.

"I'll take you for a spin sometime if you'd like. It runs like a beaut, and the leather seats are softer than you can imagine." He slid his hands into his pockets. The little smile again played across his face.

He wanted to take her for a spin? "Did you come all the way over here to ask me out for a driving date?" *Oh, no.* What a stupid thing to say. She'd never gotten the knack of conversation, to say nothing of flirting. And was that what this was? A flirtation? If so, what about Jake? She felt a blush creep over her neck and cheeks.

Pappas, meanwhile, appeared to have the grace not to notice her gaffe.

"Why not?" He smiled at her.

He had asked her out. Sort of. "It sounds like fun." She'd never noticed the dimple in his left cheek when he smiled. Maybe because she hadn't seen him smile much until now.

"Actually, I heard about your accident," he went on. "I was passing by and wanted to see how you were doing. Looks like you're up and around, anyway."

"I am. I'm kind of achy, but I feel a lot better today than I did yesterday. As long as I don't touch my head." Her hand stole to the bump on her temple.

"Frost told me you think someone tampered with your brakes. And this would have been while you were at the fair?"

Cam nodded and repeated her story about how her brakes had worked perfectly on her way south. "But what I don't get is why anyone would want to do that to me."

Pappas nodded like he was thinking. "I'll work on it."

"But why? Aren't you on the murder case?"

"We don't always know what's related to what. Something like this could end up being connected. I don't know how yet, but the rule is to exclude nothing." He stared beyond the barn for a moment and back at her. "For example, the murderer might think you saw something. Or overheard a conversation that would implicate him. Or her."

Cam gazed at him, the horror of the logical next step dawning on her. "I wasn't meant to survive the crash. Is that what you're saying?"

"That is one possible scenario, yes."

Cam shivered despite the sunlight. Pappas moved toward her and stopped. It felt like he had meant to put his arm around her and then had thought the better of it.

"Do you think I'm still in danger?" She hugged herself. "Am I a walking target for the killer to aim at?"

"I would recommend caution, Cameron. Go about your business, but keep your door locked and your phone with you. And don't do anything silly, all right?" Concern knit his heavy brows together.

Cam cleared her throat and stood tall. "Going to the county fair is hardly silly. But I promise. If you promise to find this maniac. And soon."

"Deal." He gave her a thumbs-up gesture and walked to his car. Before he climbed in, he called, "Let's get that joyride in one of these days."

She waved as he pulled out, hoping there was, in fact, some joy coming along soon. But that pale band on his ring finger. Was he just recently divorced? Or maybe even still married? He seemed much friendlier toward her now than he had last June. She already had an overcontrolling man in her life. Did she also need one on the rebound?

Chapter 19

Cam worked here and there alongside the volunteers for the next couple of hours, being careful not to bend down. She sat for a rest every twenty minutes or so. She found herself looking over her shoulder at odd noises and startling at the least thing. She wished she'd told Pete about Preston's disappearance.

Her feelings were at odds with the weather. It had turned out to be a sunny day with a mild breeze, perfect for ripening the pumpkins and winter squashes where they lay in the field and for sweetening up the apples. Deep purple eggplants and reddening peppers hung from branches, although the first frost would spell their end. She set one younger shareholder to sift through the potato beds to be sure they hadn't missed any tubers at harvest time the week before. Lucinda and another volunteer took on the final weeding in the lettuce and greens beds.

Cam joined Diane Weaver in her assigned task of picking up windfall apples. "I know it's a bit backbreaking, but I can take them over to Cider Valley Farm and put them through their press," Cam said. "I hate to waste them in the compost if we can get juice from them."

"No problem. It's great to be out in the fresh air."

"What do you do for work, Diane? I know a lot of people can't get away on a weekday morning to work on a farm."

Diane was silent for a moment. She picked up another handful of apples and laid them in the wooden box Cam had supplied her with earlier. "I'm a consultant. I can fix my own hours, within reason." She stood to stretch.

"What do you consult about?"

"I work for the government." Diane bent to pick up more apples from the ground and did not elaborate.

Cam let the subject drop. She was grateful for the free labor and didn't really care what her volunteers' day jobs were. She watched Diane's eyes fix on a field beyond and to the left of the small apple orchard. Cam followed the trajectory to see Wes Ames bent over a row of Brussels sprouts.

"Have you known Wes long?" Cam asked, remembering the look Wes had shot Diane on Saturday.

Diane paused again. "I don't actually know him. I've heard him speak about the Old Town Hall at meetings, that's all."

"When he was leaving Saturday, he gave you kind of a dirty look."

"Oh, we might have been on opposite sides of an issue once or twice." Diane's laugh seemed forced. "Nothing personal. Has he been a subscriber long?"

"This is my first year of having a CSA, actually. But his wife, Felicity, signed them up early last winter, and they've been active members. He told me she's away helping her sister right now."

"Interesting."

Cam started to work alongside Diane until she realized bending down to pick up apples was not the best thing for her head. She spied Alexandra at the compost piles and strolled in that direction instead.

"Thanks once again for tackling compost duty," Cam said to

Alexandra. There was plenty of new material to add almost every day now. "The weather is still warm enough to cook it down if it's turned often enough."

"No worries. It's great exercise." Alexandra stuck her pitchfork in the ground.

At a sudden rustling from the grapevine behind Alexandra, Cam whirled but saw only a squirrel chasing another up a nearby tree.

"So Madeline didn't have any news about Preston?"

Cam shook her head. "No news. I put the poster up all over town and on this road, too." She patted the phone in her back pocket. "No calls yet, either."

Alexandra reached out an arm and squeezed Cam around the shoulders. "He'll show up. I'm sure of it."

"I hope so," Cam said, tears pricking her eyes. "I can only hope so."

As the sun reached its apex, she wandered the fields and asked each person working to keep an eye out for Preston. Most expressed their sympathy. All the volunteers knew the farm cat, and several had grown quite fond of him. She also made sure everybody knew they were welcome to pull up as many cornstalks as they wanted to take home for fall decorations. A sheaf of cornstalks next to a bale of hay and a couple of pumpkins was apparently an obligatory decoration in town. Cam herself didn't bother. She had all the cornstalks she'd ever want to see a few short yards away.

She headed out to the field where Wes was working. She gave him her spiel about Preston.

"You know cats," Wes said. "He's out catching songbirds somewhere. He'll either be back or he won't. He's an animal, isn't he?" He didn't meet Cam's eyes, and he didn't sound as if he cared if the kitty was found or not.

She thought about how he'd reacted to Preston on the most recent pickup day, almost as if the feline was disgusting. "You don't like cats, do you?" She stuck her hands in her back pockets. Certainly some people were not cat people, but she'd rarely encountered a person who appeared to actively dislike them.

"I wouldn't go that far." Wes bent over a stalk and began to hack at it with the machete-like knife he held.

The knife wasn't one of hers. He must have brought his own. Cam shivered as she wondered why. At least today he didn't seem stoned.

"It looked like you were enjoying yourself at the fair yesterday," she said.

"I was." He straightened and arched his lower back into his hands. "It's one of the perks of being retired. You can have fun when you choose to, not when the boss tells you to."

Wes turned his back on Cam and began whacking the stalk with excess force. Green chips flew every which way until the plant split. Wes tossed it on the wheelbarrow full of other stalks and threw the knife in on top.

"See you Saturday," he called over his shoulder as he marched toward the barn.

Cam followed him at a stroll.

As they filed back to their cars, Lucinda and the woman she'd been working with paused to say good-bye to Cam.

"Hey, *fazendeira*. Any news about Bobby? He still in jail or what?"

"I've been so worried about Preston being gone and about what happened to my brakes, I almost forgot about Bobby."

The other woman, a local named Fiona, said, "Bobby Burr is in jail? He's the talented carpenter, right? I was going to call him about an addition to my kitchen."

"I think he's in jail. I haven't heard anything about him getting out. I'm sure they'll realize soon enough that he isn't the killer."

"Killer?" Fiona covered her mouth with a pale hand, her eyes wide. "You mean he's in jail for his stepmother's death?"

Cam nodded. Fiona must have been hiding under some rock if she didn't know this biggest local news story of the season. Who was the real murderer, anyway? And would he attack again before Pappas arrested him? Or her?

Chapter 20

After the volunteers left and Cam headed for the house, all she wanted to do was curl up and take a nap. Her head pounded, her stomach growled, and her heart ached with no Preston at her side. Instead, she took a deep breath and washed her hands. She poured a glass of milk. She cut a piece of cheese to go with the last of Alexandra's muffins and took her lunch to the computer desk. No new e-mail about Preston. No messages. She decided to post a notice on the farm's Facebook page and the farm Web page. She had to cover all the bases. She even sent out a tweet using the hashtag #lostcat and linked Preston's picture.

She called Sim's shop, but the mechanic didn't respond. Cam caught up on some paperwork and paid a few bills. It had been a productive morning with the volunteers, and her body was rebelling against doing any more physical work. She checked the farm's Web site again and noticed a new comment from Neela was up for moderation. Neela, one of her enthusiastic locavores, was a software engineer who lived in town with her husband, Sunil. Cam opened the message.

Can we have a volunteer day on the weekends, please?
We want to help but cannot be there during the workweek.
Thank you!

Cam shook her head at her own cluelessness. Of course she should have a volunteer day on the weekends. Lots of people had to be at their own workplace on Wednesdays. She was lucky she got the turnout she did on a weekday morning. And if she called for volunteers on Saturday mornings, that solved the problem of scrambling to get the harvest in before the noon pickup time. Or maybe she should make half the share be "pick your own." She tapped the desk next to the keyboard. So many decisions.

She was about to reward herself with a quick nap when she remembered how she'd felt when Lucinda asked about Bobby. Sure, a few things had happened to Cam in the last day or two, but he was her friend. She wasn't being much of a friend back.

Cam pressed Susan Lee's number on her cell. To Cam's amazement, the lawyer picked up. Cam asked her if there was news about Bobby.

"I just got called to the court. They're about to hold his hearing."

"What evidence did they have against him?"

"I can't talk about the evidence." The lawyer's voice was tight.

"Can he have visitors?" Cam had brought Lucinda a few personal items while she was jailed for a few days last spring. Lucinda had been very grateful for the gesture. "Does he need anything?"

"So far I'm the only one allowed in. I'll let you know when that changes."

Cam thanked her.

"Cameron? One more thing. You need to call off your friend Simone. She's only making trouble. For Bobby and for herself."

"I don't really know her very well. But what do you mean? What has she been doing?"

The phone emitted a noise, and Susan seemed to drop off. A moment later, she said, "I have another call. Catch you later." The call clicked off.

Cam disconnected, too, but kept her eyes on the phone in her hand. What did she mean about calling off Simone? Cam hoped Sim wasn't doing anything rash. She called the auto shop, but again Sim didn't pick up, and the call never went to voice mail.

As she stared at it, the phone rang. She checked the caller ID. "Ruth?"

"I heard you were in an accident. Are you all right?" The concern in Ruth's voice came through loud and clear.

"I appear to be." Cam told her about her brakes failing and the crash.

"You were lucky."

"I'll say." Cam went on to outline her thoughts about tampering.

"Did you tell somebody at the station?"

Cam said she had. "You're not on duty?"

Ruth replied that she was headed out to work in an hour. "Why?"

"I spoke to Susan Lee. She said my mechanic, Sim Koyama, was making trouble about Bobby. Do you know what's going on?"

"I heard she was hanging around the station all morning. Demanding we let Bobby out of jail. Not the most effective tactic, really."

"Is she still there?" Cam asked.

"No, I heard she left. I hope she behaves herself."

"Good. Maybe now she'll get my truck back on the road. Hey, Ruthie," Cam said. "Any chance we can get together to hang out sometime soon? We haven't really talked in a while." Cam had been meaning to follow up with Ruth about where her husband, Frank, was. Judging by little Natalie's remarks at the market, he wasn't around.

"I'd like that. I'm single parenting it these days—"

"Yeah, I gathered that."

"But let me talk to my mom. She loves taking care of the girls. Maybe Saturday night?"

They said good-bye and disconnected. So Frank was gone and probably off to get in even deeper trouble with his militia friends than he had been last spring. Good riddance, in Cam's mind, but it couldn't be easy for Ruth.

Cam finished up her paperwork and lay down for a nap. She managed to sleep for twenty minutes. She had just gotten up and brushed her teeth when someone knocked at the door. She checked the window before throwing open the door.

"Bobby," she said, smiling. "You're out."

Bobby Burr wasn't smiling, but he wasn't in jail, either. He stopped a yard away and stuck his hands in his pockets.

"Yeah, I'm free. For now, anyway. For what it's worth." He almost spat the words out.

"What do you mean, for what it's worth? They must have realized you didn't kill Irene. You're not happy about that?"

"They said they didn't have enough evidence to hold me. And essentially threatened it was only a matter of time until they do. I continue to be a 'person of interest,' as they put it. And they charged me with assault. I wasn't going to attack them with a crescent wrench!" He looked disgusted with the world. "You bet. I'm real happy."

Cam didn't blame him for feeling bitter. "When did you get out?"

"An hour ago. I called Sim, and she met me at the garage, where my van has been. I wanted to let you know." He shook his head. "Listen to me. I've been talking to the police for too long. I feel like I have to explain my every action."

"Well, I'm so glad they released you. Did you know Sim was doing a Free Bobby Burr campaign? I don't think the authorities liked it much, but maybe it helped."

He raised his chin along with his eyebrows. "She's a good friend, but she's a little nuts."

"She must have been ecstatic to see you."

Bobby nodded.

"Hey, can I get you anything?" Cam asked. "A beer?"

"No, but thanks." Bobby looked at her and laughed, his face lightening for the first time. "I knew there was a reason I came by. I'll definitely take you up on that beer another time. For now, I have a big job starting and I'm already late."

"Don't worry. It might sound dumb, but I'm sure they'll find the real murderer soon." She reached out and patted his arm.

He squeezed her shoulder in return and walked back to the white van with more spirit in his step than before. Cam hoped that spirit was never quashed again.

Chapter 21

She did some searching online. She located diagrams of the engine compartment for her year and model of truck and printed them out. It was such an old model Sim might not have the information on hand. She also printed out a schematic of what brakes and brake lines looked like and stashed it all with her wallet and phone in a knapsack. It was time to head into town.

She coasted her bicycle down the long hill to Main Street. As the trees and houses flew by, she panicked for a moment. What if her bicycle brakes failed, too? She pressed the levers on the handlebars and was infinitely relieved when the brake pads pressed in on the wheels exactly like they were supposed to.

At Main Street, she turned left and rode into the lot at SK Foreign Auto. The bay door was closed, as was the office door. The only two cars parked on the side of the building had weeds growing up around their wheels. She checked her watch. Three thirty. She had assumed Sim would be at work after leaving the police station, so she hadn't called ahead. Cam looked around. Where was her truck? She had asked for it to be towed here. Had there been some mistake?

She dismounted and parked the bike. She peered around the side of the building. No truck. She walked all the way around the back. Nothing there but a pile of rusted mufflers and tire rims in a forest of waist-high ragweed and goldenrod growing up through cracks in the pavement. She sensed a sneeze coming on, just looking at the allergen-producing growth. She finished her circumnavigation in the front, at the window in the bay door. She rubbed a spot of dirt off the glass with her fist. A ray of sunlight shone over her shoulder and into the garage. Her truck sat on the right.

Cam let out a breath. At least that mystery was solved. But not the one of what had gone wrong with her brakes. She'd asked Chief Frost to check, but if Sim had been gone all day, he couldn't have gotten access. Where was she, anyway? Cam tried the reception area door, but it was locked, as she expected.

A cloud scudded across the sun with a chilly breeze in tow. She had to find out what had gone wrong with her truck. The brakes going out had nearly killed her. It was time to take matters into her own hands. Maybe Sim didn't lock the back door. Cam walked around to the rear of the building again.

Faded green paint had peeled off the old wooden door. She tried the knob. It felt loose but didn't turn. Cam cursed. She stepped back and narrowed her eyes.

There could be another way in. Cam thought of detective books she had read where the use of a simple credit card was all a private investigator needed to spring a lock. That wouldn't really qualify as breaking in, would it? She shed the knapsack and extracted a credit card from her wallet. She looked around—she wasn't in eyesight of any windows from the neighboring buildings—and pushed the card into the slot where the door latched as she turned and pulled the knob with her other hand. But nothing happened. She removed the card and tried sliding it down, as if swiping it in a machine for actual credit. The door wouldn't budge. She cursed again. So much for getting PI procedure from a novel.

A grimy window was set into the wall next to the door. Cam tried to lift the sash, but it didn't move. She wasn't quite ready to start breaking glass to get in. Using a credit card would have been one thing; vandalism was quite another. She had one more idea before she gave up. Maybe Sim had hidden a key in case she locked herself out. Or maybe she'd hidden one for Bobby. Cam ran her hand along the top of the trim around the door and smiled to herself as her hand closed around a key. Maybe she should have thought of that first.

Some security. Sim must put a lot of trust in the good nature of the town residents. Surely the shop held a number of expensive tools and equipment.

Cam inserted the key into the lock. It wouldn't turn. She jiggled it. She pulled it out a hair and tried again. She turned it over and tried again with no luck. She kicked the bottom of the door in frustration. Why leave a hidden key if it wasn't for this door? She pulled the key out and examined it. The metal looked corroded and dirty. She spit on it and rubbed it clean with a bit of the hem of her shirt, glad she hadn't dressed up more than donning a clean long-sleeved T-shirt for her visit with Albert. She extracted a ChapStick from the pack and rubbed a bit of the waxy substance first onto her pinkie and then onto the key, which was as close to oiling the lock as she was going to get.

This time it had to work. She was already going to be late for her beer with Albert, but she couldn't repress the urgency she felt to examine her truck. Cam slid the key in, edged it a millimeter back and forth twice for good measure, and turned. She felt the lock release. She whistled her relief, opened the door, and replaced the key on the trim before grabbing her pack and entering the shop.

She made her way to the heart of the establishment, a large

room capable of holding three vehicles side by side. A wide workbench lined the back wall, with a ten-drawer red metal tool chest on wheels next to it. Shelves above the workbench held boxes of supplies. Two racks supported new tires on the wall opposite the door into the office.

Cam's old Ford was the only vehicle inside. The clouds that had scudded past the sun earlier now fully occupied the sky, and the filtered light from the dirty bay-door window kept the interior dim. Cam didn't want to bring attention to herself, though, and decided not to turn on the overhead lights. She looked around the workbench until she found a big flashlight. She lifted the truck's hood and propped it open. She'd worked on her old Volkswagen bug in a car co-op during college, so she knew her way around an engine a bit. But even this older-model truck, the smallest of its kind, carried much more sophisticated systems than her vintage VW.

She extracted her printouts from her pack and set the ones for the engine compartment on top of the radiator. She studied the schematic of the brake system and what was in front of her. She found the brake fluid reservoir. It was nearly empty. According to the diagram, it sat on top of the master cylinder. She traced the four lines coming out of the cylinder until they disappeared too deep in the compartment to see. She groaned. She'd have to get underneath the Ford, concussion or no concussion. How nice it would be if Sim were here and could put the truck up on the lift. But Cam wasn't about to try that maneuver herself. With her luck she'd get it halfway up and it would fall down on her.

She scanned the shop until she located a flat platform on small wheels. She lowered her back onto it, flashlight and schematic in hand, and slid under the front of the truck. It was easy to spy the metal lines leading away from each wheel. The front left line looked intact, as far as Cam could tell. She slid over to the right, lifting her head to get a better view. A piece of metal grazed her forehead as she passed under it. She swore and lowered her head flat again. The headache was back. She tried to get the light in a good position to check the right line. It appeared fine, too. She pushed with her feet until she was clear of the truck and scooted to the back. The bed was higher than the engine compartment, so maybe she wouldn't scrape her head back here. She took a deep breath before sliding under again.

As she played the light over the left rear line, she noticed a darker spot. She reached up to touch it. It was rough and damp. Bringing her hand close to her face, she sniffed the fluid on her fingers. She laughed softly. She had no idea what brake fluid smelled like. She rubbed her fingers together. The fluid was oily. She put the light directly on the rough spot and felt a stab of cold. The area wasn't just rough. It was an opening in the sealed system. Someone had definitely hacked at the thin metal with something like a saw or a file. The hole had caused the brake fluid reservoir to empty out. A braking system without fluid or pressure could not stop a car. And this was not a case of wear and tear. This had been perpetrated with malicious intent designed to put Cam out of commission.

She slid over to the right to examine the final line, and the chill she felt in her gut became more widespread. Cold air crept around her neck. She heard a rustle. She froze. And switched off the flashlight. She listened with all her senses alive. Had somebody followed her in? Or maybe it was a resident rodent. The room reverted to silence. She dared to breathe. She peered up at the brake line again.

Suddenly the overhead light snapped on.

"Police! Come out from under there," a female voice commanded. "Hands first."

Chapter 22

Cam reared her head up and cracked it on the frame of the truck's bed. She cursed and lay back down again. Not what she needed—a second injury on top of the one from her accident.

"Now!"

"I'm coming. Don't Taser me!" She stuck her hands out. She managed to scoot herself out with her feet and pushed up to a sitting position.

"Cam?" Ruth Dodge stared at her. She lowered the gun she was pointing at Cam with both hands. She shook her head. "What are *you* doing here?"

"Hi, Ruth."

"Cameron Flaherty?" Chief Frost entered from the office.

"That's me," Cam said with a rueful smile. "I can explain everything."

"Well, I sure hope so." He pointed to her. "Why don't you start right now?"

Cam looked from one officer to the other. "I needed to take a look at the brake lines. I hadn't heard from you or from Sim all day."

"How did you get into the shop?" Ruth was clearly in work mode. Her expression didn't look a bit friendly.

"Sim hides a key out back." Cam shrugged.

"Same one she told us about," Frost said. "Ms. Koyama might as well leave her shop open if she's going to tell the universe how to get in."

Cam didn't think he really needed to know she had discovered the key on her own. Without Sim's permission.

"You came down to check out the brake lines, right? You should see what I found," Cam began.

"Actually, a passing citizen reported seeing a flickering light through the window," Ruth said.

"So you haven't looked yet? I told you about the tampering this morning, Chief." Cam couldn't believe he had waited this long.

The chief cleared his throat. "We were waiting for Ms. Koyama to get back to us. Which she did only an hour ago."

"She wasn't here? Where's she been all day?" No wonder the shop was closed so early. It sounded like Sim hadn't ever opened it for the day.

"I'm not at liberty to divulge that information."

"Anyway, I can show you. The rear brake lines both have a small opening in them. It's rough. It looks like it was done deliberately. No wonder the truck didn't stop."

"We'll take care of it. For now I need you out of here." Frost gestured toward the office door, which stood open.

Cam boosted herself up and found a clean red rag to wipe her hands on. "Just a second. I need to get something out of the cab." At Frost's frown, she said, "I won a ribbon at the fair. I want to show it to my great-uncle."

"Go ahead."

She dug through the wreckage in the cab until she found the ribbon. As she walked out, she glanced back. Ruth and Frost were conferring, Frost pointing to the truck, Ruth writing something in a notebook. They didn't look up.

*   *   *

Albert clinked his glass of ale with Cam's in his room at Moran Manor. He'd proffered two squat water glasses for the beer, saying they would have to do. He sat, as usual, in his recliner, a red plaid lap blanket over his knees, with his usual stack of books threatening to topple off the small table at his elbow.

"I'm sorry I'm late." After the police's questioning she had stopped off at the Food Mart to pick up the beer and then visited the guest washroom at the residence to clean up her hands and face.

"It's fine. Here's to your health, Cameron," he said. He sipped the brew and smiled. "Very fine. Very hoppy."

Cam stretched out in her chair and sipped her own. "They grow their own hops right at the brewery. I was thinking I should get some good rootstock and start some myself next spring. What do you think? I could train them up the south wall of the barn."

"Far's I know, you don't get much of a harvest the first year, and they don't weigh but diddly-squat. But if hops are what you have a liking to raise, you should go ahead."

"True, the flowers are lighter than paper, but they fetch a pretty good price per ounce."

Albert set his glass down on the end table next to his chair. He leaned forward and took Cam's hand. "How are you holding up, my dear? You look a little peaked."

"The accident was tough. I'm not completely recovered from it." Her hand went up involuntarily to the lump on her head.

"Tell me how you think it came to happen."

Cam relayed the story again of getting her brakes checked by Sim on Monday and how they had functioned normally before she arrived at the fair.

"I told Chief Frost I thought someone had tampered with the truck. I wasn't sure he believed me, so I stopped by the shop on my way over here."

"Had Sim taken a look?"

"I don't think so. She didn't call me about it, anyway, and she wasn't there. I sort of found a key and let myself in."

Albert raised snowy eyebrows that could have served as ski jumps for tiny elves, but he didn't interrupt. Cam went on to tell him what she had discovered.

"Are you sure the sabotage was deliberate?"

"It had to be, Uncle Albert. It looked like someone sawed at the lines or took a rough file to them. The fluid had leaked out. The reservoir in the engine compartment was empty, too. No way my truck would stop." Cam stared out the window at the memory of the truck picking up speed, her brakes not responding, the Civic in front of her not hearing her horn, finally—

Albert touched her knee with his hand. "Cameron, come back. You survived the crash safely, now, didn't you?"

Cam took a deep breath. She nodded. And laughed to herself.

"What's funny?" Albert asked. He leaned forward in his chair and smiled encouragingly.

"I was flat on my back under the truck at Sim's. An hour ago. I'd just seen the cut in the second line when all of a sudden . . . busted! Ruth and Chief Frost showed up. They thought someone had broken into the shop. I had to talk myself out of trouble."

"And how did you manage that? It doesn't sound like you had permission of the owner to enter, did you?"

"No. But I told them I had used the hidden key. Which was true!" Cam protested.

Albert shook his head. "Now, what would your parents say?"

Cam looked at him. They both broke out laughing at the same time. "They'd say, 'Whatever you need to do, dear. I'm off to catch a plane.' As always."

Albert smiled and nodded.

"Anyway, I told Chief Frost I needed to check the brake lines since they hadn't done it. They let me go, but I'm glad they knew me."

"I'm glad, too. Now, what about the fair? Did you bring me a couple of blue ribbons?"

"Not exactly." Cam pulled her mouth as she reached into her bag. She held up the red ribbon for Albert to see. It now sported a crease and a smudge of dirt from being tossed about in the truck during the accident. "Second place for the Sun Golds."

"Not bad for your first time out."

"But they shafted me on the garlic braids. At the end they said I was disqualified because I incorporated a string in the braid. But the rules didn't say I couldn't!"

"Now, that doesn't seem quite fair, does it?"

"I'm going to write them a letter about clarifying the guidelines."

"Good idea." Albert nodded. "Something else is bothering you."

"You mean besides a murderer wandering around out there?"

Albert waited with the patience of the aged.

"I haven't seen Preston since yesterday morning." Cam rolled the hem of her shirt between her fingers until it caught on her dirt-roughened skin. "He's never stayed out this long."

"What do you think has happened to him?"

"At first I imagined him having a bad encounter with a predator in the woods. I've heard fisher cats out there, and I saw one running along the border of the woods at dusk last week."

"They have a terrible cry. Sounds like a baby being tortured." Albert frowned.

"I know. And they are voracious hunters. I've seen pictures of their teeth. We have foxes and coyotes, too, as I'm sure you know. Anyway, I looked everywhere on the farm. I drove up and down the road and didn't see him. I posted signs with his picture on them everywhere. Madeline hasn't seen him, and nobody has called me."

"He's a good-natured cat, your Preston."

Cam's eyes began to well. She wiped them with a fast gesture and took a deep breath. "Alexandra suggested maybe someone had taken him. I can't understand who would do such a thing. Or why."

Albert's frown turned to wrinkles of concern. "You need to be careful, Cameron. If what you say is true about your brakes, why, the same person could have taken your cat. What's next?"

"But why me?"

"Maybe the murderer thinks you're getting too close."

"I've told a couple of people I think Bobby is innocent. But I'm leaving the investigating to the police this time, I swear." Cam glanced out the window. "I gotta run, Uncle Albert. I have to get the chickens in before dark."

"You won't stay for dinner?"

Cam shook her head. "But I will use your phone book. I'm going to call Port Taxi. I'm not up to riding my bike uphill all the way home."

"A wise move."

Chapter 23

The flashlight barely penetrated the corners of the dark chicken yard where Cam pointed it. She hoped she'd gotten all the birds in. When she'd arrived, several of them were already in roosting position on the edge of the feeder, eyes closed. These girls seemed bound to their internal clock, or that of the sun, more likely. Cam had to lift each one up in turn and put her in the coop, the last one complaining bitterly and pecking at her hand. Rescue hens were more of a responsibility than she had expected. She latched the coop door and tested it.

As she trudged to the house, she called for Preston. He could have been at a neighboring house and gotten shut in a shed accidentally. Maybe he'd made friends with the tabby across the road. She called again, not daring to let her hopes rise, not being able to help it when they did. He didn't appear.

As she approached the back of the house, her motion-detector light illuminated a large bouquet of pink carnations in a vase on her doorstep. Cam narrowed her eyes for a moment. Someone had delivered flowers anonymously last spring, but they had turned out to be trouble. She retrieved the little florist's envelope from among the blooms. The card inside read, *Please forgive me. And congratulations. I miss you. Med kärlek, Jake.*

She heaved a big sigh as the key snicked into the lock. What was she going to do about Jake? Cam hefted the vase with a little too much force. Water sloshed on her pants. She cursed as she set the vase on the table. She took heavy steps into the kitchen and leaned on the counter. Her stomach griped about its empty state, and her entire body ached from yesterday's blow.

First things first. She put pasta water on to boil and got out a jar of the summer's pesto she'd blended up from handfuls of farm-grown basil and garlic, plus pine nuts, salt, and olive oil. Marie had taught her the recipe, one she'd gotten from her brother Jimmy, who had been the U.S. consul to Florence, Italy. Cam opened a bottle of a California Central Coast pinot noir and poured a generous glass. She arranged salad greens on a plate, adding slices of a Brandywine tomato that had ripened on the windowsill. She ground pepper and drizzled olive oil over the plate.

As she worked, she fretted over how she was going to get along without her truck. She had Jake's delivery to make tomorrow. She couldn't afford to keep taking taxis around the rural roads of town, and Sim hadn't made any progress fixing her brakes. If the police were even going to let her work on the truck now. Cam wondered where Sim had been all day. She called one more time, with the same zero results.

She threw in half a box of farfalle—the pasta Ruth's twins liked to call "bow ties"—and let it cook. She set out a place mat and silverware and had finished draining the pasta when the phone rang. She threw some olive oil on the pasta so it wouldn't stick and grabbed the phone.

"Cameron?" A gruff male voice spoke.

"That's me."

"Howard Fisher here. Heard you had an accident."

"Yes, I did. Where'd you hear the news?" Cam was pretty sure he didn't go looking for local news on the Internet, but she could be wrong.

"Your truck beat up pretty bad?"

"A little. Why?"

"Could loan you a vehicle. If you wanted. Till you get yours back and all."

Cam barely knew the man. And he wanted to loan her a car? "I appreciate the gesture, Howard, but I'm sure you need the vehicles you have."

"Nope. Vince ain't driving right now. Got another ticket. You can use his Jeep. It's only fifteen years old. Runs okay. If you want."

A Jeep would solve her transportation problem for the moment. "Yes, I guess I could use it for a couple of days. Thanks very much, Howard."

"I'll drop it off in the morning, early. You can run me home."

Cam was about to thank him again when the phone clicked off. She hung up the receiver. How different small town life was from the city. Nobody would have offered to loan her a vehicle in Cambridge. She shook her head and resumed preparing dinner, tossing the pasta with a quarter cup of pesto. She grated fresh Romano onto it and brought it to the table.

Her cell phone rang as Cam took the last bite. Feeling restored, she checked the caller ID. Jake. She hesitated for a moment before pressing the SEND button.

"Hi," Cam said.

"Hi, yourself."

She heard the bustle of a manic kitchen in the background. She looked up at the wall clock. Seven. It had to be in the middle of the dinner rush at The Market.

"Thanks for the flowers," Cam said. "They're very pretty."

"I wanted to apologize for being a jerk the other night. Again."

His deep voice triggered the rush of pure lust in her that it always did. She took a deep breath to steady her voice. "Thank you."

"And I read in the *Daily News* you won a ribbon at the fair. I expected no less. Congratulations. I'll put it on my menu. You know, 'Greens from Award-Winning Farm.' "

"That would be awesome publicity. Thanks." Cam wondered if she should tell him about her accident but decided not to. It would sound too much like begging for sympathy. Begging wasn't an activity she wanted to get used to doing.

Something crashed, and Jake muttered to himself in what Cam was pretty sure was Swedish swearing.

"I gotta go. I'm sorry."

"No problem. I'll bring your delivery over after lunch tomorrow as usual. Right?"

"Thank you. We'll talk more then."

Cam said good-bye without agreeing and disconnected. She wasn't sure she was ready to talk, if it would result only in the same roller coaster of feelings and reactions the two of them had been on since they'd met. There was no question they had a strong physical connection. But a relationship that complicated her life like this one did? She didn't think she could handle it and be a solo farmer, too. And there was Pete. She had to admit to herself she found him intriguing. And attractive. But she doubted dating a state police officer would be any easier than a jealous chef.

She stowed the rest of the pasta, cleaned up the kitchen, and worked on the computer for a bit, checking e-mail and paying bills. She opened a new file and made notes on which crops had thrived this year and which had not. The ones customers at the market had particularly exclaimed about and the ones that always went unsold. The produce that had been popular with her subscribers and the offerings they had complained about getting too much of. Kohlrabi had tended to end up in the swap bin, for example, with nobody swapping it into their bags.

She shut the system down, made sure the door was locked, and headed up to bed. As she paused at the landing, her eyes met Preston's forlorn dishes at the bottom of the stairs, one brimming with dry food, the other full of clean, untouched water.

Chapter 24

Despite a clear sky, temperatures threatening November towered over the morning. Cam awoke with a headache and a sore body. Still, work called. She threw on a jacket and a knit cap before she let the chickens out. She watered the seedlings and returned to the house for a second cup of coffee and to warm up a little. A car horn beeped from the driveway. Startled, she checked the clock. It wasn't even eight. *Right.* Howard had said he'd bring the car by early, and he was a farmer, too. She stuck her wallet and phone in her jacket pockets and grabbed her keys.

She climbed into the passenger seat of the fifteen-year-old car, a beat-up Jeep Wrangler, and greeted Howard.

He nodded without making eye contact as he turned the vehicle around and headed out.

"How are things at the farm?" Cam asked. "I saw Vince at the fair. Did he win for that big pig he was grooming?"

Howard's mouth turned down in a scowl. "No. Judges are prejudiced. Gave the ribbons to those rich kids down to Hamilton. What do they know about raising swine?"

"Too bad. Vince sounded pretty hopeful when I talked to him. How did he take it?"

"What don't kill you makes you stronger."

"My garlic braids didn't win, either. They disqualified me for something they didn't even include in the rules."

Howard nodded like this news did not surprise him.

Several minutes later they turned into the Fisher farm. Howard left the car pointed toward the road with the engine running. He ambled toward the back of the farm.

"Thanks for the favor," Cam called as she climbed into the driver's seat. "I'll get it back to you as soon as I can."

Howard raised a hand and disappeared into the barn. Cam was about to drive away when she spied the edge of a large animal carrier almost out of sight on the wraparound porch of the house. It was of green and gray plastic, with vents and a handle on the top. Cam's heart raced. It looked a lot like the carrier she took Preston to the vet in. She threw the Jeep back into neutral and pulled up the emergency brake but left the engine running.

Barely able to keep herself from running, she strode to the porch. She rounded the corner. When she was a few yards from the carrier, she whispered, "Preston!" but heard no response. She glanced at the house windows but didn't see anyone looking out.

As the morning light slanted across the porch, it angled through the slits on the sides of the carrier. Cam's heart turned to ice. She couldn't see a furry shape. It must be empty. It must be their own cat's carrier, or maybe that of a small dog. She heard the tiniest of sounds. She took the side stairs in two steps. She bent over and peered into the carrier.

Preston lay flat on the bottom. He barely cracked an eyelid at her. She didn't know if he was sick or drugged or starved. Or all three.

A loud crack sounded behind her. She flinched even as she whipped her head around. Her heart thudded in her throat. Was Howard back with his rifle? She let out a breath. It was just a branch that had crashed down from the old maple. She turned back to Preston.

She lifted the carrier and ran back to the vehicle. She set the carrier on the passenger seat and closed the door firmly but as quietly as she could. She looked around. As far as she could tell, no one watched. She didn't trust herself to go after Howard and confront him. She had to get Preston to safety. She climbed in the driver's seat and drove off, spinning gravel as she went.

She kept driving until she was back in a more populated area of town. She pulled over at a wide spot and killed the engine. Anger and questions roiled in her from head to toe. Her hands shook as she unlatched the door to the carrier. In Howard's own car.

"You're going to be okay, Mr. P." Cam reached in and stroked his head and back again and again. He finally opened both eyes and mewed, lifting his head a few inches. He laid it down again and closed his eyes.

Now what? She hated having to drive Howard's car, but she had to get Preston to a veterinarian. She couldn't very well take him back to his old vet in Cambridge, but she hadn't yet taken him to an animal doctor since she'd moved to Westbury a little over a year ago. Albert and Marie had had a dog and must have used a local vet, but the dog was long gone and their vet might be, too. Cam snapped her fingers. Ruth had a cat. She must know of someone. Cam pressed Ruth's number on her cell.

When Ruth picked up, Cam asked her about a vet.

"Why? Is Preston all right?"

"No. I hadn't seen him since Tuesday morning. Today Howard Fisher loaned me his Jeep—"

"What? Why'd he lend you a car?"

"I don't really know. But it solved my problem of the truck being in the shop, and I thought he was being neighborly."

"Okay. How does this relate to Preston being sick?"

"After I dropped Howard at his farm, I caught sight of an animal carrier that looked a lot like Preston's. It was almost out of sight on the porch of the farmhouse. I checked, and Preston was in it. But he's sick or drugged or something. I think Howard must have kidnapped him!" Cam heard the anguish in her voice.

"Now, Cam, why would he kidnap a cat? You just said he was being friendly by offering his car to you."

"I know."

"There's probably a good explanation. Like Preston wandered over there through the woods and they didn't know whose cat he was."

"Maybe. It's true, our properties abut way at the back. But why would he put him in a carrier?" Cam didn't believe Preston had strayed so far for a minute, but now wasn't the time to argue. "I have to get him to a vet, and I don't know of a good one. Who do you take your cat to?"

Ruth told her to call Mill Pond Animal Hospital. "They've only been open a year, but I like them a lot. Particularly Dr. Melissa. It's Thursday. She's probably in today. They're on Main Street, on the right. On the way up the hill to the pond as you head out of town."

Cam thanked her. "Hey, any idea when I can get my truck back? Do you know if Sim has shown up?"

"The staties haven't exactly cleared Simone of suspicion for the murder, you know."

"Really? Why not?"

"You know she was seen arguing with Irene, don't you?"

Cam was silent for a moment. "I saw them, actually."

"Anyway, we checked your brake lines. They were definitely cut. You were right."

Well, yeah. "I have to get the Ford back. I don't feel comfortable keeping Howard's Jeep a minute longer than I have to."

"Let me check with the chief. We took pictures and all. Maybe you can convince Sim to get back to her job."

Cam agreed to try, after she got Preston looked at, and disconnected. What a mess. She decided to drive to the animal hospital instead of calling ahead. Preston was an emergency. They'd have to treat him. She gave him one last stroke, trying to keep her ire from transmitting to the poor fellow. Even if Ruth's idea was correct, who would leave a beautiful animal languishing in a cage? Had it been Howard? Or someone else in his family? Cam was determined to find out.

At the animal hospital, Dr. Melissa, a congenial woman with a dark braid hanging down her back, took a sample of Preston's blood and said she'd check it for drugs. She also confirmed that it was Preston, not that Cam had any doubt, by scanning the identifying chip Cam had had a vet insert after she'd gotten him from the shelter as a kitten.

"His heart sounds fine," the doctor said. She squirted a dose of a nutritional supplement into his mouth and stroked his throat to make him swallow. She offered him a small dish of water, which he lapped up.

"I don't think he's sick, but he is certainly dehydrated and hungry, and possibly drugged."

As the vet examined Preston, Cam took a closer look at the carrier. It wasn't Preston's, after all. It didn't have the Merrimac River Feline Rescue Society sticker on top that his did, and it was missing the scrap of lamb's fleece she kept inside, which had been a kind of blankie for him when she'd adopted him as a kitten.

By the time Cam walked out with him, Preston had regained some energy. As she drove home from the animal hospital, Cam thought longingly of walking along Mill Pond to the boulder on its edge where she liked to sit and think. But getting Preston back to familiar surroundings and nutrition was more important right now. She reminded herself to make time for the pond, though. It was a place that restored her like almost nowhere else.

Cam brought the carrier into her house and set it on the table. She opened the door and petted Preston. He purred as she ran her hand through his white ruff. He pushed himself up and stepped daintily out of the carrier onto the table. She picked him up and set him on the floor in front of his food and water dishes. When he looked up, asking to be petted while he ate, Cam knew he was going to be all right.

She stroked him and paced into the kitchen and back. The crunch of Preston eating was sweet music, but it didn't help her know where to start getting on with her life now that he was safe. She felt like a blizzard of complications and obligations threatened to bury her and suffocate her. She needed to confront Howard about Preston. She needed to get her truck back and find out if Sim had been at the fair. She needed to do all the work a farm demanded: harvesting, weeding, nurturing. She needed to make a delivery to Jake. And if she could figure out who killed Irene, that would be good, too. But how could she get any of it done? And which to tackle first?

A faint buzzing started up in her right ear. She stopped moving. When this had happened in the past, she'd heard Great-Aunt Marie's voice in her mind. This time was no different.

Cammie, you can do whatever you put your mind to.

Cam pictured the tiny woman standing in her violet-flowered dress at the kitchen counter, making out a list in her precise, flowing handwriting. Sometimes Marie would laugh as she wrote. She'd look over at Cam having a snack at the table and say, "Well, bless me. I already hung the clothes on the line this morning. I might as well add it to my list so I can cross it off." And she would do just that.

Cam knew what she had to do first. Having a list in hand had quieted her mind since she was a child. She used to mimic her great-aunt by making her own to-do list, even when the only items on it were "Read book. Eat lunch. Play."

Pencil and paper in hand, she set to work. Several minutes later she added one final item at the end. There. Now to start crossing them off.

Chapter 25

Cam drove the Jeep to Sim's shop and turned into the parking lot. The garage door was closed, but her motorcycle sat out front. Cam opened the reception door, glad to find it unlocked. The room was empty. She stuck her head into the garage itself.

"Sim?"

"I'm over here." The voice came from the far corner.

Cam walked over to where the mechanic perched, cross-legged, on the workbench. "What's going on?"

Sim's face was pale, and her black hair stuck up in spikes that looked inadvertent, not styled. She looked at first surprised to see Cam. Then her face hardened.

"I'm depressed," she muttered. "Bobby's out, but they still think he killed Irene."

"Hey, at least he's free. And he's working, which is more than you're doing."

"So what?" She turned her face away from Cam.

"I really need you to fix my cut brake lines so I can start using my truck again." Cam planted herself in Sim's path so Sim would have to meet her eyes. "Somebody tampered with them. That's why I couldn't stop in Middleford. I thought you were going to look at them yesterday, but you didn't seem to be at the shop all day. Where were you?"

Sim shook her head. "I'm sorry I didn't get a chance. I had some business come up. How did you find out they were cut?"

Cam reddened. "I found your hidden key and let myself in and checked for myself." At Sim's look of anger, Cam rushed on. "I tried all day to reach you. I needed to know the cause of my accident. And the police saw my flashlight, and they dropped in, too." It had been a touch more confrontational than dropping in, but Sim didn't need to know that.

"Yeah, I got a message from the chief. I didn't call him back."

"Ruth Dodge told me this morning the police are done checking the truck. You're free to work on it. You must have other jobs waiting, too, right?"

"I do." Sim looked back at Cam. "I guess you're right. I'm not going to get Bobby's name cleared by sitting here in a funk. That's the justice system's job."

Cam raised her eyebrows as Pete Pappas appeared in the doorway from the reception area. "Speaking of the justice system."

Sim whirled. "Not him again!" Her eyes narrowed.

Again? Cam wondered how many times Sim had already spoken with Pappas.

Pappas called a greeting to them. "Just the two I was hoping to find," he added with a broad smile.

"Good morning, Pete." Cam smiled back. "This is perfect. You are on my list to call." Calling him had in fact been the final item Cam had added to her list an hour earlier.

Sim cast Cam the kind of look you give a person in the grocery store who keeps talking to herself. The kind of look that shouted, "You're nuts! Wanting to talk to a detective is worse than skinning your knuckles on a hot manifold."

The way Cam figured it, she had nothing to lose and everything to gain by talking with Pappas about progress in the murder case. Plus, he was kind of cute. But she wondered why Sim didn't want to talk with him. Surely she wasn't a credible suspect for the murder. Or was she?

"Ms. Koyama, you've been hard to locate lately. You apparently were not at your shop all day yesterday or half of Tuesday."

Cam noticed Pappas again looked somewhat more put together today than he had last Friday on the farm. It struck her it had been an entire week since the dinner on her farm. And the murder. He must be getting a lot of pressure to solve it.

"I'm self-employed. I can work when I want to. Is that a crime?" Sim stuck hands on hips and lifted her chin.

"I wanted to follow up on a couple of details regarding your whereabouts after the dinner last week." He checked a small notebook in his hand. "You said you went to visit your sister in Amesbury and spent the night there after dropping Bobby Burr off at his home. Correct?"

Sim nodded without speaking. Cam didn't even know she had a sister. But really, she didn't know much about Sim at all.

"We checked the number." His voice softened. "The woman who answered said she is not your sister. She said you weren't with her that night."

Cam gazed at Sim. What had she been thinking, to lie to the police?

Sim turned her head to the left with a sharp movement and to the right. She opened her mouth for a moment. She looked at Cam, her eyes pleading something Cam couldn't read. She took a deep breath and let it out.

"Yeah. I just said that so you wouldn't be on my case."

"Where were you really?" Pappas leaned against the door-jamb.

"I was by myself at home."

"You went straight home after the dinner?"

"I dropped Bobby off at his house, and, yes, I went straight home. I practiced for an hour and went to bed."

"Practiced?"

"I play the drums in a band. So I practiced. Played my drums."

"Could a neighbor have heard you?" Pappas asked.

She shook her head. "I use a practice set. It basically doesn't make noise. It's pads hooked up to an app. I can listen to it amplified on headphones, but it doesn't bother anybody else." She pursed her lips.

"You argued with Irene Burr at the dinner."

"And who didn't? Look, she was a jerk of the highest order. But I didn't kill her!"

Pappas checked his watch. "I have to run. We'll be talking again." As he walked away, he called, "See you, Cameron."

Cam touched Sim's arm. "Why don't you work? It'll take your mind off all of this. And I do need my truck, you know."

Sim nodded. "I guess."

Chapter 26

As Cam drove along Main Street back toward the farm, she realized she hadn't asked Sim if she'd been at the fair. She could do it later, when she picked up the truck. An early model Prius in front of her slowed and pulled into the parking area in front of the Old Town Hall. The beige hybrid with the THINK GLOBAL, EAT LOCAL bumper sticker belonged to Wes and Felicity. Was Felicity back from her sister's? She glimpsed Wes craning his head around. He didn't park in front but continued around the side of the building to the back. Cam didn't know there was a parking area back there.

On a whim, she turned her steering wheel sharply to the right, earning a honk from the bumper-hugging driver behind her, and parked in front of the classic hall. She'd been forgetting to ask Wes how Felicity's sister was doing. And she'd love a peek into the nonpublic spaces in the building. Maybe Wes could fill her in on its history real quick, even though she didn't really have time for a tour. Living in a semirural town where half the buildings were more than a century old, with some of them built before the country was even a country, had quickened Cam's interest in local history and antique buildings. The plaque on the Old Town Hall read WESTBURY MEETINGHOUSE, BUILT 1855.

The white clapboard building featured the graceful ten-foot-tall windows of any self-respecting New England meetinghouse, windows that also made it an expensive nightmare to heat in the winter. Wide double doors at the top of even wider granite steps were painted dark green, as were the exterior shutters. She knew each window also had interior shutters on its lower half. A golden rooster sat atop a small cupola.

Cam tried the front doors, but they were locked. She strode around the side where Wes had driven. At the back corner she spied the Prius and a door to the building propped open behind it. The back hatch of the Prius was also open, facing away from her. In it she glimpsed a rectangle of greenery that looked like a flat of seedlings. He must be on his way to the farm to ask her to grow something in her hoop house now that the weather was getting colder. Cam had had one other customer ask if she could raise a particular kind of green, which Cam had been happy to do.

"Hello?" Cam called out at the entrance but didn't get a response. Inside the entryway one short flight of steps led up and another led down. She figured the flight up probably led to the back of the stage at the end of the large first-floor meeting room. Light shone at the bottom of the lower flight, so Cam followed that path. She turned a corner into a large and depressingly institutional multipurpose room. Folding chairs lined dingy khaki-colored walls, and a couple of laminated posters rested against the wall in a corner, the outermost one displaying a poem titled "Serenity Prayer." Cracks in the wall plaster radiated in every direction. The air smelled vaguely of mold. High casement windows let in almost no light, particularly on a gloomy day like today, but the insufficient overhead fluorescent lights weren't much help.

At the far end appeared to be a door to a kitchen and another labeled FURNACE. The latter was open an inch. She walked through the room until she could see Wes wasn't in the kitchen.

"Wes?" No answer. She'd have to try the main level. He must be up there cleaning or something. He was the town maintenance person for the hall, after all. She had turned to go when she heard a few quick footsteps behind her.

"What are you doing here?" Wes scowled, his eyes like icicles.

"You were right in front of me on Main Street, and I saw you drive in here. I've been forgetting to ask how Felicity and her sister are doing. And I love old buildings, so I thought maybe I could grab a quick look."

"A look?"

"I've never seen anything except the main meeting room during Town Meeting."

"Sorry. I'm busy. We can do that another time." He gestured toward the exit. He kept his arm extended and started walking toward the door, effectively moving her along ahead of him. "By appointment. Sorry, Cam. It's been a rough day. Anne—Felicity's sister—is doing pretty well. Thanks for asking. But I miss Felicity."

"You must." Cam smiled when she reached the steps. "I do, too. She's such an enthusiastic volunteer."

Wes accompanied her around to her car. "See you Saturday." He raised his hand in farewell.

As Cam drove home, she couldn't figure out why Wes had scowled at her. Wes seemed different lately. It must be because Felicity was out of town and she served as his anchor, his calming influence.

After she arrived home, she made sure Preston was still indoors and looked healthy. She had locked his cat door before she left to make sure he stayed inside. One look at him nestled on a blanket in the corner of the couch assured her he wasn't going to be asking to go out any time soon. And his deep purr when she petted him was enough to satisfy her that he was going to be all right.

She headed out to harvest, her thoughts focused on what to do about Howard Fisher. She had to confront him about Preston. She would also have to return his Jeep after Sim repaired her truck. She had begun to cut mixed greens when Lucinda walked up.

"Need some help?" Lucinda's hair was wilder than ever in the damp air, and her eyes sparkled as she shoved curls back off her face.

"How do you stay so cheerful all the time?" Cam sat back on her heels.

"It's in my genes, I guess. Or my culture. Brazilians are pretty happy people."

"You're lucky. But sure, I can always use help."

"I grabbed scissors on the way out." Lucinda knelt and began clipping at the other end of the bed. "Any news about Preston?"

"The best news," Cam said. She told Lucinda about finding him that morning and about having to take him to the vet. "He's in the house now. I think I'll keep him in for a few days. Or at least until he demands to go out."

"Fisher stole him." Lucinda's eyes flashed. "I'll go beat the crap out of him. People can't go around stealing animals."

"It might not have been theft. And I don't think beating him up is necessary." Cam sighed. "Maybe it's innocent. Ruth said Preston probably wandered off and got lost."

"Ya think?" Lucinda stared at Cam.

"I don't know. But why would Howard have taken him? And his son, Vince, is a nice kid. He wouldn't have taken a cat, for sure."

"Well, if you need backup when you go talk to him, you call me. I'm pretty tough."

Cam nodded, smiling to herself. Lucinda was tough, and she

was a good friend. She was happy to have the Brazilian on her side. Cam's cell buzzed in her pocket. Sim was on the other end, saying the truck would be ready in the early afternoon.

"I'll pick it up at the shop. Thanks," Cam said, then disconnected. "That was Sim. Could I get you to help me return the Jeep to Howard this afternoon?"

Lucinda nodded. They worked in silence for several more minutes. When Cam remembered they were harvesting for Jake's restaurant, her mood darkened again.

"Lucinda, I need some advice."

"I'm it." Her friend couldn't have looked more delighted. "Call me Dear Lucy."

Cam explained about Jake's jealousy and his sliding back and forth between affection and near hostility. "I'm not sure I can take it anymore. I mean, I like him when he's nice. And we really click physically."

At Lucinda's grin, Cam blushed. "Well, we do! And I want to be able to work with him. But I'm not sure I can handle the fireworks and the hot, then cold, then hot. It's exhausting."

"Do you trust him?" Lucinda cocked her head.

Cam looked at her for a moment. "You know? I don't. I don't trust him to trust me. And that's important." She frowned. "But I'm not sure how to end our relationship without making him even angrier at me. And I want to work with him. I need those sales, and he needs the local produce. I think."

"You're gonna be all right. You're smart. You'll figure it out." Lucinda walked over and rubbed Cam's shoulder. "Now, what else do we need to cut for this crazy chef?"

Chapter 27

As it happened, Jake was out when Cam made her delivery two hours later. She left the vegetables with the sous-chef and started the drive back to Westbury. It was a relief not to have to confront Jake, even though she knew she'd only postponed the inevitable. As she drove, she thought about Pete's invitation to go for a spin, and how attractive the prospect seemed. She shook her head. If she was about to embark on some kind of undefined something with Pete Pappas, she sure had better end things with Jake first, or he would finally, in fact, have cause to be jealous. The bigger question was whether she wanted to pursue other men or work through the issues with Jake. Maybe the wiser course was to simply settle for the life of a celibate farmer. She wouldn't be the first in history to do so.

Cam made a decision. She pulled into a gas station near the highway. After she topped up the Jeep's tank, she pressed the numbers for Jake's cell phone. She half hoped that he would answer and prayed with the other half that he wouldn't. At the sound of his voice on the message, she let out a breath.

"Jake, I missed you with my delivery. Hey, will you come to the farm for a quick lunch tomorrow? Say, eleven thirty? Let me know." She quickly disconnected. She'd better be ready by to-morrow with whatever decision she hadn't yet made.

Lucinda was waiting at Sim's shop when Cam drove up. She paid Sim, thanking her, but the mechanic didn't seem to want to chat, so Cam excused herself.

"Catch." Cam threw the truck keys to Lucinda. "Follow me. I guess we're doing this on the fly."

"I like flying," Lucinda said after she caught the keys. "I'm your copilot."

Cam drove Howard's Jeep slowly down the road to the Fisher farm. She hadn't decided how to approach Howard. Innocently? With an accusation? She wondered if she should have told some-body at the police station. She remembered she had told Ruth, who hadn't taken the kidnapping idea seriously. She checked the mirror. At least she had Lucinda as backup. Cam would be glad to be rid of this vehicle, this obligation to a man she no longer trusted. Make that *another* man.

She parked next to Howard's dusty truck, which sat to the left side of the farmhouse. She left the key in the ignition. Lucinda pulled Cam's truck around so it was facing toward the road and hopped out.

"Let's walk out back. He's probably working," Cam said.

Lucinda replied with a thumbs-up fist. "I got your back."

"Howard?" Cam called as they neared the ramshackle barn. The area in front of it featured mostly packed dirt with a few lan-guishing lilac bushes to one side and a parched, weedy perennial garden to the other with only a few tired asters adding color.

"Hello?" she called again. No one appeared, so she pulled open the wide sliding door at the front of the barn.

The mid-afternoon light revealed an interior clogged with junk. Rusty farm equipment, discarded cardboard boxes, odd bits of white PVC pipe, empty feed bags, a broken wheelbarrow. Nowhere was the semblance of order Cam had grown accustomed to in the barns of working farms she had visited and her own. The path weaving through the mess was barely wide enough for one person to navigate, and the sides were high enough to make it almost a tunnel.

Lucinda gave a low whistle. "Looks like a hoarder show I saw."

"He must keep his working tools somewhere else," Cam said in a low voice, shaking her head. "Come on. Maybe he's around the back."

As they walked between the lilacs and the barn wall, Howard emerged around the corner of the barn. Once again he carried a rifle. He pulled to a halt directly in front of them.

"What do you want?" He spied the open barn door, and his face darkened. "What were you doing in there?" He waved the gun at them.

"Hey." Cam threw her hands up, palms out. "Calm down, Howard. I returned your Jeep. I wanted to thank you."

"Oh." He lowered the gun. "Yeah. Glad you could use it."

"I filled the tank, too."

"Appreciate it." Howard didn't meet Cam's eyes.

Cam raised her eyebrows at Lucinda and tilted her head toward the front of the property. Lucinda started walking in that direction, with Cam close behind. As they approached the truck, Cam turned. Howard had stopped near the back of the house. Vince rode down the drive on a bicycle. He braked near Cam and smiled at her.

"Hi, Ms. Flaherty." He stood astraddle the bike and slipped a pack off one shoulder.

"Hey, Vince." He must have come from school. "How are you?"

"It's all good."

Cam returned her eyes to Howard, suddenly glad both Vince and Lucinda were nearby. "By the way, Howard. When I was here this morning, I saw my cat in a carrier on your porch. I took him home. How did he get there?"

"I don't know what you're talking about." Howard stood with his arms at his sides, holding the rifle in one hand, his chin in the air.

"Are you sure? It was my cat, Preston. He wasn't doing too well. I hadn't seen him in two days."

"No idea. You must be talking about some other cat."

"But, Dad—" Vince darted his eyes to Cam and back to his father.

"Shut up, Vincent." Howard glared at the young man.

"No, it was definitely my cat," Cam said. "I had his chip checked by the vet."

"Like I said, I don't know what you're talking about."

Vince looked at Cam and seemed to steel himself. "I told him—"

"Vince!" Howard bellowed. "Go do your chores."

Vince looked like he might speak again. Cam smiled at him with encouragement.

"Now!" Howard pointed to the back of the property, where Cam had seen the pigs.

Vince shook his head and rode away. As he disappeared around the back of the barn, he turned back and mouthed "Sorry" to Cam.

Lucinda cleared her throat. "I have an appointment, Cam. Can we get going?"

Cam nodded. "Well, thanks again for the loan, Howard. I left the carrier in the Jeep."

Howard put the shooting end of the rifle on the ground and leaned both hands on the butt end. He kept silent as they climbed into the truck.

"Close one," Lucinda said.

Cam steered the truck down the road away from the farm. "We didn't really learn anything, either."

"Howard's got major problems. And it sure seems like he took your cat. But why?"

"If I can ever talk to Vince alone, I might find out the real story."

"Good thing for him his father didn't see him say he was sorry. Poor kid, huh? And no brothers or sisters?"

"I don't think so."

Poor kid, indeed. Cam knew he'd had a run-in with the local police for speeding and driving an unregistered car. He'd always seemed polite and cheerful when he delivered manure from a horse farm where he sometimes worked to Cam's farm for compost. With a father like his, keeping a positive attitude could be a real problem. She wondered what his mother was like. Cam had seen her only once, and it had been in town, not on their farm. Howard hadn't brought her to the farm-to-table dinner. Maybe they were divorced by now. Or maybe she kept house and cooked for her men, although most farms used all the person power they had on hand.

The overcast day had brightened a little but was still chilly and raw. As Cam pulled up at Sim's shop to let Lucinda off at her car, the pangs in her stomach made her realize she'd never had lunch.

"Buy you early dinner at the Grog?"

Lucinda agreed and said she'd follow Cam there. A burger and a draft IPA sounded perfect, and it would get Cam home in time to bring in the chickens. Maybe if she and Lucinda put their heads together, they could come up with some way to sort out the events of the last week.

Chapter 28

The Grog had been a fixture in Newburyport for as long as Cam could remember. She'd first come to the pub as a child with Albert and Marie after a morning of bird watching on Plum Island. She'd drawn on the paper place mat with the provided crayons and demolished the child-size burger and fries. The restaurant welcomed regulars at the bar, as well as families in the dining room. The walls between the wooden booths were high enough to keep conversations private, but if you wanted to perch on a bar stool and schmooze with the stranger next to you, that was welcome, too. Cam had done both over the years. She'd also listened to live music downstairs on a Saturday night, although she hadn't made it to a single concert since the growing season had launched itself with a vengeance.

She and Lucinda slid into a booth near the bar and perused the menus.

"Looks like the most local food I'll get here is the clam chowder. And an Ipswich ale," Lucinda said.

"I'm going to try the Green Head IPA from Newburyport Brewing Company. It's right here in town, even more local than Ipswich."

"Good idea."

A waitress stopped by, took their beer orders, and said she'd give them a minute to decide on food.

"How's your year of being a locavore going, anyway?" Cam asked. Lucinda had decided the previous spring to try to eat only local food for a year, an idea she'd gotten from a Barbara King-solver book in which she described her family's efforts to do the same.

"I've had a few slipups, but it's mostly good. Local food is out there if you look for it. Milk, cheese, meat, and fish. Your produce, of course. And wine and beer." Lucinda smiled and raised her eyebrows. "I finally decided to give myself a pass on coffee, though." She raised her shoulders. "What can I do? *Sou brasileira.* Coffee's in my blood."

"I think you can be excused." Cam smiled back.

The waitress brought two full pints and listened to their food orders: the Middle Street Cuban sandwich for Cam, clam chowder and a salad for Lucinda, but only after she'd asked if the greens came from a local farm.

"How do you say 'Cheers' in Portuguese?" Cam asked.

"*Saúde.*" Lucinda lifted her glass.

Cam repeated what she'd heard Lucinda say, which was something like "sow-OO-gee," and grimaced. "I was terrible at foreign languages in school. My engineer's brain couldn't do it."

Lucinda laughed. "That was close enough."

They clinked glasses, and each took a sip.

"Lucinda, I can't help thinking about Irene's death. Pete—"

"Oh, it's *Pete* now? You guys getting to be good pals?"

"No!" Cam felt the telltale blush creeping up her neck. "No, he only asked me to keep my eyes out for him. Anyway, he said they searched Irene's house. But what if they missed something?"

Lucinda rummaged in the slim shoulder bag she used as a

purse. "Ta-da!" She held up a ring holding two keys. Off it also hung a little red rectangle that looked like a miniature Oriental rug. "Irene's keys."

"Oh, my." Why were her friends always proffering other people's keys? Cam held out her hand, and Lucinda dropped the keys into it. "Are you thinking what I'm thinking?"

"If we go over there and look around, we'll get in big trouble with your boyfriend Pete? Yes."

"It was sort of the first part of that."

"Listen, *fazendeira*. You go get yourself in whatever hot water you want. Me, I just got legal. I'm not doing nothing to put my immigration status in danger."

Cam stuck the keys in her bag. She took another long swig of the Green Head and thought an India pale ale had never tasted so good. Newburyport Brewing was a fairly new microbrewery, but they seemed to be on top of their game. As she felt herself start to relax, she realized how much stress she'd been under in the last week. Maybe this wasn't a good time to hash things out. The police had to be making progress in finding Irene's real killer. She didn't have to use Lucinda's keys. She could sit here and have a girls' afternoon out with her friend. And not worry about anything except enjoying good food and company.

She took another sip and closed her eyes for a moment, savoring the hops on her tongue.

"Hmm. That was interesting," Lucinda said in a low voice.

Cam opened her eyes. "What was?"

"Bev Montgomery just walked by. Lady looks terrible."

"Was she by herself?"

"Yeah."

"I don't think she's too well," Cam said. "Albert's going to try to convince her to sell her farm and move in where he is. She's not very young."

"She can't possibly manage her farm all by herself, right?"

"Right." Cam nodded as she threw her hands out to the sides in an "It's obvious" gesture. Her left hand collided with a waiter passing with a tray of full beer glasses. Cam's shoulder and arm took most of the spills.

"I'm so sorry!" the young man said. He halted, eyes wide, mouth pulled down in chagrin. He balanced the edge of the tray on the table and proffered a cloth napkin from his apron pocket. "I, I . . ."

Cam laughed. "I was the one throwing my arms around. Don't worry about it." She swabbed off her arm. "And charge me for the spilled beer if you need to." The waiter shook his head and returned to the bar.

"I'm going to go clean up. Back in a flash," Cam said, heading for the ladies' room in the far corner of the restaurant. She shook her head and laughed at herself as she pulled the heavy door open.

When it shut behind her, the room stayed dark. The last time she was here, the bar had installed motion-detector lights and they had come on automatically. She waved her hand around, but the lights didn't come on. She felt around for a switch, but the wall near the door was smooth. She heard breathing.

"Wow, this is weird," she called to whoever was in there. "The lights aren't working." But there was no response.

Cam froze. Why didn't the person answer her?

It was darker than a darkroom. Her eyes weren't adjusting. She couldn't see a thing. Something creaked. A hint of barnyard scented the air.

"Who's there?" Cam called. No response. Cam stood next to the exit, so she knew the creak hadn't come from the door. She should get out of here. Her feet felt like blocks of ice. Her heart thudded in her chest. Where was the door handle? She felt around where she thought it should be, but couldn't find it.

A raspy voice said, "I knew you'd come in here sooner or later."

Cam knew the voice. "Bev?"

"Is our newfangled farmer a little bit scared?" Bev Montgomery's voice singsonged like a failed horror-movie actor's.

"I'm not scared, Bev," Cam said, hoping her voice didn't reveal how nervous this was making her. "Why don't you switch the lights back on, though?"

"Only when I'm good and ready," Bev growled. "You seem to do whatever you want to do. Steal my customers. Steal my hens. It's my turn now."

The lights blinked on. They nearly blinded Cam. She wanted to squeeze her eyes shut, except that Bev Montgomery stood a scant yard away, pointing a pistol at her. Bev's eyes were wide and wild.

Chapter 29

"Bev!" Cam's voice shook. "Put it down." Her heart sank. She had been through this once before with Bev and had managed to wrest the gun away. But they had been outside on Cam's farm. The gun had been in a bag, not pointed at her. And Bev was a lot closer this time.

Her steel-gray hair looked like she'd been cutting it herself, and she must have lost twenty pounds since last June. But it was her eyes that gave away her desperation.

"I thought you'd come to the Grog. You wouldn't take your illegal-alien friend to a fancy place like The Market."

"You were following me?" Cam didn't bother to tell her Lucinda was, in fact, not in the country illegally. She knew of Bev's activities with a militia group that sought to expose undocumented workers.

"And what if I was? You've been putting me out of business ever since you moved here," Bev accused. "It was your fault my son was killed, and now I don't have anybody to help me."

Cam opened her mouth to deny it.

"Be quiet and listen." Barb waved the weapon in Cam's face. "You lured away my business, and now you've stolen my chickens."

"But as soon as those hens get healthy and start laying again, I'm going to bring you eggs every week."

"Those are *my* hens! You people had no right to take them."

Cam fought to keep her voice calm. "You have friends who want to help you, Bev. My great-uncle Albert, for one. He was speaking of you yesterday, in fact."

Bev sniffed like she didn't believe Cam. "But not friends who will do farmwork for me." She glared and kept the gun leveled at Cam's chest.

"Maybe not. Albert thought you might like to move where he's living. It's a really nice place."

"I'm not moving anywhere. I'm not selling my farm." Her face reddened, and her breathing sounded erratic. "Those developers, they want to turn it into some cheap housing. You, of all people, should understand."

Cam nodded. She thought fast and furious. She had less and less hope that Bev would calm down and listen to reason. Hoping someone would come in and rescue her wasn't going to cut it, either. She ducked with a quick move and brought her head up sharply under Bev's hand. The gun went flying as Cam grabbed both of Bev's hands with her own. Cam took a deep breath when she heard the weapon fall to the floor without discharging.

The exit door swung open and thudded on Cam's back. Cam pushed Bev farther into the restroom to let the door open and, letting her hands go, sidled around behind her, where the gun had landed.

"Oops, sorry," said the young woman who came in. She gave the two an odd look but headed for a stall, checking her artfully arranged hair in the mirror as she passed.

Without taking her eyes off Bev, Cam bent down and picked up the gun. Bev's face paled, and she looked as if she might collapse.

"Are you going to shoot me?" Bev whispered. She stood without moving, her arms at her sides, all her anger apparently drained, and her will, as well.

Cam made sure the safety was on and stowed the weapon gingerly in her bag. "Of course not. Come on." Cam knew Great-Uncle Albert would want her to assist Bev. "Let's get you some dinner and some help. All right?"

Cam told Lucinda that Bev was going to join them. After ordering for Bev, Cam phoned Albert, who said he'd call a friend of Bev's. Lucinda looked impatient to hear the story, but Cam put her off with hand gestures and eyebrows. Bev sat with slumped shoulders and didn't speak, but she ate like it had been a while since her last good meal. By the time they were finished with their food, pink light slanted through the windows on the street. They waited outside until the friend fetched Bev.

Standing on the sidewalk, Cam watched the two walk slowly down the street. She faced Lucinda and explained in detail what had happened in the restroom.

"You were lucky on that one, *fazendeira*," Lucinda said. "The woman is nuts! She could have shot you right there in the bathroom."

"She's out of energy and out of hope. I think it was her last gasp at wishing she could get her old life back. Maybe now she'll be more willing to sell the farm. And to quit coming after me, as if I'm the source of all her problems."

"Are you going to tell the police?"

"I don't think she's going to be a problem again, but I'll give Ruth a heads-up."

"What about the gun?"

Cam groaned. "Crud. I'll lock it up at home and think about it later."

"You sure have a thing for getting in crazy situations, you know?"

Cam nodded as she checked the sky. The afternoon clouds had lifted on the horizon in time to showcase a band of spectacular sunset. "Sailors' delight. I gotta run home and see to the chickens."

"I'll check in with you tomorrow." Lucinda headed for the municipal parking lot.

"Thanks for backing me up at Howard's today," Cam called. She strode toward her truck, which she'd had to park a couple of blocks away. When her bag bumped more heavily than usual against her hip, Cam put a hand to her mouth and slowed her pace. Wouldn't that top off the day to shoot herself in the leg?

Chapter 30

Cam locked Bev's gun in a cupboard under the stairs at home, wondering what in the world she was going to do with it. At least it was safe there for a while. She dialed Albert on the house phone and talked with him at greater length about Bev. He assured her he'd make sure she was cared for. After they said goodbye, Cam checked her cell phone. Jake had left a message accepting her lunch invitation. Lunch tomorrow was on, then. She didn't foresee it being an easy conversation. And the first task, of course, was to figure out what she planned to tell him.

She poured a glass of white wine and paced the length of the downstairs, from one end of the kitchen through the eating area to the far end of the living room and back. She and Jake had a real spark together. He was taller than she and made her laugh. It was easy for them to talk food and farming together. But there was much about life they had never talked about. She had no idea if he was interested in raising a family. She knew he had immigration issues. She was well aware of his jealous streak and control issues.

Cam knew she wasn't the best at social interactions, but she had a core of self-confidence about her strengths and an interest in overcoming her difficulties relating to all kinds of people. And she knew it wasn't healthy for one person to want to control another's relationships. She sipped her wine and paced some more.

Finally, she refilled her glass and sank onto the couch. She made a special effort, using a trick her friend Tina had taught her, to shut away all the concerns and questions in her life in a mental box. She visualized locking it and putting it on a shelf.

The trick seemed to work. Preston jumped up on her lap and, under her ministrations, purred himself into oblivion. Cam spent the rest of the evening on the couch with her cat and a book and adjourned to bed for a deep and restful sleep.

Sure enough, the red sky at night brought a sunny, clear morning to the next day, although the temperature was again seasonably cool. Cam yawned as she laced up her boots before going out. It was so early, she'd caught sight of the nearly full setting moon from her bedroom window when she'd first opened her eyes. She had a list of items to harvest for the Saturday share pickup the next day, plus the usual tasks of chickens, weeding, tending seedlings, and so on. If she worked hard this morning, maybe she'd have time to take a walk around Mill Pond this afternoon.

Then she thought about the list of concerns she'd made the day before. She sure hadn't found Irene's murderer, but many of the other items had been ticked off.

She stuffed her phone in her pocket and reached for the key to the door. Preston ran over to his food bowl and looked up at her. Cam smiled and petted him for a moment as he ate. Her heart swelled with gratitude that she had found him, that he was all right, and that he was her feline companion. She wondered if she'd ever have a child of her own. Could she find her way along the path to intimacy with a partner and not blow it? If so, and if they were in agreement about wanting a child, she suspected this kind of loving feeling would be amplified a thousandfold. For now, a full heart and a sweet cat were enough.

Cam opened the back door to head out to her tasks. Preston streaked by her. The heart full of love instantly turned to one of fear. What if he disappeared again? She wasn't sure she could take it. She called him, and he paused near the big tree in the yard. He looked back at her, as if to say, "Aren't we going out to work and play like we always do? You work, and I play."

Cam took a deep if slightly shaky breath, locked the door behind her, and followed a now ambling cat toward the barn. She let the chickens out and stood back, watching them. They already seemed stronger and more energetic than they had earlier in the week. She was starting to be able to tell them apart. One, who was growing new feathers, seemed to be a leader of some kind. This one was usually first down the ramp in the morning, sometimes flying out, and a clutch of others followed her around. Cam called her Hillary. In contrast was Her Meekness, always the last to emerge from the coop, often last in line for food, occasionally pushed around by the bossier hens. Maybe Cam should name her Pea Brain. She was acquiring new feathers, too. Preston didn't seem the least bit interested in the girls, for which Cam was grateful. The last thing she needed was a predator for a pet. As long as Preston stuck to voles and mice and stayed within the bounds of the farm, they'd be in good shape.

After two hours of physical work, the mental box Cam had so carefully stowed away the night before sprang open like Pandora's. It brought with it a share of angst that went way beyond worrying about Preston. Questions roiled in her brain even as she weeded the beds of dark green kale in the mild sunshine. Why hadn't Pappas made any progress in the case? Why had Wes behaved so oddly at Old Town Hall? What did Sim have to hide that she felt compelled to lie about the night of the dinner, and what had she done on Wednesday instead of working in her shop? How did Howard come into possession of Preston, and why did he react so belligerently when Cam asked him about her cat? What did Vince know that he hadn't been able to tell Cam? And how in the world was she going to be able to end things with Jake, if breaking up was even what she wanted?

Cam shook her head. She tried without success to corral the thoughts back into their box. They were taking over her mind and her day. In the absence of pen and paper or yesterday's list, which was probably in the laundry basket, she pulled out her phone and brought up a text editor. Sitting back on her heels, she tapped in a list. Was there any of it she could control? Anything she could do?

She saved the file. On second thought, she deleted the item about Jake, saved the file again, and pressed the numbers for Detective Pete. Most of these concerns were in his bailiwick. One of them was clearly in hers. Several they might be able to work together on. Which made her heart beat a little bit faster. Which reminded her of her impending lunch with Jake.

When Pete answered, Cam asked if they could meet and talk this afternoon.

"Sure. When is good?"

"How about three o'clock?" Cam asked. "Do you want to take a walk around Mill Pond? I mean, to talk about the case?"

When Pete took a moment to respond, Cam was suddenly afraid she'd overstepped the boundary of casual, friendly interchange.

"Sounds good. Meet you in the parking lot there?"

Cam agreed, relieved. She told him she was going to e-mail him the list of issues she'd come up with. "Just so you know what I'm thinking about."

He thanked her and hung up.

She stared at the scissors in her hand and then at the Red Russian kale in the bed at her feet. She had a harvest to bring in. She bent over and resumed cutting, placing handfuls of the sturdy stalks in a bucket with a few inches of water in the bottom.

She wondered if Pete had any idea what she was really thinking about. Did she?

Chapter 31

Cam spread a cloth on her market table under the big maple in the yard. She brought out napkins and silverware. She strode back into the kitchen. The wall clock read 11:20 a.m. She threw a handful of kalamata olives onto the rest of the pesto pasta, to which she'd added chopped cucumber, diced sweet red pepper, some chunks of goat cheese, and two diced tomatoes. Now she whisked together a vinaigrette with olive oil, an herbed red-wine vinegar, Dijon mustard, and a pressed clove of garlic. Pasta salad on a bed of greens would have to do for lunch.

She glanced down at her clothes and groaned at her usual dirt-stained shorts and worn-out T-shirt. She ran upstairs and pulled on a red embroidered Mexican blouse and black capri pants. She dashed some water on her face and hand-combed her hair as she padded back down the stairs in bare feet. She might be hosting a breakup lunch, but she didn't have to look like she didn't care.

She glanced out the window. Jake was climbing out of his Cooper Mini. The convertible top was down, and his pale hair stood up from the wind. He wore his usual weekday attire of black-and-white checked chef pants and a black T-shirt. In one hand he grasped a paper bag. Cam, suddenly nervous, walked out to meet him.

He greeted her with a buss on the cheek and stood back. "Some hard cider to go with lunch," he said, extending the bag. His smile was a pale version of its usual megawatt beam.

"Thanks." Cam tried to make her voice brighter than she felt. He seemed as nervous as she did.

Jake frowned. He reached a hand out and touched the bruise on her temple as lightly as if he were wielding a butterfly's hairbrush. "What happened?"

His look of concern made her want to cry. She took a deep breath instead.

"I had a little accident on Wednesday. I'm fine."

"You didn't tell me." Accusation mixed with sadness in his voice.

"Don't worry. So, how about a glass of cider?" She set the bottle on the table. "Perfect for an alfresco lunch. I'll get some glasses." She was about to head for the house when she looked at the table again and laughed, her tension instantly dissipating.

"What's funny?" His voice was tentative, as if he was unsure whether he should even ask.

"I was going to tell you to sit when I saw I forgot the chairs." She rolled her eyes and laughed again. "Will you get some out of the barn?"

He smiled, his tension apparently also gone, and gave a little salute. "Yes, ma'am."

In the kitchen, Cam loaded a wide wooden tray with glasses, plates, the pasta, a bowl of greens, and a serving spoon, and balanced it with care as she returned to the yard. Jake now sprawled in a lawn chair that appeared as if it might give way under his weight. She didn't feel anywhere near as relaxed as he looked. The tray shook, and she barely got it onto the table without a catastrophe. When she placed the glasses next to the cider bottle, she knocked the bottle. It tipped over, shattering one of the glasses. Jake had already opened the bottle, and now hard cider fizzed over the tablecloth and into the pasta bowl.

Cam swore and stepped back as Jake leaned in from his chair, grabbed the bottle, and set it on its base.

"Look what I've done," Cam muttered. "Ruined everything."

"No, you haven't." Jake mopped up the cider with a napkin. A thin line of blood ran down the back of his left hand.

"You're cut!" Cam lifted his hand.

"It's nothing. Just a scratch."

"I'm so sorry. I'm a complete klutz."

"Not a klutz. You're a beautiful and talented farmer." He drew her toward him until she sat sideways on his considerable lap. He wrapped his arms around her.

Cam tried not to melt into him. She was supposed to be breaking up with him. A total body embrace had not been part of her plan.

"I've missed you," he murmured into her ear. "We're always fighting these days. I want to fix that." He stroked her hair with one hand.

Cam pulled away a little. She sat up straight and looked him in the eyes. "I'm not sure we can. You don't trust me. I can't—"

"Wait." He gave her a rueful look. "Let's eat lunch and I'll tell you a story. Give me that much?"

Cam nodded. She moved to her own chair. She picked up all the pieces of the glass with her fingertips and wrapped them in the sodden napkin. She checked the pasta salad. It looked like only a little cider had made it into the bowl, and the broken glass had fallen in the other direction. She stirred the pasta and tasted it.

"Well, we still have lunch. I'll claim it was meant to have hard cider vinaigrette all along." She gave a wan smile.

"I'll get another glass," Jake said, grabbing the napkin full of glass and heading for the kitchen.

"And a couple more napkins," Cam called after him.

After he returned, they ate in silence for a few moments, until Jake declared the salad a masterpiece.

Cam laughed. "At least it isn't ruined."

"Okay." Jake sipped the cider. "Here goes. I know I have trust issues." He surrounded the last word with finger quotes. "My last girlfriend had several affairs while I was with her. She lied about all of it." He frowned into the distance.

"What rotten behavior. How did you find out?"

"Oh, you know." He waved a hand. "Once she left her e-mail open. With another one, I saw them at a bar. She kept apologizing, saying she wouldn't ever go out on me again. The last one, well, I thought something was up. I actually followed her."

"What was her name?"

Jake cleared his throat. "Camille."

"Really? Did you call her Cam, too?" *How strange was that?*

"I did. Funny, huh?"

Cam nodded. She took a bite of salad.

"But there's more. I learned not to trust long before that. My mother . . . Well, I am adopted. My brother and sister are my parents' birth children. And my mother never treated me the same. My dad, he was great. We were all three his children, all alike. But my mom, it was like she wished she could get rid of me."

She laid a hand on Jake's knee. "That's terrible."

"It's made it kind of hard for me to trust women with my feelings. Look at me. I'm a successful chef, I own my own place, I'm in my thirties. And I'm single. You never wondered why?"

She shook her head. "That's not really how my brain works."

"Anyway, I'm not trying to excuse my behavior. But when I see you with other men, when somebody like Bobby Burr flirts with you, I get crazy."

"I know. But the craziness is what I have a problem with. I can't operate like that. I have enough trouble with relationships as it is. For reasons different than yours." Cam shook her head. "If I can't have other friends, male friends, without you thinking I'm going to betray you, I don't see how being with you can work."

Jake gazed at her without speaking.

"I love working with you," Cam continued. "It's great to have a business partnership. And you know we've had a spark between us—"

"I know." He covered her hand on his leg with his own and squeezed. "And it's a good spark. Will you give me one more chance?"

She sat watching him. Preston appeared and rubbed against her knee. She looked down at him, her uncomplicated, trusting friend, and rubbed his neck. She looked up again and nodded.

Jake beamed. "Dinner Monday, then? I'll make it extra special."

She nodded again. What had she done?

Cam cruised down Main Street, near Westbury High School, at a quarter past two. She thought classes were out for the day at around this time, and it looked like she was right. A line of yellow school buses idled single file in front of the main building. The school marquee urged the Westbury Eagles on to victory against the Ipswich Tigers, and half the cars in the parking lot seemed to be decorated with green and white. There must be a big football game on tonight.

Cam hadn't been involved in the pep or sports scene at her high school in Indiana, except for running cross-country. She had captained the math team and had been active in 4-H. She used to watch Friday night football games from the stands with her science-minded friend Cindy, but neither had screwed up the courage to attend the fifth-quarter dances afterward. The two had gone out for ice cream and had had sleepovers where they did each other's nails and fantasized about dating various non-geeks at the school. A fantasy it had remained.

She shook the memory off. It was half her life ago. She pulled to the side of the road and killed the engine. Teenagers began pouring out of the buildings. Student-piloted cars started to pass by. A large number of junkers. Older cars likely passed down from no-longer-driving grandparents. A few SUVs. The occasional sports car, clearly a sweet-sixteen gift from Daddy. The school district included families headed by factory workers, farmers, teachers, doctors, and investment professionals, and pretty much the whole income range in between. The students' rides reflected the mix.

Cam kept her eyes trained on her rearview mirror. When she saw a skinny kid wheeling toward her on a bicycle, she stepped out of the truck and leaned on the hood, out of the way of traffic.

"Vince," she called when he approached.

His eyes, previously focused on the pavement, swung up to meet hers. He veered out of traffic and screeched to a halt right beyond her.

"Ms. Flaherty. What are you doing here?" He looked around quickly and back at her. The pack on his back looked laden with books, and his bike helmet hung by its strap off the right handlebar.

"Think your helmet hanging there is going to protect your brain?" She smiled to buffer the remark.

"What's going on?" He glanced at the traffic going by. "I have to, like, get home."

"I sensed there was something you wanted to say yesterday. When we returned the Jeep." She tried to keep her tone casual. "About Preston, maybe?"

"I told him," Vince muttered, looking at the small ice cream and burger joint across the road.

Cam waited, not wanting to interrupt. A car of young people drove by with all the windows down. She heard cries of "Vincent!" trail after it. A hand waved out of the passenger side as the car rounded the bend before disappearing out of sight.

"I told him we had to let you know." Vince straightened and met Cam's eyes. "My father took your cat. Or found him. I don't know why, or where. But when I told him we had to call you, he wouldn't listen."

"What day was this?"

Vince concentrated. "It musta been Tuesday. Yeah, I had my bio exam that day. Tuesday afternoon."

Cam thought back. She had been in the hospital, getting checked out after the accident.

"I tried to take care of him, Ms. Flaherty. I gave him water. He's such a cool-looking cat. But he just lay there. Like he'd been drugged or something."

"Why didn't you call me?" Cam searched his face.

Vince hung his head. "Dad said he'd beat me if I did. I wish I'd a stood up to him."

"Does he beat you a lot?"

Vince nodded, gazing across the road again.

Cam's heart went straight out to the boy. Well, more of a young man. Her own father had been distant, not really present in her life. But he was always kind, without a cruel bone in his intellectual body. She gazed at Vince's left hand, where it lay on the bicycle seat. The pinkie finger was bent at an odd angle. She hoped it wasn't from his father breaking it.

"But why? Do you know why your dad kept him? He must know Preston is my cat."

"Oh, he knows, all right. He said something about giving the cat back when the time was right. I think he wanted you to, like, like him. But that so doesn't make sense."

"No, it doesn't." Cam had another thought. "Vince, has your dad said anything about losing the farm?"

"Dude." His eyes were wrapped in anguish. "If you only knew."

Cam waited, hoping she was projecting as much warmth as she felt for the teen.

"He's, like, nuts about this letter he got. He didn't really talk to me directly about it, but I heard him yelling at somebody on the phone. Something about Dad being adopted."

"Had he ever mentioned it before?"

Vince shook his head. "You don't understand, Ms. Flaherty. We're not like a regular family. We don't talk about anything at home."

"Not even with your mom?"

Vince shook his head fast. "You don't really understand." He glanced at the watch hanging off his spindly wrist and looked back at her with desperation. "Man, I gotta get home."

"Thank you so much for talking with me. It helps to know you tried to look after Preston."

"No worries. And Ms. Flaherty?"

"Yes?"

"I'm sorry. Really."

Cam nodded. Vince slapped the helmet on his head and clicked the fastener under his chin. He rode off without waving.

Chapter 32

Mill Pond was as smooth as a mirror this afternoon. Cam sat on top of one of the picnic tables with her chin in her hands, elbows resting on her knees. After talking with Vince and picking up groceries at the Food Mart, she had arrived a few minutes early to meet Pete. She had shoved her phone and keys in her pockets and had strolled down the winding path from the parking area. She figured he'd call her if he saw her truck in the gravel lot or he'd walk down to the pond. She tried to shush the butterflies in her stomach. She was meeting Pete Pappas to talk about the murder. It wasn't a hot date. If she were honest with herself, though, she felt drawn to him and thought it was mutual.

Even here, within sight of Main Street, the pond was a peaceful refuge. It got a lot quieter once one started along the path through the trees circumnavigating the water, or up one of the other ones that wound through the woods and around the edges of meadows and fields. When she was walking, Cam could pretend she was hiking in Maine or even in southern Indiana. She had cross-country skied here last winter. Tina had come up from the city, and the two of them had bumbled their way along the paths, laughing at themselves, enjoying the fresh snow, inhaling clean, cold air.

Now the sun shining through the colors of a New England fall dappled the pond like an Impressionist painting as Cam sat and gazed. Her focus was anywhere but present, though. Vince had said that Howard took Preston so she would like him. It didn't make sense in any universe she could imagine. Maybe Howard wanted to seem the hero by returning the cat. She shook her head. It was a puzzle she couldn't figure out. At least not now.

Another puzzle was what to do about Jake. She'd given him one more chance but against her better judgment. She didn't know why she hadn't insisted they revert to being friends. She liked things clear. On or off. Black and white. That was why she'd been attracted to software engineering in the first place. Elegant ways to arrange ones and zeroes and make them do your bidding felt like a very safe world compared to the confounding fog of interpersonal relationships.

She checked her phone. While she'd been musing, twenty minutes had gone by. Pete was late. She frowned. He seemed like he would be the punctual type. She pulled her phone out, about to press his number, and thought better of it. He'd show up. At least she had a lovely place to sit and wait, although the air was cool here in the shade of a tall fir tree. She had left her sweater in the truck, and the light blouse wasn't as comfortable as it had been at noon. Neither were the sandals.

Cam rose and walked down to the pier jutting out over the water, where the sun shone without impediment. She sat at the far end, hugging her knees. She had suggested this meeting as a way to let Pete know what she was thinking about the case, but also to follow up on what had seemed like a bit of romantic advance on his part. But now that she had not broken up with Jake and had, in fact, committed to a date Monday night, things were muddy. And she wasn't the type to date two men at once. It didn't seem honest, although she knew others did it.

She gazed into the water, which smelled aquatic in a clean, fresh way. Small fish darted to and fro, and she could see the posts supporting the pier all the way to the bottom. She wished she had the same kind of clarity.

A footstep on the wood resounded the length of the pier. She craned her neck around. Pete Pappas stood at the other end. Hands in his pockets, he looked like he had a week ago, when he had come to inspect the remnants of the farm-to-table dinner scene. Wrinkled shirt, hair not smoothly combed, wearing dirty sneakers instead of his usual polished oxfords. He walked the length of the pier and sat cross-legged next to her.

"What's happening?" Cam cocked her head at Pete. "You're not your usual spiffy self," she said and then rued saying it. She had no business addressing his state of attire.

"Yeah. I know." He nodded slowly, staring out at the pond. "Sorry I'm late."

They sat without speaking for a few minutes. Cam's dark shirt and pants soaked up the sun and warmed her. Pete hefted a pebble that lay on the pier, pulled his arm back, and lobbed it way out in an arc. It splashed the quiet surface, and its effect rippled out until the largest circle reached them.

"It's all circles," he muttered.

"What?"

"Everything is connected. This murder case. I know it's all tied together. I can't seem to tease apart the circles. And this?" He gestured at his clothes. "It's connected, too."

Cam raised her eyebrows in what she hoped was an inquisitive look. She didn't trust herself to speak and blunder away what seemed to be an impending confidence.

"My marriage is falling apart. I guess I should say it *has* fallen apart. My wife moved out last week. And she took Dasha, our dog."

"Oh, I'm so sorry."

"Don't be. We'd been miserable for years. And at least we didn't have children. Except Dasha."

"Doesn't sound like much fun."

"And it's not helping me solve this case. Which, as my boss so kindly reminds me, is getting colder by the day."

"Do you want to talk it through?"

Pete nodded. "Walking as we talk might help."

"Come with me to get my sweater. And I think I have some sneakers in the truck, too. One of the walking paths starts from the parking area and leads back here."

"You're on."

A couple of minutes later they strolled down a wide mowed path between a field of dry cornstalks and a brushy area. Cam sneezed.

"Gitses." Pete smiled at her.

"What?" Cam cocked her head and frowned as she smiled.

"Means 'Bless you' in Greek."

"Oh. Well, thanks." Cam sniffed. "I'm allergic to grass. And I'm a farmer. Go figure."

He cleared his throat. "You know this is not strictly kosher, me talking about the case with you."

"Because I'm a suspect?" Cam clasped her hands behind her back.

"I have ruled you out as even a person of interest." He glanced over at her. "It's not an insult, mind you. It's a technical term. Seriously, I can't see why you would want to murder someone who had to be one of your richest customers, even if she was a little prickly. No, talking through a case with a civilian is not the way we're trained to operate. But I figure you circulate among these people in a way I never could. I feel sure there are things you've heard or seen that might help me find the murderer."

"I don't know. I'll do my best. Let me start by telling you about Preston."

Cam spent a few minutes catching Pete up on Preston going missing and on finding him at Howard Fisher's. She told him about confronting Howard and Howard's anger.

"You shouldn't have gone there alone." Pete looked at her with worry etched all over his face.

"I didn't. Lucinda was with me. And I was glad she was." She went on to describe her meeting Vince after school a little while earlier. "He seemed to think his dad took Preston so he could give him back. When the time was right. I don't really get it."

"It's information. It might connect later."

"Poor kid. Said his dad beats him, which was why he was afraid to tell me the truth about Preston."

Pete shook his head. "I wonder if the school knows, if anyone has notified social services."

"I don't know."

"I'll make a note to check into it. Now, do you think Howard had any reason to kill Irene?"

"I don't know. Lucinda said she saw his truck driving away from Irene's one time." At Pete's quizzical look, Cam went on. "Lucinda cleaned house for her."

"Interesting."

"She was supposed to call you and tell you. Did she?"

He shook his head.

"I heard something else about Howard from my great-uncle," Cam said. "He told me Howard's business is in jeopardy, that he might lose the farm."

"I wonder if it's true."

"I asked Howard, and he said he isn't losing the farm. He wasn't too happy about my asking, either."

Pete stopped in his tracks and pointed to a large bird swooping over the open field. "Marsh hawk. See the white tail patch? And how it tilts back and forth as it swoops?"

"Cool," Cam said as she watched the hawk. "I don't know much about bird watching."

"But you do know something about Sim Koyama." He resumed walking, as did Cam. "She seems to be a bit unstable this week."

"I only met her for the first time at the dinner, you know. She and Bobby are good friends, and she's worried about him. That's what she says, anyway." They followed the path into the trees as it wound uphill over roots and between large rocks.

"She was seen disagreeing with Irene Burr several times," Pete said. "Rather vociferous disagreements, I might add."

"I guess she might have killed Irene." Cam turned up her right palm. "But why? I mean, we all have people we don't get along with, right?"

"Maybe she's convinced of Bobby's innocence because she's the murderer."

"I don't think so. But tell me more about Bobby. He came by the other day and said he'd been released but that he's still a person of interest."

"We have a reliable witness who places him at the pigsty."

"So what if he was there? Maybe he argued with Irene, and she fell in by accident."

"Why wouldn't he call for help, then? And it wasn't an accident. She was hit on the head before she died. And it wasn't from the fence."

Cam shuddered. "Is there any other evidence against Bobby? Don't you have to have DNA and fingerprints and everything?"

"Leave the CSI to us, Cam." Pete cleared his throat again. "You're right, though. We didn't have enough to arrest him. Yet. It's the reason we had to let him go. But we're working on it.

And speaking of working, I was thinking about that note you said you found and lost."

"I told you—"

"I know. I'm afraid I didn't take it seriously. I'm sorry. Can you remember what it said?"

"Something about 'or I'll tell what I know.' "

"Interesting. I hope it turns up soon."

They had been strolling in single file. He put a hand on her shoulder for a moment and caught up with her, and they continued side by side.

Picturing the pigsty and its malnourished residents, she shuffled through the leaves on the path. Her toe caught in a hidden root, and she launched forward.

"Whoa!" Pete snapped his arms around her waist right before her knee hit the ground. He pulled her back up.

Cam found herself standing with her back to Pete. His arms encircled her waist with a light touch, and his face warmed her left cheek.

"Gotta watch your step, Flaherty," he murmured.

Cam didn't move. It felt so comfortable, so right, for his arms to be around her. And Pete calling her by her last name was far more intimate than when he'd first addressed her as Cam.

A rasping blue jay flew at an angle directly in front of them and broke the moment. Cam opened Pete's arms and twisted away to face him.

"Thanks for the rescue." She tried to smile through the power of the moment.

Pete looked at her face and closed his eyes for a moment. He reopened them. "Right, where were we? What else do you know?" He resumed walking without meeting Cam's eyes. "Have you seen anybody acting oddly? It could be anyone, anywhere."

"Do you know Wes Ames?" Cam asked, wondering if she'd ever regard Pete as only a friend and colleague after today.

"I remember he's a customer of yours. Petite, friendly wife?"

"Right, except she's out of town for a few weeks. Wes seems . . . I don't know . . . off somehow. And he was arguing with Irene the night of the dinner."

"I heard. About the fate of the Old Town Hall, right?"

"Speaking of which." Cam went on to describe her encounter with Wes at the Old Town Hall. "He was jumpy and kind of angry. I'd never seen him like that before."

Pete walked in silence for a minute. "Do you happen to have a customer named Diane?"

"I do." Cam didn't even try to hide her surprise at the question and the sudden change of subject. "Why? Do you think she killed Irene?"

"No." Pete laughed. "I don't. Her name came across my desk recently, and I wondered."

Cam stared at him. Not only for the sound of his deep, throaty laugh, which she was pretty sure she'd never heard before, but at the prospect of Diane having anything to do with illegal activities.

"She seems like a perfectly upstanding citizen to me," Cam said. "Her check for her share didn't bounce, she volunteers on the farm, and she cans her own tomatoes. She's a consultant of some kind with a flexible schedule. I don't really know anything else about her."

Pete made a halting gesture with his hand. "That's plenty. Thanks." A little smile stayed on his face as they walked, though.

Cam shook her head in confusion but decided it would be better to watch where she walked than to quiz Pete about Diane and risk tripping again. She wasn't sure she could handle another rescue today.

Chapter 33

Cam sat in a lawn chair in a last spot of late-day sunshine outside the chicken enclosure. Preston sat next to her, doing his Sphinx imitation. During the rest of her walk with Pete, they had chatted about non-murder-related topics—movies they liked, his three brothers, her quirky parents, how they'd gotten into their respective professions. They'd kept it light and easy. When they'd parted in the parking area, he said to call him if she learned anything new, and made her promise to be careful.

It had been a pleasant afternoon. The part where she tripped had been particularly nice. But Cam reminded herself of two red-flag points. The first was that she had a date with Jake on Monday night. The second was that Pete was a man on the rebound and he was not yet divorced. It didn't matter how much she liked that he didn't whine about his situation and didn't dwell on it. It was irrelevant at this time to feel a strong attraction to him both physically and intellectually. She needed to be content to be friends with him and to help him on the investigation if she could.

"Hey, Cam!" Ellie's voice intruded on her thoughts.

Cam turned to look behind her. The teenager rode around the corner of the barn on a bicycle. She was breathing heavily, her cheeks rosy, a smile splitting her face. She pulled to a stop next to Cam's chair, unclipped the helmet strap under her chin, and hung the helmet on the handlebar.

Cam greeted her. "You look happy."

"I got my Locavore badge! I wanted to show you." Ellie dismounted, letting the bike fall to the side. She wore a gray hooded sweatshirt with a yellow GS emblem on the left chest. What looked like a pre-distressed numeral twelve decorated the front of the hoodie, with a small nineteen embedded in the top of the one. The right leg of her skinny jeans was rolled up at the ankle, above a leopard-print sneaker with neon-green laces.

"Congratulations, Ellie. You worked hard for it."

"We had our troop meeting after school today. I, like, finished the requirements in the summer, but it took this long for the badge to come through." She rolled her eyes as she dug something out of her pocket. She proffered a plastic sheath holding a colorful cloth patch bordered in orange. "Do you think it's a radish or a beet?" The reddish orb had its aboveground greenery attached.

"Good question." Cam peered at the leaves. "I think it's a beet. A radish would have a lighter-colored root and would taper into it more."

"I think you're right."

"Grab a chair. Unless you have to get home?"

"No. I told my mom I was coming by here. What a killer hill you live on, Cam. This is the first time I've ridden my bike all the way up here."

Cam laughed. "Where's an attic? At the top of the house. And this is Attic Hill."

"How are the hens doing?" Ellie knelt by the fence and stuck her finger through one of the openings. Hillary marched over to check out if food might be part of the deal. When she pecked at Ellie's finger, the girl laughed and withdrew it.

"Her name is Hillary," Cam said.

Ellie stared at Cam. "Do you mean for Hillary Clinton? Awesome. My mom worked on her campaign for president."

Cam knew Myrna Kosloski suffered from multiple sclerosis. Being wheelchair bound didn't let her get out much. But she wasn't surprised the former surgeon had been active in a political campaign for a strong female candidate, and there was a lot a person could do from a desk and a phone.

"Omigod." Ellie giggled. "She's the hens' fearless leader, right? That is *so* the right name."

"I thought so, too. I hadn't realized they were going to have personalities. So how's high school treating you?" Cam hadn't had a chance to chat with Ellie since the summer ended.

"Some good, some bad. It was pretty confusing at first. Lockers, seniors. You know. But I'm in advanced math, and I made the cross-country team, which is a bunch of fun kids."

"Aren't you on the soccer team, too?"

"That's the traveling team. It's with the town, not the school, and it's only on weekends. Well, we're supposed to practice every Tuesday. But Coach Molise doesn't like it when I miss cross-country practice. I guess this'll be my last year playing soccer. But it's okay. I love running."

"I'll bet you're fast." Cam had noticed most of Ellie's recent growth seemed to be in her legs, which looked longer every week.

"I'm trying to talk up Girl Scouts at school, too. Make it cool, instead of nerdy. I brought a couple of new girls to the meeting today. I think they're going to join."

"Would that be a Girl Scout sweatshirt you're wearing?"

"Totally. See?" She pointed to the small nineteen and the big twelve. "Founded in nineteen twelve. Not a bad design for a nerdy group, right?"

"I like it. So, any boys on the horizon at school?"

"Chill, Cam!" Ellie refastened her fine blond hair in a scrunchie. "Well, there is one kid I kind of like. He's a junior, so he's wicked old. But he's nice. And he doesn't try to, like, play Mr. Big Man or anything."

"Name?"

"Vince. His dad is the pig farmer who was at the dinner last week. You know, their farm is where Ms. Burr died. Poor Vince."

Cam watched Ellie stroke Preston. She had a crush on Vince Fisher.

"Do you ever go to see him at the farm?" This could be worrisome. She didn't want Ellie anywhere near Howard's temper.

"Uh, no." Ellie stretched the negation into three syllables while she wrinkled her brow and raised her eyebrows as only a teen could. "We just, like, get an ice cream after school and talk. Once we rode our bikes to Mill Pond and walked around."

Cam had had no idea Mill Pond was date central for old and young and everyone in between. The spot of sun they sat in suddenly turned to shadow as the sun sank behind the woods beyond the farm.

Ellie stood. "I have to get home. See you tomorrow. I'll come early to help, right?"

"I'd love it. Thanks, Ellie. And congratulations again on your badge. You're great."

Ellie fastened her helmet and rode off with a wave.

Cam shoved herself up out of the chair and shooed all the hens into their coop. Sunset ate away at the light earlier each day. In a couple of weeks the clocks would change, and they would plunge into the short, dark days of a northern fall. She wondered

229

if the chickens' internal clocks were linked to the actual sunset or to the same time every day. She guessed she'd find out.

She made sure the coop door was securely fastened and puttered in the barn for a while, setting up the farm table for the next day's distribution, assessing what still needed to be harvested, putting away tools.

She felt unsettled as she walked to the house. The dusk gathered like a dark dream. While it was great to see Ellie learning, growing, falling in love, even, it made Cam feel all the older. This life she'd taken on, running a farm solo, was a hard one. It was not so different from any other farmer's the world over, but it varied in every respect from her previous safe, sedentary job as a software engineer with a condo in the city and clean fingernails around the clock.

As Cam unlocked the door to the house, she wondered if she'd ever have a teenaged daughter like Ellie. Was she even cut out to be a mother? Cam's own mother was sweet but had been as distant as her father. Her only real role model for maternal nurturing had been Great-Aunt Marie. And what man would want a socially unskilled woman like herself? Jake appeared to, but Cam wasn't sure she wanted him in return. Pete? Maybe, but they would have to get to know each other much better, and he had a few details of his own to work out first.

Cam flicked on the lights and called Preston. When he ran in, she relaxed into relief from tension she hadn't realized she was holding. She locked the door behind them.

She pushed back her chair two hours later. She'd cut an acorn squash in half and baked it. She had thrown together a quick whole-wheat couscous stuffing with sautéed onions and chopped steamed kale, rosemary, and pine nuts, and had filled the scooped-out halves, topping them with grated sharp cheddar. A few more minutes in the oven, time enough to pour a glass of wine, and it was dinner, with enough left over for several more solitary meals.

She was halfway through both her dinner and reading the *Boston Globe* when the house phone rang.

She greeted Great-Uncle Albert.

"I wanted to tell you I got a ride over to Bev Montgomery's today," he said. "We had a long talk, and I think she's agreed to sell the place. A lady here passed recently, so her room is available." He laughed. "Death is the only way rooms come open, I'm afraid. At any rate, Bev said she'd take it."

"I'm glad to hear it." And maybe in assisted living Bev would also get some of the mental health attention she needed.

"Say, did Preston ever turn up?" Albert asked.

"He's back."

"Wonderful, dear."

"I forgot to tell you last night. I'm sorry. And you might not think it's so wonderful when you hear where I found him." She relayed the story of the previous morning.

"Oh, my. Why would Howard keep Preston?"

"Vince said something about his father wanting to wait to give him back so it would look like he had rescued Preston instead of taking him."

"The whole thing is a shame. Howard Fisher has had his troubles, I must say."

"He seems to be passing them on to his son, unfortunately. I spoke with Vince after he got out of school yesterday. He said his father beats him regularly."

"That's a crime. Has somebody reported him?"

"Detective Pappas said he'd look into it."

After they'd finished talking, she thought a little harder about why Howard would want to play the nice guy by pretending to find Preston after having kept him nearly starved for a few days. Because he thought Cam was being overly critical of the way he tended his pigs? Or that she was suspicious of him? For what? The murder?

She shook her head. She returned to her dinner and her paper. Maybe she'd call Pete to talk some more when she was done eating. Maybe he was sitting home alone on a Friday night, too.

Chapter 34

She awoke the next morning with a fleeting dream memory of her feet traversing a frozen lake. When she opened her eyes, the gray light and the sound of dripping eaves through the open window played backdrop to her bare feet outside the covers. Cam groaned as she grabbed for the quilt, curled her feet and head under it, and prayed without hope to get back to sleep. She lay listening to the rain as her feet gradually warmed. She never did call Pete last night. It would have seemed too personal. She didn't really have anything pressing on the case to talk with him about, after all.

Rain was the worst possible condition for a last-minute harvest. The greens would be sodden. Any fungus on the bean plants would be spread by picking in the rain. Possibly worst of all, she and any volunteers would be soaked and chilled before the first shareholder even arrived. She cast a glance at the clock and groaned. It was already seven o'clock. This was major sleeping in for a farmer, especially on pickup day, but she was both too cold to get out of bed and too reluctant to start the workday.

When she'd warmed up enough, she sat, slid her feet into slippers, and rolled out of bed. She took a deep breath and straightened her back. This was her life right now, like it or not. A hot shower, a bowl of oatmeal, and a mug of French roast later, she suited up in old jeans, an old fleece sweatshirt, wool socks, and rain gear. She ventured forth, Preston at her side. The digital thermometer on the porch read forty-three degrees Fahrenheit. A little below normal for the middle of October, but not unheard of. Preston, with his double layer of fur, was unfazed by the rain. He ambled by her side, paused to sniff the chicken enclosure after she entered it, and headed back to sit under the eaves of the barn.

Cam wasn't sure how the birds would react to the rain. She opened their door. They wandered out and started pecking, rain or no rain. She realized they would need a cover for their food, so she rummaged in the barn until she came up with a discarded piece of plywood and a couple of boxes to prop it on over the feeder.

She felt completely inadequate with respect to these fowl. She remembered with relief that Alexandra would be there later to pick up her share. Maybe she'd even come early to help harvest. Cam could ask her then what to do about hens and rainy days. Alexandra had also promised to build a covered run with DJ this weekend. It seemed more like the girls needed an entire covered housing complex, but that was definitely not Cam's area of expertise. And would they build while it was raining?

Grabbing scissors and a big basket, she trudged over to the salad area. She grew the lettuces and tender greens as close to the barn as she could. Woodchucks and rabbits loved to munch nearly mature heads of lettuce right to the ground if they got a chance, and she'd had her share of heartbreak when going out to cut lettuce on market morning, only to find flat green stumps instead.

Earlier in the year, Cam had spent some time researching effective solutions short of poisoning every critter in sight. After the new barn was completed, Cam had set up an area fenced in by a wire that was powered by a small shocking device. The wire ran from the device, mounted inside a corner of a barn window, out to the salad garden. She'd stretched it around the area one foot up off the ground. She'd wrapped the wire around a narrow fiberglass post at four-foot intervals. All she had to do was keep weeds from growing tall enough to lean against the wire so that they wouldn't short out the electricity.

She'd touched the live wire once so she could understand the effect on the small mammals, not that she was anywhere near their size. The shock was unpleasant but didn't knock her out or anything. She fervently hoped it would deter the varmints from browsing through some of her most valuable crops. Somehow, possibly from being shocked once, Preston had figured out this area was one to stay away from. She supposed she could have built a permanent wire fence, sinking it into the ground to prevent the critters from digging under it, but then she would be stuck with that size of garden. The electric-wire method was a lot more flexible.

Now Cam stepped carefully over the wire and set to work cutting bunches of mesclun in the rain. It wasn't a downpour, so the leaves stood mostly erect, and most weren't lying in the wet soil. She remembered her arugula beds being poisoned last spring. It had taken a while to find the culprit.

She'd filled the capacious market basket and stood to stretch her back when she spied a slight figure in a lime-green rain jacket approaching.

"Now, that's dedication," Cam said when Ellie drew near. "Thanks for coming."

"I said I'd come help. It's just rain." Ellie smiled. "It's what we say in cross-country. We train in anything except lightning. Rain doesn't hurt you."

"Well, I'm glad to have you. You didn't ride your bike in this, I hope."

"My dad dropped me off."

"How are your running times, anyway?" Cam asked.

"I'm getting there. I'm only a freshman. But we have this girl, Chelsea, a junior? She might go to states. She's wicked fast."

"I actually ran cross-country in high school. It was the only sport I had any interest in."

"You did?" Ellie's eyebrows rose.

"Don't look so surprised. I figured it was a good use of these ostrich legs." Cam gestured vaguely at her extra-tall rain pants.

"Were you any good?"

"I placed once. I tripped a lot, too. I'm actually too tall to be a great runner. Or at least that was my excuse." Cam laughed and shook her head.

"You should come to one of our meets sometime."

Cam gazed at Ellie, thinking of Myrna, who couldn't possibly navigate the grassy fields or wooded areas where the meets would be sure to start and finish. "I'd like to. Can I find the schedule online?"

Ellie nodded. "On the high school Web page. Click the Sports tab. We're down at the bottom." She rolled her eyes. "Of course. So, what's my first, like, job this morning?"

"Why don't you take this basket back to the barn and see if you can make it presentable for the shareholders? The greens are pretty wet, but I don't think they are too dirty. Maybe spread them out in several baskets for an hour or two so the greens will dry out a little. Watch the fence!"

"Got it." Ellie leaned over the wire, hefted the basket, and headed back the way she'd come. Cam looked around, trying to remember what else she needed to harvest out here. She could set Ellie to cutting herbs when she reemerged. It would have to be a small share this week. Fortunately, the subscribers' agreement stated that shares would go down to half portions in the fall. She realized with a start that they had only a month left to go for the summer shares. And the winter shares would start in December. *Yikes*. Did she have enough started in the greenhouse to sustain cutting all winter? And could she keep it warm enough?

Cam heaved a sigh as heavy as a peck of carrots. She turned when she heard voices behind her. Ellie and Bobby were walking toward her. Bobby wore a Red Sox cap and had the collar of a canvas jacket, dark with moisture, pulled up around his ears.

"Look who I found," Ellie said, smiling.

"Did you come out here in the rain to volunteer?" Cam asked Bobby.

He shook his head. He shifted his eyes to Ellie and back to Cam, as if sending Cam a message.

It took her a moment. "Ellie, can you cut herbs next? You know the routine."

Ellie walked off, nodding.

"What's up?" Cam faced Bobby.

"They took Sim in for questioning."

"Oh, no. But I saw Pete yesterday and—"

"Oh, so you're on a cozy first-name basis with the statie who accused me of murder?" Bobby pulled his mouth down in disgust.

"I thought Detective Pappas had already questioned Sim." Cam ignored the jab. "Twice."

"It's some issue with her alibi. But so what? Same as with me, they can't possibly have any actual evidence. I'm betting they'll let her go. I wanted to let you know."

"Thanks. I appreciate it."

"I *thought* you and she were friends. Like I thought you and I were friends. But maybe you're better friends with old Pete, there." Bobby's look changed to one of worry. "If you are, I hope you can convince him to leave Sim alone. She didn't kill Irene any more than I did."

Alexandra didn't show up early to help, but with some degree of scrambling and no small dose of ingenuity, Cam and Ellie managed to assemble enough produce for the shares. Ellie's father, David, came promptly at noon, picked up the family's share, and whisked his daughter away to get warm and dry. The rain had finally stopped, a brisk wind moving the front through. Cam could even spy traces of blue in the western sky.

She dashed to the house before anyone else arrived, stripped off every piece of her wet clothing, and pulled on a dry outfit, socks, and work boots. She grabbed a granola bar and munched it as she headed back to the barn. She was in time to greet two customers getting out of their cars.

By two o'clock only half the shareholders had taken their produce. Cam checked the clock on the barn wall. Usually, things were winding down by now. Maybe people were out of town, leaf peeping. She had no idea.

Lucinda walked slowly through the door, hands in her jeans pockets, a cloth bag slung over her shoulder. She didn't smile at Cam.

"Hey, what's up?" Cam asked.

Lucinda poked through the salad greens like she wasn't sure she wanted to take any of them. "You know I said I had to find another cleaning job, now that Irene is gone?"

Cam nodded.

"Then I thought, I got my green card. Maybe now I can be a librarian again, like I was in Brazil. The heck with scrubbing toilets."

"Absolutely. Did you find something?"

"Nada." She shook her head. "Nobody wants me. Not even as

an aide, a shelver." She picked up a squash and threw it into the bottom of her bag. The bag slipped off her arm and fell, the squash rolling out and toward the wall of tools. She swore but let it roll.

Cam approached her. "Rotten luck. How many libraries did you talk to?"

"All the ones around here. They don't like immigrants, I guess. Westbury was actually the most friendly, but they want me to get more training in this country. I have a degree in library science! But it's in Portuguese. Not good enough for them." She spat out the last sentence.

"I'm really sorry, Lucinda. Don't give up."

Wes rushed in, carrying Felicity's market basket. He greeted Cam and set to work. Checking the blackboard where Cam listed all the items and how much to take of each, he threw three leeks into the bottom of the basket, selected a squash, added a bunch of kale, frowning all the while.

"How's it going, Wes?"

"Good. In a hurry today." He finished his order, gently laying the salad greens on top. "Felicity is coming home tomorrow. I have some cooking to do."

Diane Weaver entered the barn. Two men Cam had never seen before flanked her. She walked straight up to Wes. He tried to move around her, but one of the men grasped his arm.

"Wesley Ames," Diane began. "You are under arrest for growing, selling, and distributing non-medicinal *Cannabis sativa* over the amount of one ounce with the intent of making a profit."

Chapter 35

The other man moved in and deftly relieved him of his basket while the first cuffed Wes's hands behind his back. He struggled for a moment and then stood quietly. The color drained out of his face as he gazed above Diane's head.

Diane went on speaking, but Cam didn't pay any attention. She stared at the scene. Wes Ames, growing and selling marijuana? Diane arresting him? In her barn? The world had gone topsy-turvy.

Right before they led Wes away, his head snapped toward Cam.

"Call Anne Kennedy in Elmira, New York. Felicity's sister. Please."

The anguish in his eyes tore at Cam. She nodded.

Diane saw them out the door and turned back. She walked up to Cam. "I'm so sorry to do this here. We had information that led us to believe he was about to destroy his operation."

"Who are you?" Cam stared at Diane, this normal-looking woman who said she was a consultant, this person who took pride in canning her own tomatoes.

Diane stood a little straighter. "I'm an undercover DEA agent. We've been following Wes for a while. He had established a rather large marijuana factory in the back basement of the Old Town Hall." She raised her eyebrows. "It wasn't exactly altruism for the town that made him not want Irene to buy the property."

The flat of seedlings. The way Wes had seemed alarmed to see her and had hurried her out of the basement the day she'd stopped by. His arguments with Irene. Cam wondered if the clicking of things falling into place in her brain was audible.

"This explains a lot. Does Detective Pappas know about it?" He had to. That was why he had asked her about Diane during their walk.

"He does."

"Did he tell you what I told him on Friday? About my run-in with Wes in the Old Town Hall basement a few days ago?"

She nodded.

"It all makes sense now, but it didn't at the time," Cam said. "Poor Felicity. I wonder if she knew anything?"

"As far as we know, she didn't. We've done some checking around." Diane smiled, but it was a professional smile and not a particularly cheery one.

In the distance Cam heard the four flat, slow blasts from the municipal siren, indicating a fire. And again. And again. On-call firefighters would be jumping into cars all over town and driving from every direction, flashing lights on, toward the firehouse. A minute later the faint wail of an engine's siren started up. She sniffed. When she caught a whiff of smoke in the air, she shuddered. She'd been trapped in a fire not once but twice in her life. She never wanted to experience it again.

Diane dragged a vibrating phone out of her jacket pocket. She turned away to answer it.

"I'm on it." Her eyes darted to Cam. "Thanks." She stabbed a button to disconnect. "Do you mind assembling my share for me? I'll pick it up later. I have to run. Old Town Hall is on fire. The bastard must have triggered the fire to destroy evidence."

"How could he trigger a fire?"

Diane shook her head. "I don't know." She hurried out of the barn at a near run.

Lucinda moved next to Cam. "Holy manure. I always thought Wes was a little *doido*." She made a circular motion with her finger next to her head. "You know, funny. But growing pot for a business on town property? He really is nuts."

Cam nodded. This upped the stakes for his being a suspect in Irene's murder, too. It was one thing to want to save a historic building for town functions. It was quite another to have a profitable business threatened. But why hadn't he grown the pot at home? Maybe he hadn't wanted to involve Felicity.

She glanced at his overflowing basket. She'd promised to call Felicity at her sister's. And if Felicity was coming home, as she surely would be now, she should have the food.

"Can you watch the shop for a few minutes? I have to go look up Felicity's sister and call her."

"You can find the number on your phone, you know. It ain't called smart for nothing."

"I know. I'd rather have the privacy, though. Back in a flash." At least Wes's troubles seemed to have taken Lucinda's mind off her own, Cam mused as she walked to the house. An idea hit her like a spring thunderstorm. Cam smiled, her own mind taken off Wes's troubles for the moment.

Her step returning to the barn was much less lively. Felicity had dissolved into tears at the news. Her sister Anne had had to take over the phone. Anne assured Cam they would call a lawyer. She said they would be leaving Elmira shortly, but it was a seven-hour drive. Before Cam hung up, she volunteered to leave the basket of food at Felicity and Wes's house, telling Anne nothing was overly perishable, especially with today's cool temperature.

Cam had never been to their house before but had the address

242

in her files. She could go right after the last shareholder showed up. She smacked her head as she walked. Tomorrow was market day again. The market manager had offered her a table for the rest of the season, and she had accepted. How in the world would she get everything done in time? Then she remembered her idea.

Alexandra was in the barn.

"Yo, Cam. We didn't forget about the run."

"No worries. Besides, I didn't expect you to build anything in the rain."

"DJ's outside communing with his little girlfriends." Alexandra tilted her head in the direction of the chicken area. "They look great."

"I think they're really responding to good care in their new home. I wouldn't go so far as to say they're happy, but who knows? Maybe they are."

A subscriber Cam didn't know well approached. "I saw you have chickens now," he said. "Good move. When will you include eggs in the shares?"

"Uh . . ." Cam looked at Alexandra. The young woman took over the conversation, to Cam's relief, and began to tell the man about the hens' gradual return to health, when they could be expected to start laying, and the value of the rescue organization. Cam imagined Alexandra would have a new recruit before the afternoon was over.

Cam walked out to the hen area. DJ stood in the enclosure, next to the coop, looking like he was checking the construction. She greeted him.

"How's it holding up?"

He turned and smiled. "Looks great. So do the ladies. They're learning how to live like chickens again. Did you see how their feathers are already coming back?"

Cam nodded.

"We'll build the covered run right here for now. It'll be light-weight, just two-by-twos and chicken wire. You'll be able to move it easily whenever you rotate the hens around the prop-erty."

"What if they're out when we want to move them?"

He raised his eyebrows a few times, channeling Groucho Marx. "Ve haf our vays," he said with a big smile that produced a dimple in his left cheek.

Cam smiled back. It was hard not to around this engaging young man. "I'd better get back inside. Make sure you give me a bill for your supplies."

He said he would and bent down to stroke Her Meekness's tiny head.

Alexandra was finishing filling her bags when Cam reentered the barn. Alexandra left the bags by the door and headed out to work with DJ. The barn was now empty of subscribers, except for Lucinda. Cam checked the sign-in list. There were still a half dozen shareholders to go.

"Lucinda, I have a proposal for you." Cam leaned against a thick post bisecting the main area.

Lucinda had retrieved the dropped squash and was shifting it from hand to hand, back and forth like a ball.

"I'd like to hire you. I can't pay too much—I'll have to check my books—but I really, really need some extra help. And you volunteer so much, you should be paid instead. I know it's not being a librarian, but it's also not cleaning up other people's messes. What do you say?"

"But I volunteer because I like it. You don't have to pay me."

"I want to. Let me at least offer you all the produce you want and something more per hour. We can work out a schedule. If I don't get more help around here, I'm going to have a nervous breakdown or a failed farm. Or both. And I don't want either to happen."

Lucinda stared at the squash in her hands. She shifted it back and forth a few more times. She raised her eyes to Cam. And nodded, breaking into a big smile.

"I'll do it, *fazendeira*. But one thing?"

"What is it?"

"If a library job comes through, I gotta take it. Deal?"

"Deal." Cam walked over to Lucinda and extended her hand. Lucinda took it, and they shook. Lucinda held out her arms to Cam. They exchanged a quick hug.

As Cam greeted a latecomer at the door, she reflected that Lucinda was about as opposite from her as possible in terms of being comfortable around people both physically and socially. Maybe a few of Lucinda's habits would rub off on her.

Chapter 36

By the time Cam came back from leaving Wes and Felicity's basket at their house, it was almost five o'clock and the clouds had blown clean through. Lucinda had stayed to do some harvesting for the market, but her car was gone when Cam drove in. Alexandra's bike and DJ's borrowed truck were there, and Cam heard sounds of hammering coming from behind the barn.

She took a few minutes to tidy up the barn. She checked the subscriber sign-in sheet. Five households hadn't made it over to get their shares, which put her ahead for items she could sell at market tomorrow. She'd made it clear at the start of the season: if shareholders didn't show up or make prior arrangements, the vegetables reverted to Cam. The number of no-shows, of course, didn't include Diane. Cam had asked Lucinda to assemble her share and leave it on the table.

Speak of the devil. Diane rushed into the barn. Her normally neat cap of dark hair was a bit flyaway, and she wore a smudge on her left cheek.

"Sorry about earlier, Cam." Diane spread her hands out. "We should have taken Wes at his home, before he even got here. I hope we didn't offend any of your customers."

"It was certainly a shock. I haven't heard any complaints, though."

"Good." She glanced around. "Is my—"

"Your share is in those plastic bags on the table there." Cam pointed. Lucinda had left a slip of paper next to the bags with Diane's name on it.

"Great. Thank you."

"So being a subscriber was only a front for getting closer to your suspect?" Cam shoved her hands in her back pockets. She didn't much like being a tool for anyone.

Diane stopped. She faced Cam. "I am very devoted to eating locally. I love your produce. I do have a life outside my job, Cam. Please believe me."

"All right. I hope there won't be any more busts in my barn."

"I hope not, too."

"What happened with the fire at the Old Town Hall?"

Diane let out a little breath. "It turned out to be a shorted wire, and between the fire department and the sprinkler system, the damage was pretty slight."

"Nobody was hurt?"

Diane shook her head. "Thank goodness."

"And so it wasn't Wes trying to destroy evidence, after all." Cam raised her eyebrows.

"No." Diane had the grace to look chagrined. She looked relieved at the same time. She picked up her bags, said good-bye, and left.

A last ray of sun slanted through the clerestory window high above the door. The familiar barn smells of dust, motor oil, and bits of dried manure mixed with the pungent scents of garlic, earthy potatoes, antique apples. Cam caught a trace of freshly sawn wood, so different from the dry-timber bouquet of Albert's antique barn before it had gone up in a terrifying conflagration. Cam gazed at the neat array of tools hanging on the back wall, next to three stacks of empty bushel baskets standing ready to hold the next harvest. It had been one more exhausting day as a farmer, and it wasn't over yet. In this moment of grace, though, she knew she was lucky to have her health, a sturdy old house to live in, a job.

"Cam? We want to show you something," Alexandra called from outside.

The two young people had gotten a lot done in a hurry. A structure made of two-by-twos now enclosed an area about ten feet out from the coop doors. The section closest to the doors was human height, and the rest came up to about half that high. A thick roll of chicken wire lay on its side next to a six-foot ladder.

"You've been busy." Cam tested one of the upright supports. It barely moved. "So you'll run the fencing over the top and the sides?"

"That's it," DJ said. "We'll come back tomorrow and finish the job, if it's all right with you."

"Of course," Cam said. "Can I offer you both something to drink? I'm sure ready."

"I'll feed the hens," Alexandra offered.

When Cam came back from the house with three full glasses of beer and a bowl of tortilla chips on a tray, the hens were pecking away at their dinner. Hillary shoved Her Meekness out of the way, but DJ grabbed a handful of the feed and led the smaller hen into a corner to eat in peace.

Cam set the tray on the bench behind the barn. "Beer's here," she announced.

DJ dusted off his hands and joined her and Alexandra.

After they clinked glasses and Cam took a long swig, she sniffed. "It's getting a little smelly out here."

DJ laughed. "Part of the deal. We have to keep up with raking the yard when you have the coop here next to the barn and with changing the straw in the coop. But every bit of it can go into the compost, and it'll feed your next round of crops."

"We? You mean *I* have to," Cam said, wrinkling her nose. She was certainly no stranger to manure and didn't mind the odor when she had a fresh load delivered. But having the smell around all the time was different.

"We'll help, right, Allie?"

Allie? Cam thought Alexandra was adamant about not being called by any nickname, even Alex.

Alexandra nodded, apparently not noticing. She stretched her legs out, caressing DJ's foot with hers.

Oh. So that was why she didn't mind being called Allie.

The three sat and chatted until the afternoon started turning into evening and the temperature cooled. Most of the chickens had already made their way into the coop to roost. DJ shooed Her Meekness up the ramp and latched the door behind her.

"Thanks again, you guys," Cam said, collecting the glasses. "I'll be at market in Newburyport in the morning, but you're welcome to come and work even if I'm not here."

"We'll do it." Alexandra fetched her share bags from the barn and followed DJ to the truck he'd borrowed. She hefted her bike into the back and slid into the cab with him. He gave a little honk as they drove off, and Cam waved back.

Her thoughts turning to dinner, Cam was headed toward the house when a truck drove up the drive. She peered in the dusk. Were DJ and Alexandra already back? Maybe they forgot something.

She took a closer look. It was Howard Fisher. Her heart thumped in her chest. What did he want? He'd better not have his rifle with him. She patted her pocket and was relieved to find her phone right where she wanted it. She moved closer to the house, until the motion-detector light flashed on.

Howard's driver's-side door complained of rust and age as it opened. Howard climbed out, carrying a flat package. He had left the lights on and the engine running.

"Hey, Howard. What brings you here?" Cam stayed in the pool of light.

"Brought you something. We butchered Buddy, our big fella, today. Here's some chops for you." He extended the package.

Cam didn't know how she could refuse, so she took the packet wrapped in white butcher paper. "Thank you. But why—"

"Just wanted to show no ill will and all." Howard looked at the ground. "And my boy told me I should bring the meat. Sometimes he's right about stuff."

"He's a good kid. And he's always very polite, you should know. Unlike some teenagers these days."

"His ma's doing." He cleared his throat. "I'll be going. So's you know, there's more pork where that came from, if you should want any."

Cam barely had time to call out her thanks before he drove off. She gazed at the packet in her hand. She was completely confused by the meaning of Howard's gesture. He wanted to show no ill will? Maybe he felt bad about taking Preston.

The next question was, did she want to eat Buddy for dinner? She was hungry enough to. And he hadn't been the one to gnaw on Irene's body. The thought of Irene brought the thought of the killer. Who was still out there. She glanced around quickly as she unlocked the back door.

When she called Preston, he dashed toward her from around the corner of the house. She didn't blame him for hiding from the man who had snatched him only a few days earlier. Cam flicked on the lights and locked the door behind both of them.

As she started unwrapping the chops, she reflected that it was a good thing Alexandra and DJ had already left. They surely would have accosted Howard about how he treated his animals. Maybe Cam wouldn't tell them she was having part of the big fella for supper.

Chapter 37

Two pork chops were broiling under a rub of olive oil, fresh rosemary, and garlic when the doorbell rang. Cam whirled. Who could that be? Whoever it was knocked several times.

"Who is it?" Cam called.

"It's me," Ruth's voice called.

Cam flung the door open. "Hi. What are you doing here?"

Ruth raised a single eyebrow. "We arranged this. Right? We haven't visited in a long time and all?"

"Oh! Would you believe I forgot?" Cam shook a rueful head. "I'm really sorry."

Ruth sniffed. "As long as it's dinner for two I smell, you are forgiven." She extended a bottle of red wine with a smile.

"It is! Two pork chops are broiling, and I already baked a pan of Beauregard sweet potatoes. I can always extend the salad."

"Pour me a glass of wine and explain why you're making dinner for two for one."

Cam laughed. "I already have a pinot noir open." She slid a glass out of the stem holder under the cabinet and poured for Ruth. "I make extra so I don't have to worry about cooking the next day. The life of a single person, you know."

They exchanged cheers. Ruth took a sip.

"Wait. I thought you were going to confirm with me about your mom babysitting tonight," Cam said. "That's why I didn't realize you were coming over."

It was Ruth's turn to smack her forehead. "Oh, yeah. I guess I'm the one who slipped up."

"As Great-Aunt Marie used to say, 'All's well that ends well.' "

Ten minutes later, after they'd begun to eat, Ruth put down her fork.

"I'm a single person now, too. I mean, a single parent."

"I wondered. Where did Frank go?"

"He took off about a month ago. Gone to play militia, I guess. I haven't heard from him. And the girls miss him something terrible."

Cam patted Ruth's hand. "I'm really sorry."

"Don't be. Our marriage had been on the rocks for a while, as you know. If I weren't mopping up the kids' tears, I'd be feeling pretty happy. I don't even know what to tell them."

"A tough assignment." Cam grimaced. "What do you say?"

"Daddy's on a trip, and I don't know when he'll be back. It's the truth."

"Have you tried to find him? You must have resources at the station."

Ruth shook her head. "I'm letting it sit for now. Waiting to see how long he stays away. Could be forever." She picked up her fork again.

"I can babysit now and then, if it would help. Those two would probably push me around something wicked, but it would be fun. You'd come home and find all three of us eating candy and jumping on the beds."

"Thanks." Ruth laughed. "I needed that image. Hey, sorry to put a damper on dinner. I haven't really talked about this with anybody but my mom so far."

"No problem. At least you have a mom you can talk about stuff with. Mine? I hear from her twice a year, and she never has any idea what's going on in my life. And doesn't really ask, either." Cam shrugged. "But I'm used to it." Cam gazed down the hallway. She caught sight of the locked cabinet and clapped her hand on her forehead. "The gun!"

"What gun?" Ruth drew her brows together.

Cam almost pushed her chair over rushing to the cabinet under the stairs. "Bev Montgomery threatened me with a gun at the Grog on Thursday." She grabbed the key from where she'd left it next to a stair baluster and unlocked the cabinet.

"And you didn't report this?" Ruth's voice rose.

"Calm down, Sergeant. Bev was harmless, as it turned out, and Albert got a friend of hers to take her home. After I got the gun away from her, that is. I meant to call it in and just forgot."

Cam showed Ruth the weapon where it still sat in safety. Ruth agreed to leave it there for now, under lock, and she'd fetch it the next time she was on shift.

They spent the next couple of hours eating, drinking, and catching up. Relaxing as if life were simple and things like violent death and disappearing husbands happened in an alternate universe.

After Ruth left, Cam washed the dishes, moving as she cleaned to a Brazilian CD Lucinda had given her. She had no idea what the lyrics were, but not knowing made the music itself more enjoyable. Not that she would have danced to it or anything else in public, but in the privacy of her own house, she didn't mind trying out a little corporeal self-expression.

When her cell phone rang, she turned the sound down on the CD player and checked the ID. Bobby Burr. She dried her hands on a dish towel, threw it over her shoulder, and answered the phone.

"Cam? It's Bobby. I'm outside your door. I called so I didn't freak you out. Can I come in and talk to you?"

Cam checked the clock. Nine forty-five. Late, but not too late to see what was up with him.

"Sure." She unlocked the door and welcomed him in. He looked somber but, in contrast to a week ago, well rested and as if he'd been showering and doing laundry regularly.

"Seems like déjà vu, sort of," Cam said.

"What are you talking about?"

"Didn't you knock on my door last Saturday night? You know, the night after I saw you out in the field, when you got spooked and split."

"Yeah. Sorry. I was freaking out." He tilted his head in a "What can you do?" gesture, extending his hands to the sides and smiling. "I heard you talking to somebody, and I couldn't handle it."

"I was actually on the phone with an old friend. What's going on?"

Bobby's smile faded. "Sim's missing."

"Oh, dear." Uh-oh. First, Bobby went missing, and now Sim. "Sit and tell me about it." Cam gestured at the table. "Glass of wine?"

Bobby hesitated for a moment and then said, "Why not?" A smile toyed with his mouth but never quite arrived.

Cam poured a glass for each of them.

"So what do you mean, she's missing?" She sat opposite him. "How long has she been gone?" She tried to think of the last time she'd seen Sim. It must have been Thursday, when she'd picked up the truck.

"We were supposed to get together tonight." He took a sip. His hand shook, setting little waves going in his glass before he set it down. "I hung out at the Thirsty Whale for two hours, waiting for her. I went to her apartment. She's not there. She doesn't answer her phone."

"Did you try her cell? Did you check the garage?"

"That *is* her cell. Us hipsters don't have landlines, Cam." He tried at a smile again, but sad eyes and down-sloping eyebrows canceled out the effect. "I went by the garage. She's not there. I'm afraid she's in trouble."

"Why do you think she's in trouble?"

"It's just a feeling."

"What happened after they called her in for questioning this morning? Did they keep her?"

He shook his head. "No. They didn't have any reason to."

As far as Cam was concerned, she didn't know Sim well enough to know she wouldn't kill anyone. But Bobby obviously had faith in her.

"She's the one who suggested getting together tonight," he said.

"Hey, I'm sure she's fine," Cam said. "She must have gone out with friends or something."

"Maybe." He drank down half his glass and stared into it.

"Can I ask you a question?"

"Go for it," Bobby answered without looking up.

"Are you and Sim dating?" Cam shut her eyes at once, again putting her foot into it. What a delicate way to ask him. She reopened them to see Bobby looking straight at her and starting to laugh.

"No! Why would you—" He squinted at her. "Are you a little bit jealous?"

It was Cam's turn to object, although maybe she was, a little. "You seem so worried about her, that's all."

"We're buddies. We actually served in the navy together a few years ago. Most people don't know about that. But it makes a superglue bond between you that never breaks." He tilted his head, and his eyes flashed at Cam like the old Bobby was back. "Anyway, she prefers women. So there's no threat there, Ms. Cam."

The air felt supercharged, like the ions of lightning were about to break loose. Cam felt her cheeks pink up. She cleared her throat.

"So how's your new job?"

Bobby threw her a look Cam couldn't interpret. "It's fine. It's a job."

"I'll be sure to let you know if I hear from Sim."

"You don't think I need to report her missing?" he asked.

"I don't think they would let you. Not until twenty-four hours have gone by. I read that somewhere. Plus, you're not family. I'm not even sure you'd be allowed to after twenty-four hours."

"That's dumb."

"I don't think anything's wrong. You'll see. She'll call you tomorrow and say she forgot or something." Cam hoped she sounded more comforting than she felt. She had no idea if Sim was fine or not.

"I have a bad feeling about this." Bobby shook his head.

"To change the subject, is there going to be a service for Irene?"

He heaved a huge sigh. "Detective Pappas says they can't release her body yet. And frankly? I don't really care."

"Did she have any other family?"

"Nope. She had a sister, who died years ago. I'm it. If you can call me family." He pressed his lips together and shook his head again. "So I guess I should start figuring out what to do."

"Did she go to any particular church?"

"Irene?" He snorted. "No way. This'll be a one hundred percent secular deal, I can assure you."

"If you need help, call me." She didn't know one thing about planning a funeral or, more realistically, a memorial service, but Great-Uncle Albert would. And how hard could it be?

"I appreciate it." He stood. "Thanks for the wine, Cam, and for trying to reassure me about Sim. You have a good night."

Cam walked him to the door and stepped out onto the porch as she said good night. She sniffed the clear night air, hoping it wasn't frost she smelled. October 18 wasn't too early for temperatures to dip below freezing, but she was pretty sure frost hadn't been forecast for tonight. She leaned against the doorjamb. The grass, the barn, the perennial flower bed—all were bathed in a silvery light from a perfectly full moon high in the sky. She thought back to an article she'd read in the *Natural Farmer* about names for full moons. The harvest moon had been in September. She shivered. That lovely orb up there was the blood moon.

She hurried back in and locked the door. The light and warmth inside dispelled the ominous feeling that had come over her a minute before. She realized she still had the dish towel hanging over her shoulder and laughed at herself. *Nice look, Flaherty.* Thinking about Bobby, she used a corner of the towel to wipe the speckled Formica countertop. That moment of supercharged air was a little unsettling. Her life was complicated enough juggling Jake and Pete. She needed to be sure Bobby's flirtations stayed in the distance, right where they belonged.

At least he wasn't still in jail, although Pete had alluded to finding more evidence against him. Pete. She supposed not hearing from him for a whole day was a good thing. If Sim didn't reappear tomorrow, Cam should probably let him know.

She yawned as she pushed the junk drawer closed. The day had been long and busy. She couldn't wait to fall into bed, since tomorrow morning promised to be equally as busy. The drawer wouldn't quite go in. She gave it another push. It was stuck somehow. She tugged it open and saw a slip of paper half caught between the drawer and the slider. She wiggled it loose and smoothed it out on the countertop.

Her eyes widened. It was the lost note. The threatening invitation to meet in the woods. So that was where it had gone. Some evil person hadn't snuck in and taken it, after all.

Cam took it to the table and sat. She read it again.

MEET ME IN THE WOODS AT ELEVEN, OR I'LL TELL WHAT I KNOW.
YOU KNOW WHERE.

A little bell rang in the back of her head. The writing looked familiar. Where had she seen it? She checked through her mental hard drive but came up with nothing. She yawned again. Her brain's search engine was too tired for thinking. She'd fire it up again tomorrow and see what results she got. And tell Pete she'd found the note. She tucked it under the corner of the flower vase so it wouldn't go traveling again.

Chapter 38

The gong rang out, signaling the start of market. Cam locked the legs of her market table into place and set it upright. She was extremely, frantically, abysmally late. Not a great way to start her second appearance here. She snapped the market cloth over the table and started hauling buckets and baskets off the truck. She was arranging bags of cut mesclun when her basket of herbs plopped onto the table at her elbow. Cam looked up.

"Thought you might want some help." Pete Pappas winked at her. "Should I continue unloading?"

"Um, sure." She wanted to ask him what he was doing there. She wanted to hug him for helping, and maybe for other reasons, too. She wanted to grill him about Irene's murder. She decided the wisest course was to just keep setting up.

An older woman in a denim skirt, striped socks, and hiking boots asked about the leeks. By the time Cam finished selling her a bunch of three, plus a bouquet of rudbeckias, nasturtiums, and asters, and two bundles of rosemary, Pete had unloaded the truck and was arranging buckets full of produce on the ground in front of the table.

"You are a godsend," Cam said.

"Not really. I'd say I was a Pete-send." He smiled as he stuck his hands in his back pockets. He wore jeans again, but they were clean and pressed, as was his tucked-in plaid shirt.

"Well, thank you. I was wicked late this morning." She yawned. "Excuse me. Life's catching up with me." She eyed him. "Are you here detecting or shopping?"

"A little of both, I suppose. Any news from your world?"

"I'm not sure if you'll count it as news, but Bobby Burr stopped by last night. He's worried because Sim didn't show up for a drink with him. A drink she had invited him to."

Pete frowned. "He's still a person of interest in the murder, you know. You might not want to be alone with him."

"I suppose. But he doesn't seem like a killer to me."

"Famous last words, Cam. But why is he so concerned about being stood up for a drink?"

"Sim didn't answer her cell, either. I doubt it's anything, but I think everybody's on edge. I know I'm kind of spooked with the killer still out there. "

"I'm doing my best."

"I'm sure you are. Speaking of that, he also told me that you, or somebody, questioned Sim yesterday morning. Do you really think she could have killed Irene?"

"As I said, I'm doing my best."

Okay, don't answer me. Cam straightened the farm's business cards on the table. "By the way, I found the note. Remember I said the tent guy had given me a piece of paper he'd found on the ground the day after the dinner?"

"Ah, the purported threatening letter." He raised his thick eyebrows. "Where did you find it?"

"Not purported!" Cam frowned at him. When she saw the baker two tables down glance over at her, she lowered her voice. "Late last night I found it stuck in a drawer."

"I'd like to see it. Although it'll be no good as far as physical evidence goes. What did it say?"

"It said something about meeting in the woods, or the writer would tell all. I'm happy to turn it over."

"I'll call you later about picking it up." He surveyed the crowd, whistling a tune Cam couldn't recognize. Without looking at her, he said, "I enjoyed our walk on Friday. It was nice to get out. With you, I mean."

"I did, too," she said in a soft voice.

This week's musicians were setting up near the market manager's table, which sat in front of the old tannery building, now a successful mini-mall housing local businesses. A woman tuned an electric guitar, another fiddled with the drum set, and a third did a mike check. All three wore skirts of varying lengths with cowboy boots.

Pete stayed at Cam's side as she sold kabocha and Hubbard squash, explained that the leaves at the ends of the Brussels sprout stalks were tasty and sweet when stir-fried, offered recipes for kale chips and shallot-pepper jelly.

"Shouldn't you be out dusting for fingerprints somewhere?" Cam leaned sideways toward Pete, then wondered if he'd think she was trying to get rid of him. Foot in mouth, as usual.

"That's what the crime-scene techs do. Not part of my job description, thank goodness. I prefer to use zee leettle gray cells, you know." He pointed at his head.

Cam laughed. She'd had a frantic morning—waking up late, scrambling to get the harvest together and loaded onto the truck, racing over to Newburyport—but all seemed well with her world now.

"Cells that need to be fed. I'll be right back." Pete strolled toward the baker.

Cam was smiling, watching him buy pastries, when Jake

walked up from the opposite direction. He followed her eyes. Uh-oh. Here was trouble.

"Morning, Cam." He loomed in front of her, not smiling at all.

"Good morning, Jake. How are you?" She didn't trust herself to say more.

He took a deep breath. "It's a lovely day." He mustered a smile. "Who is your friend?" He raised his eyebrows in Pete's direction.

"You must remember Detective Pappas?"

Jake's frown suddenly registered recognition. "Now that you mention it. He looks different."

"It's a Sunday." Pete looked different to her, too. But did he really? Or was it because he was relaxed and kind of flirtatious with her?

Pete strolled back toward Cam's table, carrying two coffees and a white bag with the bakery logo on it. He checked out the other tables and exchanged what looked like pleasantries with several vendors. He arrived at Cam's spot as he smiled at the Herb Farmacy vendor across the aisle. He set the food down and finally looked up.

"Ah, Mr. Ericsson. Pete Pappas." He smiled and extended his hand to Jake. "I'm not sure we actually met last spring, but without you Cam's attacker might have eluded us."

Cam held her breath. She had no idea if Jake was going to be civil, turn icy, or explode. She'd promised to give him one more chance. This had suddenly turned into the test for that. It struck her, though, that it was more like the alpha males circling each other for the reward of the female. In the wild, Pete wouldn't stand a chance. Jake was almost a foot taller and weighed perhaps twice as much. But here wily Pete had offset the physical challenge with a compliment that had to arise from feeling secure in his position. What had she gotten herself into?

"Call me Jake." The chef extended his hand and cleared his throat. "How's the investigation coming along?"

Touché, Cam thought. *Point to Jake.*

"Slowly but surely." Pete smiled, but it didn't include his eyes.

Jake lifted his empty cloth bags with one hand. "I'll be off. Lot of tourists in town this weekend, leaf peeping. It's going to be a busy day at the kitchen. Enjoy your breakfast." He leaned over and brushed his lips on Cam's cheek. "See you tomorrow night."

"Nice to meet you, finally, Jake." Pete lifted his cardboard cup of coffee in farewell.

Cam glanced sideways at Pete, but he was peering into the pastry bag and didn't seem to react to the kiss. As far as she could tell.

The market was nearly at its end. After Pete had finished his coffee and pastry, he'd said good-bye, promising to call her later about picking up the note. Now Cam's table was almost empty, as were the buckets that had held the kale and flowers. She stacked a couple of empty baskets and was stowing them in the truck behind her when someone called her name. She turned.

"Yo, Cam. Looks like I'm almost too late to do my shopping." Sim stood in front of the table, dressed as usual in all black.

"Sim! You're all right."

"Why wouldn't I be?" She frowned and crossed her arms.

"Bobby said you stood him up for a drink yesterday and you weren't answering your cell last night. He was really worried."

"He's one silly dude. I got a last-minute invite to fill in at a hot gig with my friend Elizabeth. You probably saw the posters all over town for Elizabeth Lorrey and the Rafters."

Cam shook her head. Keeping up on the current music scene wasn't part of her life anymore.

"Their drummer got the flu. So I had to head over to the Firehouse and rehearse with them beforehand. I totally forgot to call Bobby."

"He'll be glad you're fine." Cam straightened the last remaining bunch of leeks. "He did say you were questioned yesterday morning. How'd that go?"

She rolled her eyes. "They have nothing. Maybe they think I'm going to change my story and confess or something. To what? Knocking off an obnoxious woman? Sheesh. There'd be nothing in it for me. I'd lose a customer with an expensive car."

Cam wondered if she was telling the truth. And wondered what Pete knew about Sim that he wasn't telling her.

"And imagine how many murders there would be if all the obnoxious women got popped. Heck, I wouldn't even be here anymore." She flashed a wicked grin as she hefted the leeks.

Cam laughed a little nervously. "Well, anyway, give Bobby a call, would you?"

"Sure."

"I've been meaning to ask you a question all week," Cam said. "Were you at the Middleford Fair last Wednesday? I thought I saw your motorcycle heading up Route One."

"Not me." She waved the leeks. "How much are these, and what do I do with them?"

Chapter 39

When Cam got home, she greeted Alexandra, DJ, and Katie. They were almost done stapling the chicken wire to the run framework. In the house, she fixed a sandwich and poured a glass of milk. When she sat at the table, Preston approached her chair. She glanced down at him staring up at her. Cam was sure his face, with its luminous light green eyes lined with kohl above a full snowy-white ruff, could get him a gig as a feline supermodel. He didn't look worried or hungry. It was the calm, patient stare he always gave her when he wanted to sit in her lap. He never jumped up, but simply waited to be lifted. If he was keeping track on his success-o-meter, he had to know he'd scored again. She hoisted him by his ruff and his midsection onto her lap and stroked him with one hand as she ate.

The note from the dinner still sat on the table. She examined it again. Why did the writing look so familiar? On a hunch, she gave Preston one more stroke before sliding him onto the floor, murmuring, "Sorry, Mr. P."

She got up and went to her desk. The pile of her recent transactions waited next to the computer. Promptly entering which money came in and went out into her online accounting system was not one of Cam's strong suits. She rifled through the hodge-podge of invoices, receipts, bills, and farm-to-table dinner sign-ups until she found what she wanted. She took Irene's sign-up form to the table. She compared the writing to that on the note. Identical, as far as she could tell.

Now all she had to do was figure out why.

Cam pulled the truck all the way up the long, curving drive to Irene's Colonial, as close to the back door as possible. Its tasteful cream clapboards and pale green trim were complemented by understated landscaping that had to have cost her a bundle. She must have hired weekly gardeners to keep the annual flowers deadheaded, the rhododendron and weeping cherry neatly pruned, the black mulch free of weeds.

Cam shut off the engine. She fingered Irene's keys in the pocket of her jacket. Howard had written the note. To Irene, apparently. Did Cam have the nerve to enter Irene's house to find the reason for the note? Maybe it was because she didn't use her intellect in farming the same way she had writing computer code, but she felt a steel filament drawing her toward solving this problem of finding the connection between Howard and Irene.

She checked her phone. Two thirty. What if she was spotted? The house was situated so the neighbors on either side didn't have a direct view of the end of the driveway and the back door, but Cam heard a smooth engine noise like a riding mower from one direction and the voices of children playing outdoors from the other. Someone could easily see her and ask what she was doing there.

She'd better come up with a story. She couldn't very well claim to be a long-lost cousin, since people who lived in town might recognize her. She ran through possibilities. She worked with Lucinda and was here to clean and get the house ready for sale. On a Sunday? No way. She could say Irene had asked her to help with the museum plans. But why? Cam snapped her fingers. If somebody questioned her, she'd claim Irene had asked her to plant a vegetable garden behind the house and Cam had to retrieve garden design books she'd left with Irene. She swallowed. It was a long shot, a story that would have to do. With any luck nobody would see her slip in the back door, anyway.

As a dark cloud blew over the sun, she shut the truck door as quietly as she could. She tried to walk naturally to the door and exhaled a long breath once she was inside, with the door shut behind her. She whistled as she walked through the house. The decor was simple and looked expensive. Rich woven rugs sat atop gleaming hardwood floors. The kitchen could have been featured in a *Gourmet* magazine spread with its magnet-free refrigerator and empty countertops.

Cam kept walking. Her goal was an office of some kind. Irene surely had a home office. And although she knew Pete and his crew had searched the house, they hadn't been looking for the object of her search. If she found it, she'd call Pete and go home. And if she didn't, she'd still call him and go home.

She found herself almost tiptoeing. This lovely home was Irene's life, her refuge from the world. Cam was intruding on it, uninvited. She was at least as private a person as Irene and would detest someone invading her personal zone of retreat and safety. Like most others, Cam hadn't particularly liked Irene, but she'd seen the older woman's affection for Preston, and anyway, nobody deserved to be murdered.

She ventured up a wide, graceful staircase cushioned with an Oriental rug runner. The door to the right in the upstairs hall opened onto what looked like a guest suite. The one next to it was to a bathroom. After peering into a room with twin beds, she turned to the far end of the hall.

She pulled her jacket tighter around her. The air was chilly. An open door led into a large bedroom. It must be Irene's. It smelled faintly of perfume. The stark decor of the room took Cam aback. No fussy flounces topped the windows. No pinks decorated the bedspread or rugs. White carpeting, white comforter, plain white blinds, and light gray walls were broken only by black lacquered furniture and a large wall-mounted piece of rich red tapestry. A framed picture sat alone on the dresser.

Cam ventured close to the photograph. A younger Irene smiled up at a man who was an older version of Bobby. She bent over to take a closer look. The man had to be Bobby's father, the late Zebulon. He was a handsome man in his later years. His hair was dark and thick like Bobby's but cut much shorter and streaked with white at the temples. It struck Cam that she hadn't ever seen Irene smile. Not really smile, like in this picture. Irene had been happy once.

Cam straightened. A whiff of freshly mown grass wafted by. She sniffed. She followed the scent to a door standing ajar in the corner of the bedroom. It opened onto a well-appointed office. Beyond the wide desk and tall bookcases, a six-foot-tall window filled the wall. The window looked out onto the back lawn and tall firs that lined the property. It presented a lovely view. And was wide open and missing its screen. No wonder the air was chilly in here.

Two blocky shapes stuck up from outside the sill. Cam approached and cautiously leaned out for a look. The shapes were the tops of a metal extension ladder's vertical supports. A ladder that extended from the ground to where she stood, and was conveniently masked from view by the screen of trees. She shivered, and it wasn't from the cold. Someone had been in here illicitly. Way more illicitly than using Lucinda's set of Irene's keys.

There was something smeared on the third rung down. She peered at it. It looked like dirt. She sniffed the air and thought she caught a whiff of manure. But whether it was from the smear or from a nearby farmer fertilizing his fields, she couldn't tell.

She heard a rustling sound from behind her and whirled. Her heart raced. Maybe the intruder hadn't left the house. She hadn't seen another vehicle. But it could be in the garage. Or the person had walked over. Or hidden a bicycle. She fumbled in her pocket for her phone. And realized it was in her bag in the truck. All she'd brought with her were the keys. A supremely dumb move. The blood pulsed so hard in her neck, she could barely swallow.

A sheaf of papers fluttered from the desk to the floor. Cam took a deep breath and let it out. The sound was only papers in the wind. She turned back to the window and pulled it shut, turning the two locks as tightly as she could. Returning to the desk, she tried to shake off her fear.

She saw the multiline telephone on the desktop. And laughed at her nerves. Of course Irene would have a phone. Cam picked up the receiver and held it to her ear. No dial tone. And of course the service would be discontinued. That was quick. Irene wasn't even buried yet.

She squared her shoulders. She was here to search for a piece of information. Might as well get started, open window or no open window. She sank into Irene's luxurious office chair. Its black leather caressed her wrists. She swiveled and wheeled over to the low walnut file cabinet. After twenty minutes, rifling through paper file folders had gained her nothing. Irritation and frustration rattled her, making her skin itch and her stomach feel like she'd drunk too much black tea.

She'd much rather be using her smarts to search a hard drive, but Pete and his cronies appeared to have made off with what-ever computer equipment Irene owned. Or maybe whoever propped the ladder against the window took the computer. Either way, it wasn't here. A printer sat lonely at the end of the desk, its USB cable stretched out, as useless as a tomato stake in January.

Cam stood. The floor-to-ceiling bookshelf next to the window intrigued her, as bookshelves had her entire life. Now that the window was closed, she inhaled the familiar smell of old paper and ink. She fingered the titles filling the cherrywood shelves. The shelves included worn paperback mysteries, biographies, a history of Iran, a selection of children's tales. What appeared to be a first-edition *The Wonderful Wizard of Oz* was not in pristine condition but rather looked like a generation or two of children had enjoyed its tale over and over. Cam shook her head. She was here to find a document, not to investigate a library. She'd been inside Irene's house too long as it was.

Curious at the lack of a title on the spine of a slim leather-bound book sitting next to the L. Frank Baum volume, Cam pulled it out. She opened the cover and exclaimed aloud. This treasure was no book. This was Irene's late-model iPad. Cam smiled and rubbed her virtual hands in glee. A treasure, indeed, at least for a geek. She returned with it to the swivel chair and pressed the POWER button.

The device asked for a password. IPads didn't by default, but whomever Irene bought the device from must have advised her to set one. Cam knew she couldn't guess randomly for very long. The device's privacy protections would make her wait longer between each try, and after a dozen failures the password would erase itself. She typed what she'd read was the most used password: *abcd1234.*

No luck. Irene was on the old side for a computer user, which usually translated into an unsophisticated user. The kind of people who really were silly with their passwords. If they only knew how easy they were to crack. What else would Irene have found easy to remember? Her birthday? Cam didn't have a clue. Surely Irene wouldn't have gone for Bobby's name. Maybe she had hidden a written list somewhere in the office, as many people did.

Cam swiveled in the chair, surveying the room. She didn't have time to search the entire room for a slip of paper.

She thought of one last tactic. She tilted the tablet under the lamp on the desk and peered at the smudges on the on-screen keyboard. They were much heavier over the letters *J* and *G*. Cam thought about typing. How often did she ever have occasion to hit the *J* and *G* keys? But Irene drove a Jaguar. A 1990, Cam remembered Lucinda saying. She took a stab at it.

Jag1990.

Bingo. She was in. For transparency Irene got an F. Anybody who knew her could figure out she drove a semi-vintage Jaguar. But the password actually wasn't bad as far as randomness went, since it at least included both uppercase and lowercase letters and some digits. If Irene had only added a punctuation mark of some kind, an asterisk or—

"Stop geeking out," Cam told herself in a stern voice. This was not the time to be musing about the ideal password for a dead woman.

She heard a noise and froze. Outside? Inside? She swore under her breath. She had to get out of here, and fast. Whoever had left that ladder could come back any minute now. Somebody else could have a key and be heading her way. She had gained access to a portion of Irene's life, and she needed to find the information she was sure was in there. But she could drill deep into the minimalist device at home. She hadn't been a sought-after software engineer for nothing.

She glanced at the window and shivered. She clasped the iPad more firmly and headed for the door.

Chapter 40

Cam sat in her idling truck by the side of the road as she ended her call to Pete. He hadn't picked up, so she'd left him a message. She had said she'd discovered something important and ended by saying she was headed home. She'd wait to hack into Irene's file system in Pete's presence, if he wanted. The gunmetal clouds above blocked not only the sun's light but also what remained of warmth in the decline of autumn. She reached out and turned the truck's heat up another notch.

She'd go home, feed the hens, herd them in for the night. She'd wait for Pete to come and pick up the tablet and the note. She had just reached for the gearshift when her phone emitted the sound of typing followed by the bell of an old-fashioned typewriter. Somebody was texting her. She dug her phone out.

Got text from Vince, Ellie had typed. Think he's in danger at home. Can u chk?

Cam cursed and shoved the truck into gear. She arrived at the Fisher farm five minutes later. She hoped Ellie was wrong. She didn't know what she would do if Vince was in danger. She could call the Westbury police right now. But what if Ellie was wrong? Chief Frost wouldn't appreciate a false alarm. She owed it to

Vince and Ellie to check, and she'd call the Westbury police at the first hint of real harm. She parked at the side of the house and stuck her phone in her pocket before climbing out.

"Howard? Anybody home?" Cam called. No one emerged from the house. "Vince?"

She walked toward the barn. "Hello?" she called out.

"What do you want?" A gruff voice sounded behind her.

She twisted her head and torso. Howard stood frowning on the back steps of the house, a can of beer in his left hand.

She waved and said hello as she walked toward him, relieved he held ale instead of arms. "Is Vince here?"

"What do you want with him?"

"One of my volunteers, Ellie—she's friends with Vince at school—and she asked me to give him a message. She said his voice mail is full or something," Cam lied.

"He's not here."

As Howard said that, the text signal sounded again. She pulled the phone out of her pocket and looked down.

Vince is here. No prob. Sorry for alert.

Cam took a deep breath. Now what would she tell Howard? She looked up to see him staring at her.

"While I'm here, can I buy some more pork from you? Those chops were really delicious last night." At least that was true.

"Glad you liked them." His expression lightened a little, as if his face was rusty at reacting to a compliment. "Sure, you can buy some. Hey, you want a beer?" He brandished the can.

She was about to politely decline. On the other hand, this was the friendliest he'd ever been, and it was beer o'clock somewhere. Heck, it was almost beer o'clock right here in Westbury. "I'd love one."

He disappeared into the house and a moment later clomped down the stairs, carrying two open bottles. He handed one to her.

Cam stared at the bent pinkie finger on his left hand. She

forced her eyes away. She examined the label on the bottle. It was from the Newburyport microbrewery. "Nice. I'm impressed."

"Only the good stuff for guests." His eyes watered as he smiled. His rusty smile cracked a little farther open.

She thought this might be the third or fourth beer for Howard this afternoon. He seemed more relaxed than she'd ever seen him. But he was at home on a Sunday, and his speech wasn't slurred. Who was she to throw stones?

"Come on back." He lifted his bottle and chugged a good bit of it. He led the way around the right side of the barn to a shed that looked relatively new, at least compared to the listing barn and the decrepit pig areas beyond it. The door of the shed stood open. Howard stepped inside and opened a large refrigerator, revealing shelves of pink meat in vacuum-wrapped plastic.

"Look here. We got roasts," he said. "More chops. Bacon isn't ready yet. Has to cure, like the ham. I'll give you a special discount on account of we're colleagues, so to speak. Even got pig's feet, if you're into that kind of thing."

"I know my Brazilian friend, Lucinda, makes her black bean stew with pig's feet." Cam followed him in and pointed to a fat roast. "That one looks good."

He selected the roast, stuck it in a plastic bag, and handed it to her. "It's the best cut. You're going to have a fine dinner. What else do you want?"

Cam heard a noise from the sty. She stepped outside, cradling the roast next to her body, the meat chilling her fingers. At the corner of the nearest pen, a pig snuffled and pushed its head against the wire enclosure. It raised its eyes, gazing at her. Was it asking for the decency of a square meal? For freedom from maltreatment? For forgiveness for chewing on Irene? Cam took a deep breath and let it out.

"Don't worry. I know what you're thinking."

She turned to face Howard. He gazed over her shoulder at the sty.

"This meat isn't from one of them," he said, pointing at the pen. "It's from good old Buddy."

"The one that didn't win at the fair?"

"We were cheated." He scowled. "But, yeah, that one."

"Vince must have been disappointed."

"Sure. But disappointment toughens you up, you know? Boy needs to know he's going to lose from time to time."

Cam thought Vince would be lucky if he didn't usually lose with a father like this one, but she kept the sentiment to herself.

"Anyway, I'm coming into some money soon. All the animals are going to start getting the five-star treatment." Howard pulled one corner of his mouth up and gestured with his head at the pig. "Even that old sow."

"Is the money coming from Irene's estate? It must have been hard to lose your birth mother after you'd finally found her." She fingered the phone in her right pocket. "And for her to die on your own property, too."

Howard froze. He stared into the distance. "What are you talking about?"

"Well, you both have that same bent finger. It's directly inherited on the mother's side."

His eyes shifted to her. Unlike in her former dealings with Howard, this time his face was like Mill Pond on a windless day. Flat, with plenty of activity underneath.

"I learned about that trait in high school biology, if you can believe it," Cam said.

He glanced at his hand and waited a long moment before he spoke. "It's true. I knew I was adopted. But with my farm falling on hard times, I had to find her, just in case she could help me. Irene. It took some digging. Vince helped me out with the computer." He snorted. "And she was right here in town all along."

275

"Did your adoptive family tell you anything about her?"

"No. They're dead. All of them. And good riddance. That witch of a mother abandoned me to a family who never really wanted me."

"So you had contact with Irene recently? I mean, besides at the dinner?"

"What are you asking all these questions for?" He started to push past her. Despite being a couple of inches shorter than Cam, Howard was a tough fireplug of a farmer. He pinched her shoulder as he passed. She had no choice but to go along. His fingers dug into her neck.

"That hurts." Cam tried to twist out of his hold. "Let go."

He tightened his grip. He marched her along with him. Toward the back of the sty.

Cam pulled back. The sty was the last place she wanted to be. Why had she even started this conversation? She could have just paid him for the roast and driven home. *Stupid.* Her heart raced.

Howard jerked her forward, nearly dragging her. They arrived at the far corner. Wind whistled in the treetops of the woods to their left. It rustled dry cornstalks in the field stretching out behind them. And it blew the acrid stench of the manure-soaked mud right into Cam's eyes and nose.

Howard grabbed her other arm, making her face him. The top of the fence pressed into her waist.

"I had contact with Irene, all right." His face, no longer a still pool, contorted with rage. "Told me she was leaving me some of her precious money. But there were conditions."

"What conditions?" How was she going to get out of here? She clutched the bag with the roast in it. Could she clobber him with it? Not with both her arms pinned, she couldn't.

"Impossible ones." He gazed at the pigs that were gathering on the other side of the fence.

"Did you give her a note the night of the dinner?"

Howard shot her a strange look. "She slipped me that note. How do you know about it?"

"I found it the next day. You must have dropped it."

"She thought she had some magic hold on me. That she'd go public with . . ." His voice trailed off. He shook himself as if he'd been asleep, and tightened his grip on her arms.

"And you killed her so you could get her money?"

Howard stared at her. And laughed. "Aren't you the smarty-pants? You think I killed my mother?"

"I hope you didn't. But she was found right here. And if you inherit her money, you won't have a problem feeding the pigs anymore, will you?" She was sure she was blabbering but didn't know what else to do. Anything to forestall suffering the same fate as Irene.

"That's right." His face reddened.

She could smell the beer on his breath. His meaty hands pressed hard on her arms. Her stomach roiled from the combination of fear and the stench of the pigs.

"I killed Irene Burr," he spat. "I didn't mean to. She never let up, though. It was like she was poking me with a red-hot stake. I was so angry, I shoved her. Hard. She fell in and hit her head on the trough."

Cam wondered how much of this was true. Had he meant to kill Irene or not? "You should tell Detective Pappas. He'd understand."

He shook his head slowly, twice. "Not a chance."

"What? Of you telling him or him understanding?"

"Either. But you're the only one who knows. I can't let you run off and tell him, now, can I?"

"I already told the detective what I know."

"I don't believe you. All you saw was something the same on her hand and mine."

And on Vince's, Cam thought. "I don't feel too well. Let's go back up to the house and talk there. Okay?"

"No more talking." His voice flamed. "You women are all alike. You're relentless."

Howard released her right arm. He drew back his hand and punched her hard in the nose.

She cried out. The pain shot through her face like fireworks. Her eyes filled, and she smelled blood. She brought her free hand up to cup her nose.

He grabbed her left hip. He wrenched her left arm. He hoisted her over the fence and into the sty.

"No!" Cam yelled as she fell. Her right ankle twisted. Her head hit the back of one animal. She fell facedown in the muck.

Chapter 41

The pigs snuffled at her. Cam felt a warm, moist snout pushing on her calf where her pants leg had hiked up. Her heart beat in her throat. She heaved herself up on her arms. The pigs surrounded her, butting at her and at each other. One tried to lick her nose, where the blood still gushed. She pushed it away. Another bit an exposed section of her forearm. She jerked and screamed as she batted at the pig.

She had to get out of here. She rolled into a sitting position and wiped her eyes with her jacket sleeve. She shoved the closest animal away, glad for the moment it was emaciated and likely weighed half what it should. It circled around and tried to bite the back of her neck. Her nose and forehead throbbed, and she tasted blood. She glanced around. Howard was gone. But he could come back with his rifle any minute. One of the pigs pawed at an object on the ground and bit at it. The roast. Another pig tried to climb over the first. Cam grabbed the bag holding the meat and managed to wrest it away from the animal.

She pushed herself up, wincing at the pain in her ankle. She clutched the bag. The pig she'd shoved was coming in for another bite. She ripped the bag partway open.

She threw it as far in the opposite direction as she could. Most of the pigs ran toward the roast and the scent of fresh meat. She turned her back on them and hobbled to the closest fence post. One pig followed her and nudged her hurt ankle. She yelled and kicked at it. She leaned on the fence post and hefted first one leg and then the other over the fence. The post wobbled but held. The last thing she needed was to collapse the barrier and have the swine chasing her.

She made for the woods. At least there she could lean on trees to help her walk, and they provided some cover if Howard came back. To check on what would have been her mauled and eaten body. Maybe he'd just gone to fetch his rifle. To finish her off. Cam shuddered but hauled herself behind the biggest tree. She drew the phone out of her pocket to call Pete. Or 911. Or anybody who would help her and nab Howard before he hurt anyone else. Thank goodness it hadn't fallen into the sty.

She stared at the phone. She swore. The battery was dead.

She searched for the path through the woods. She knew it was here somewhere. There. If she remembered correctly, it led all the way back to her farm.

She glanced behind her. No sign of Howard. Yet. She limped toward safety, covered in pig muck, her head feeling like it had exploded, her ankle shooting pains up her calf and shin.

She heard a shot. She felt her existence shrink into a core of icy determination. He would not get her. He would not.

Chapter 42

Cam paused on the path. The shot didn't repeat. She hadn't been hit. She heard nothing but leaves rustling overhead and her own heart thudding. *Time to get out of here.*

The path forked before her. Should she take the shorter branch leading out to the road? No. She didn't want to be standing alone on a deserted rural byway, looking for a ride, if Howard drove by. But if he came through the woods, if that had been him shooting behind her, she didn't want him following her on the path to home, either. She took a few steps down the branch toward the road and wrestled off her jacket. She threw it farther down the path as a decoy and hurried back to the trail homeward.

She'd walked as fast as she could for a couple of minutes when a branch cracked behind her. Her heart rate sped up once again. She whirled to see a fisher cat staring at her. It was the size of a small dog but looked like an elongated miniature bear, its black eyes watching her. If it attacked with those sharp teeth and claws, she'd be no better off than with the starving pigs. Trying to keep the animal in sight, she glanced quickly around for a stick to defend herself with. None were at hand. She tried to rip a branch from the nearest tree, but it wouldn't detach.

The fisher cat took a step toward her and hissed. White claws curved out from the dark fur on its oversize feet.

Cam's own hands and feet numbed from fear.

It took one more step toward her, then turned and trotted back into the woods.

Cam let out a breath. She hurried toward safety on the over-grown trail with as much speed as she could muster. She tripped on a rock hidden under the leaves and went sprawling, grazing her ear on the nearest sapling as she fell. She rested there for a moment, smelling the earthy must of the ground, feeling the dry maple leaves under her hands, wishing for a soft pillow and a warm blanket. Yeah, and a pain pill. Everything hurt. But it was only getting darker and colder, and she didn't even have her jacket anymore. She managed to pull herself up and resume hurrying home.

As she did, she reran what had just happened. Howard hadn't really tried to kill her. If he'd wanted to, he'd have come back and finished her off with a single bullet. So what was that shot in the woods?

After what felt like hours, she emerged at her own back field. A row of Brussels sprouts never looked so welcoming. After she crossed the field, she looked back at the woods. That must have been where Bobby had come out that day. She shook her head and made for the house.

Alexandra and DJ were gone, but Preston greeted her. Cam's heart sank when she tried the door to the house, which, of course, she'd locked. The key to which was in her truck at Howard's. She racked her exhausted brain. Did she have a spare key hidden somewhere? A loose window? Preston meowed and reared up to rub his head on her knee. Then she remembered. She'd left a key hanging on a nail in a corner of the barn, in case Alexandra or Lucinda needed to get into the house.

A couple of minutes later Cam and Preston were ensconced

inside at last. She flicked on the lights and locked the door. Shivering, she dialed the Westbury police and relayed what had just happened. She tried to keep her voice from shaking and made sure to mention that her keys were in her truck at the Fisher farm. If Howard found her keys and drove over to finish her off, she was in big trouble.

After she hung up, she scrubbed her hands with soap at the kitchen sink and gingerly splashed water on her face and patted it dry. She wasn't ready to look in a mirror yet. She plugged in her cell phone to access Pete's number.

The house phone rang as Cam was reaching for it to dial Pete. He was on the other end when she picked up.

"Cam? You're safe?"

"I almost wasn't—" When she felt sobs bubbling up, she clamped her hand over her mouth.

"Your truck is at Howard Fisher's."

"How do you know that?"

"I'll tell you. In person. We'll be over in a few minutes. But don't let anyone else in. We don't know where he is."

"Howard?" Cam's eyes widened.

"Yes."

"Are my keys still in my truck?"

"Don't know yet. Don't open the door to anyone but me." He disconnected.

Chapter 43

Cam stared at the phone. She shivered. Maybe she wasn't safe, after all. She checked the door lock and went around closing curtains. She sniffed. And looked at her clothes. She was covered in muck and stank to high heaven.

Hobbling up the stairs, she tore off every bit of clothing and changed into a clean pair of jeans and an old, soft sweatshirt. A shower would have to wait. Grabbing a clean pair of socks, she made it downstairs again as a hammering commenced on the door.

"Cam!"

She listened. It sounded like Pete, so she peered through the curtain next to the door. And opened it.

Pete stood on the porch, with Lucinda on the next step down. Pete's face registered anguish and exasperation at the same time. Lucinda's expression turned from worry to horror.

"What happened to you?" She pushed past Pete and laid her hand gently on the side of Cam's face.

"Howard tried to kill me," Cam said. "Threw me in with his pigs. I got away, but my phone was dead. I made it home through the woods."

"In my official capacity as an employee of the state police," Pete began, "I need to tell you that you never should have gone over there in the first place."

"Ellie Kosloski had texted me that she thought Vince was in trouble at home! They're friends from school. That's why I went. If I saw anything, I was going to call the Westbury police right away, believe me. But once I got there, she texted me that it was a mistake, that he had shown up at her house. And then I was stupid enough to start talking with Howard."

Pete moved to Cam's side. "That was unwise, all right. But as Pete, I'm damned glad you're alive, Cameron Flaherty." His voice turned husky, and his eyes softened.

Cam looked from him to Lucinda and back. She suddenly felt very wobbly. She put her hand on Pete's shoulder.

"Can we sit down and talk about this? I'm not quite plowing at full capacity here." She edged over to the table and sank into a chair. Pete remained standing.

"What did he do to you?" Lucinda knelt in front of Cam.

"He admitted he killed Irene. He said he hadn't meant to kill her, but she kept taunting him, and he shoved her." *Like he shoved me.* "He punched me in the nose and threw me into the sty." Cam wondered if she was about to throw up. She swallowed hard.

"And left you in there like he left her." Pete leaned on the table and shook his head.

"Right. When I landed in the pen, I turned my ankle. The pigs came after me. It was pretty awful." An involuntary shudder rippled through her. "But I got away. A fisher cat almost came at me. And then I tripped in the woods, too."

Lucinda rose and bustled about. Within minutes she had Cam's ankle elevated and wrapped in a dishcloth holding a bag of frozen peas. She wiped hydrogen peroxide on the bite on Cam's arm and then applied some antibiotic ointment.

285

Pete's cell rang. He walked out of the room, his concerned eyes lingering on Cam before he turned his back. Lucinda brought a bottle of an over-the-counter pain reliever to the table with a glass of water and waited until Cam had downed a couple of pills. She handed Cam a steaming mug.

"What's this?"

"Warm milk with brandy in it." Lucinda sniffed and wrinkled her nose. "Your hair stinks. I'll get something to wipe it off."

Cam thanked her. She could hear Pete talking in a low voice in the living room. She sniffed the mug. The brandy fumes made her eyes water. She took a cautious sip. The smooth milk and the tang of the liquor warmed her all the way down.

Pete walked back in, holding his phone.

"Sit down." Cam patted the table. "How did you and Lucinda end up at the Fisher farm?"

Pete sat. "She called me today. I was talking with her when you left your message, in fact."

Lucinda brought a bowl of water and a couple of towels to the table and spread one towel over Cam's shoulders. She began wiping Cam's hair away from her face with a warm, wet washcloth.

"I remembered that time I heard Irene talking to somebody," Lucinda said. "I finally realized it was Howard's voice. You know how I said you have to sit with a memory sometimes before it comes clear to you?"

"We put the same pieces together as you must have," Pete said. "Howard was Irene's birth son, and she had promised to leave him money. Or he thought so." He cocked his head. "How did you figure it out?"

"I have a confession to make." Cam felt sheepish but forged ahead. "I used Lucinda's key and checked out Irene's house."

"I told her I wasn't having no part of it," Lucinda said, shaking her head.

"I found her iPad hidden in her books. I was going to hack into it." At Pete's look she hurried on. "Don't worry. I didn't. It's in my truck. But what I figured out even before then was the genetic trait she shared with Howard and with Vince. They all have a pinkie finger that bends sideways at the last joint."

"We'll have to see what her will actually says, but if he believed she was leaving him money, it would certainly provide him with motive to kill her." Pete tapped his fingers on the table.

"Somebody had been in her office before me. It's on the second floor, and there was a ladder leaning against an open window. I wonder if it was Howard. Whoever it was probably didn't find anything. I looked all over before I discovered her iPad. Which I hope is still in my truck."

"My people are over there. I'll get them to check it out."

"I thought you had a witness who put Bobby at the farm, though." Cam gazed at Pete. "Wasn't that why you had him in for questioning?"

Pete nodded, looking abashed. "The witness was Howard. Turns out he wasn't such a reliable one, after all."

"And so you both went over to Howard's after I did."

"He wasn't there." Pete frowned. "Vince said his dad had stormed out right after he got home on his bike. He said Howard grabbed a rifle and drove off in a hurry."

"I heard a shot as I was trying to get home. I didn't know if he was coming after me or what. But it was only one shot."

"I'm glad he didn't end up here," Pete said. He covered Cam's hand with his own.

Lucinda rubbed Cam's hair with a dry towel. "There. You'll need to wash it properly, but at least you don't smell like the barnyard anymore."

Cam looked up at her. "You were really gentle. Thank you." She sipped the warm drink. "What time is it, anyway?"

"Time for you to get checked out at the hospital," Pete said. "Ankle and nose and that bite on your arm."

"No," Cam said. "No hospital."

"You really should be looked at." He squeezed her hand and leaned toward her, holding her eyes with his.

"Sorry, but no. I hate hospitals, and I've already been this week. I'd have to sit in the emergency waiting area for hours. You know how it is. I'll be fine." She very gingerly felt her nose. She touched the bridge and wiggled it, which sent a new firework up into her brain, but it felt intact. "I don't think it's broken."

"I'll get you ice for the nose, too," Lucinda said.

Pete sighed. "I'm calling a friend, then. He's a doctor, and he owes me a favor big-time. He'll come over here and check you out."

Cam nodded. She sat in silence for a moment, thinking through the events of the past week. She narrowed her eyes at Pete.

"Thoughts?" Pete said.

"Maybe it was Howard who cut my brake lines. He could have done it at the fairgrounds."

"They didn't get any usable prints off the truck. We'll ask him when we find him." Pete's cell rang. He pulled his hand away from Cam's as he checked the display and connected.

"Pappas." As he listened, he glanced at her. "I see. Secure the scene. I'll be there as soon as I can." He disconnected and stood. "I have to go."

"What is it?" Cam asked.

Pete looked from her to Lucinda and back, his face set in a grim mask. "They found Howard. He's in his truck out at the edge of his property."

"Are you going to arrest him?" Cam asked.

"It's a bit late for an arrest. He seems to have taken care of it for us."

"He turned himself in?" Lucinda asked.

Pete shook his head.

"That shot I heard," Cam said, eyes wide.

Pete nodded.

Chapter 44

A few hours later, after she scrubbed herself in a hot shower until the water turned cold, Cam lay in bed. Pete had called to make sure she was all right. She had talked to him on her cell as she lay with her head and shoulders, as well as her ankle, propped up on extra pillows.

"You can sleep well tonight, Cam."

"Your doctor friend came by and treated the bite on my arm. He said my nose wasn't broken and I just need to elevate and ice my ankle. Thanks for arranging that. I couldn't face sitting in the hospital for hours."

"As I said, he owed me one."

"I still have a few Percocets from my accident last week, and I intend to take a couple tonight, so I'm sure I will have a very good sleep. I'm not so sure about Vince, though."

"I think Vince is going to do fine."

"The poor kid," Cam went on. "Howard wasn't a great father. And killing himself to escape his troubles doesn't make him any kind of role model for a son."

"When I think of what could have happened at Fisher's, you

alone with Howard, I—" Pete cleared his throat and went on in a voice as soft and deep as indigo velvet. "I care about you, Cam. Probably shouldn't, but I do."

"I'd like to keep this conversation going," Cam murmured. She said good night. She shook out two pills and downed them with the glass of water she'd brought to her bedside.

She felt safe. Irene's murderer was no longer a problem. The sadness attached to Howard's suicide, though, vied with the feeling of being secure and out of danger.

Howard had had a tough life starting from the moment of being born to a mother who didn't want him. It continued with the family who fed, clothed, and housed him, but who begrudged him happiness and welcome as one of their kin. His run of bad luck hadn't ended with becoming a farmer, as he never seemed to figure out how to effectively and humanely raise both crops and livestock. The apparent promise of funds from Irene had turned him from an unpleasant, impoverished farmer into a killer.

But questions remained. What would happen to Vince? Where was his mother? Had it been Howard who had scaled the ladder to Irene's study or someone else? Who would take care of the pigs now? She imagined the questions in a box on a barge floating into harbor. They could shelter there overnight. She didn't need to answer them tonight. Perhaps never.

Before she slipped into narcotic-induced sleep, she smiled at the thought of Pete Pappas, suitor. And she had her dinner date with Jake tomorrow night. Life was getting interesting.

Cam stretched on the back steps in the morning sunlight of a warm Indian summer day. She had neglected the hens completely the night before. She strolled out behind the barn, her ankle blessedly much improved, and found the girls had roosted themselves. The door to the coop was open, because she'd never closed it, but they all appeared to be present and were venturing out into the morning air, vocalizing away. She doled out three measures of feed and returned to the house to brew coffee.

Once it was on, she checked her face in the mirror near the door. *Ouch.* Purple and dark blue bruising covered her upper face. Her eyes were bloodshot, and even her lips were swollen. She'd slept reasonably well, astonishing herself when she hadn't woken until almost eight o'clock. She had arisen with a wicked thirst for water and had downed several glasses before venturing outdoors.

She poured a mug of black coffee. On an impulse, she added several spoonfuls of sugar and a dose of milk. What was up with that? Maybe she needed the calories after what she'd been through yesterday. Which, come to think of it, hadn't included dinner.

Her cell phone rang. She glanced at the number. Detective Pappas himself. She connected and greeted him.

"Are you up, Cam? I'm in the driveway. With breakfast."

"Come on in. Coffee's ready. And I'm hungry." She disconnected and opened the door to Pete. He carried a white paper bag and Irene's iPad in a clear plastic sheath.

"This face is something, isn't it?" Cam asked with a smile.

"How are you feeling?" Pete set his offerings on the table and looked at her from under his heavy brows.

"My ankle is much better. My nose hurts. And whatever that doctor friend of yours put on the bite seems to be working."

"I'm glad." He gestured to the bag. "I brought muffins."

Cam carried a mug of coffee for Pete and plates for both of them to the table.

"What's up with the iPad?" Cam broke a muffin in half and took a generous bite. "Mmm, carrot walnut."

"I'll tell you in a minute. First, I want to show you what we found next to Howard's body last night." He pulled a folded paper out of his shirt pocket. "This is a copy of the note he left." He spread the paper out on the table. The writing was printed letters in all caps. They were rough but legible.

MY TEMPER GETS THE BETTER OF ME, AND I ABUSE VINCE AND MY WIFE. I CAN'T HELP IT. I FEEL BAD LATER, BUT IT KEEPS HAPPENING.

THE FARM IS GOING UNDER. I CAN'T SEEM TO MAKE ANY MONEY. WE COULDN'T EVEN WIN A RIB-BON FOR BIG BUDDY.

I KILLED IRENE. BUT SHE PROVOKED ME! I USED TO BE A FIGHTER. I WASN'T GOING TO GIVE UP. WHEN CAMERON PROVOKED ME, TOO, I LOST IT AGAIN. BUT I DIDN'T WANT HER TO DIE. IRENE SAID SHE LEFT HER MONEY TO VINCE, NOT TO ME. I THOUGHT MAYBE I COULD USE SOME OF IT FOR THE FARM. BUT NOT IF I'M ARRESTED FOR MURDER. I'M TAKING MY PITIFUL SELF AWAY FOR GOOD.

VINCE AND HELEN, I'M SORRY. I LOVE YOU BOTH.

Cam's throat thickened, and her eyes welled. "What a sad note."

Pete nodded. He folded it again. "I'm glad he chose himself rather than you to shoot, though. Now, about the iPad. Our IT guy is on vacation. I'm hopeless around Apple products. I wondered if I could hire you to see what's on the device."

"You don't have to hire me. I love hacking into file systems." Cam rubbed her hands together.

"Actually, I do have to hire you. Otherwise, I wouldn't be able to use what you find. I brought a copy of our consultant contract. You qualify as an IT expert, right?"

"That's me." She read the contract and signed it. "What do you want me to look for?"

"Anything relating to the case. Any document with Howard's name on it. Irene's will. Whatever you can find." He removed the iPad from the sheath.

Cam started it and typed the password she'd discovered the day before. It was time to drill deep into the device. Apple had always been minimalist and tried to make the system easy to use for the least-sophisticated customer. In Cam's opinion, it felt like they didn't trust users with their own files. But, hey, she hadn't been a sought-after software engineer for nothing.

She searched the system. "Here you go. Her will and a couple of files named Howard and Vince."

"Can you open the will?"

She opened the file and displayed it for him to read.

He whistled. "She left a chunk to Bobby. Says it was his father's money. Everything else—the house and her business—goes to Vince. Not to Howard. Just as he said in the note."

"At least Vince will be provided for."

"How am I going to find these files again?" Pete frowned. "I wouldn't be able to hack into it, as you say, if my life depended on it."

"I'll link them to the iPad's top level so you can find them." Cam worked for a minute, then handed the device to Pete. "You're all set."

Pete thanked her. "I have to get going. You take care, all right? I'll call you later."

Cam had closed the door behind him and cleared the table when high-pitched bicycle brakes screeched in the driveway. She opened the door and raised her hand in greeting.

"Vince, Ellie! No school today?" She came down the steps to greet them.

The kids climbed off their bikes and let them fall.

"Teacher in-service day, so no classes. Sweet, right?" Ellie sauntered toward Cam. Vince hung behind a few paces, and his step was more tentative.

When she got closer, Ellie exclaimed, "Your face! Who slugged you?" She put her hands on her hips.

Cam glanced at Vince, who stuck his hands in his pockets and studied the ground. She looked back at Ellie.

"I, um, ran into a post yesterday. Just being clumsy," Cam said. "Don't worry. It doesn't hurt much today." Cam took a couple of steps and stretched her arm around Vince's shoulders. "I'm so sorry about your dad, Vince." She felt him first stiffen and then relax into her. Poor kid.

He coughed, still looking at the ground. "Thanks, Ms. Flaherty. He, well, wasn't very . . . happy, I guess you could say."

Cam squeezed his bony teenage shoulder. A shoulder that should have been hugged, not bruised. A teenager who needed encouragement, not denigration. Howard had learned that behavior from his foster father and had treated his son the same way. It was time to break the cycle of dysfunction. People could break out of all kinds of problems. Look at her. A year ago she wouldn't have had any idea how to reach out to a fellow human in trouble, at least not physically. She'd been comfortable with how to talk to a computer. Communicating with a person's psyche and emotions? Not so much.

"So, how is your mom doing? Is she around? I haven't seen her lately."

Vince looked her in the eyes and smiled. His face lit up, and his shoulders relaxed. "She's coming back later today. She's been, like, living at my uncle's up in Ogunquit. My dad, he wasn't very nice to her, either. I spent the summer with Mom, but I needed to come back for school last month. You know, so I didn't have to switch high schools."

"Vince stayed with my family last night," Ellie said in a soft voice. "Detective Pappas called and asked if he could. I mean, like, obviously." She shook her head after the manner of fourteen-year-old girls everywhere.

Vince scowled. "I should have stuck up for Mom more. I've been lifting weights lately. I wanted to get strong enough so he couldn't push us around. At least I don't have to worry about that anymore."

"I'm so glad she's coming back, Vince," Cam said. "And getting stronger is always a good thing. Even if you don't have to do it to protect yourself."

Ellie took Vince's hand. "Want to see the chickens?"

He squeezed her hand but released it. "You go check on them. I'll be there in a minute." Continuing to smile, he watched her stride away and turned to Cam.

"Ms. Flaherty, I know what happened. I want to apologize for my dad hurting you." He stood up tall. "I wish I'd stopped him earlier and—"

Cam held up a hand. "It's okay, Vince. As you said, he wasn't a happy man. As far as I've heard, he hadn't been for most of his life."

"He seemed happy when I was little. We'd feed the animals together. He taught me how to hunt. I remember making Sunday breakfast with him—" He broke off, his eyes brimming over. He gave a rough swipe to them with his flannel sleeve. "But then money got tight. He got rough with Mom and with me."

"You can't save anybody else, you know," Cam said. "You can only save yourself. You're a good person, Vince. You're kind, polite, smart. You work hard." She nodded. "And you're good to your mother. Just go forward. You'll be all right."

He smiled through wet eyes. Cam reached out a hand to pat his shoulder. Instead, she surprised herself by enveloping his slender frame in a hug, which he returned with a fierce squeeze.

"Vince," Ellie called from behind the barn. "Come see the chickens! They have a covered run and everything!"

He pulled apart from Cam, gave her a huge grin, and raced away.

Chapter 45

Jake called at four that afternoon, saying he'd heard about her encounter at the Fisher farm. He offered to bring an early date-night dinner to her house so she didn't have to drive to Newburyport. Cam accepted, although she was no longer sure about the "date" part of it. After he arrived, he puttered in the kitchen, warming and applying final touches to what he had brought.

Cam sat at her computer, catching up on bills, invoices, the farm's Web site, e-mail. She'd taken the day off from physical work, settling for a few midday hours of directing Lucinda on where to work and what to harvest. She realized she was avoiding talking about relationship matters with Jake, contenting herself with avoidance therapy: both of them working in parallel and mostly in silence.

"Your dinner, madam." Jake gestured to her dining table. Two places were set, flames flickered atop slender candle stalks, and a vase of pink roses backed up the scene.

"Looks fabulous," Cam said as her stomach signaled its emptiness with an audible rumble. "What are we having?"

"Gnocchi with local pink oyster mushrooms and crème fraîche, sautéed Brussels sprouts and shallots with a garlic–red wine reduction, and a Galician sweet potato–rosemary frittata. Except for the mushrooms, the produce is all your own."

"Yum." She filled both wineglasses with a chilled white zinfandel before sitting. She lifted hers. "Thank you for this lovely meal, Jake. And for our friendship."

Jake's brow darkened. "Is it only friendship to you, Cameron?"

She took a sip and set her glass down. She took a deep breath and blew it out. She was about to answer him when someone knocked at the door. She twisted in her chair to see Pete peering in through the window. *Nice timing, Pappas.*

Recipes

Brussels Sprouts and Shallots in a Red Wine Reduction

Serves six

Ingredients:

4 tablespoons fruity olive oil
1 tablespoon butter
12 large shallots, peeled and cut in half lengthwise (about ¾ pound)
2 garlic bulbs, cloves peeled and left whole (about 40 cloves)
2½ pounds Brussels sprouts, trimmed
1 cup red wine
1 cup chicken stock
2 tablespoons minced parsley
1 tablespoon Dijon mustard

Directions:

In a heavy casserole with a tight lid, heat the olive oil and butter over medium-high heat.

Add the shallots and garlic, and sauté until lightly browned, about 5 minutes.

Add the Brussels sprouts, toss to coat with the oil, and cook for about 5 minutes.

Pour in the red wine and deglaze the pan with a spoon.

Cook the vegetables for 5 minutes more, stirring occasionally.

Add the chicken stock and parsley, stirring well, and bring to a boil over high heat. Reduce the heat, cover, and braise just until the Brussels sprouts are tender.

Remove the Brussels sprouts from the casserole with a slotted spoon and set aside. Add the mustard to the casserole, stir, and reduce the sauce until it is enough to just coat the Brussels sprouts.

Return the Brussels sprouts to the casserole, and toss to heat and coat with the sauce. Serve warm.

To serve this dish as a casserole, cook brown rice or couscous, spread it on the bottom of an ovenproof serving dish, top with the finished recipe, sprinkle with grated fresh Parmesan or Romano, and warm in the oven for 15 minutes.

Sweet Potato Empanadas

Makes 18 small empanadas

Ingredients:
    Parchment paper, for lining the sheet pan (or butter for greasing the sheet pan)
    2 sheets frozen puff pastry
    1 baked sweet potato, medium in size
    ½ cup shredded fontina cheese
    ½ cup cooked black beans
    ¼ cup diced sweet red pepper
    2 tablespoons minced fresh cilantro
    2 tablespoons freshly squeezed lime juice

1 teaspoon ground cumin
Salt and freshly ground black pepper, to taste
Few dashes hot sauce (optional)
1 large egg

Directions:

Preheat the oven to 375°F. Line a sheet pan with parchment paper, or grease the sheet pan with butter.

Defrost the puff pastry according to the directions on the package.

Scoop out the cooked sweet potato into a large bowl. Add the cheese, beans, red pepper, cilantro, lime juice, cumin, salt and pepper, and hot sauce (if desired), and mash together with a spoon or fork until well combined.

Whisk the egg in a small bowl until frothy.

Cut the puff pastry into 3-inch x 3-inch squares on a floured surface.

Brush two adjacent edges of one of the puff pastry squares with the egg. Place 1 heaping teaspoon of the filling in the center of the square, fold it in half diagonally to form a triangle, and press the joined edges firmly together.

Place the empanada on the prepared sheet pan. Repeat the process until all the empanadas are made.

Brush each empanada with egg and bake for 13 to 15 minutes, or until golden brown. Serve at once.

Note: A version of this recipe was generously provided by Phat Cats Bistro in Amesbury, Massachusetts.